The Diary, THE DETECTIVE and the DUBLIN IRISH FESTIVAL

A Novel

With tremendous thanks to those authors who took time to contribute their writing talents in adding to this wee bit o' interstellar magic:

Arthur Cola

Sinead Tyrone

Michael E. McCarthy

Cindy Thomson

Therese Gilardi

Mark Rickerby (Copy Editor)

Table of Contents

Dedicated to the
City of Dublin, Ohio.

To the phenomenal staff along with
the extraordinary volunteers at the

~ Dublin Irish Festival ~

Sláinte mhaith!

*"There are only two kinds of people in the world:
The Irish and those who wish they were."*

~ Irish saying ~

Chapter 1: A Legend is Born

Date: Saturday, August 5, 2017.
Entry 1: Dubh Linn borróg uachtar, a grá mo chroí!
Location: Room 323 - Crowne Plaza - Dublin, Ohio.
Time: Wee hours of the morn'.

Dear Diary . . .

Where to start? I guess from the beginning, although this is really something completely new to me. I have never kept a diary before, but since I'm on to a new wee adventure, I thought maybe I should capture my thoughts. Here goes nothing.

Just a couple of days ago - on Thursday, August 3rd, to be exact - I flew into an incredible place called Columbus, Ohio. It's located right here in America. Why I am writing that down, I haven't a clue. Maybe it is part of my excitement in being here. Anyway, I didn't really know much about this city other than they had a National Hockey League team called the Columbus Blue Jackets. Since I live away up north in a place called Winnipeg, Manitoba, I know they play hockey against the Winnipeg Jets. But sure, maybe a bit more about that later.

I was brought here to participate in the Dublin Irish Festival. Dublin is a wee city which derives its name from our capital back home, and whereby everything Irish is celebrated to the fullest degree possible; much more than anything I had ever seen in Ireland, unless you were to count the Orange Parades that march through Belfast every year. Wait, that is not a celebration of anything Irish. I don't even think they consider our existence, or the fact that we have the right to breathe the same air as them. But sure, to each their own.

Anyways, since this was my first time being in this city and state, I would be remiss if I did not mention that I was met at the airport by a phenomenal lad named Mike Herriott. He was at the bottom of the stairs holding up a sign with my name on it. I felt so proud, as if I was a wee celebrity, although I am sure everyone else in the airport did not know me from Adam, or Eve for that matter. But sure, it was Mike who provided transportation services over to the hotel for those of us who were attending the festival for the very first time. He gave me an introductory look – and a fine example, I must say, of what Ohio hospitality truly looks like – and then gave me a wee tour of the city. I learned auld slow hand, Eric Clapton, lives here with his wee family!

Now, I suppose this is where the craziness of this entire journey began, and about which I am now struggling to process my thoughts in the hopes of making sense of it all. I was with a group of authors – Irish and others - who identify as being American-Irish. I am not sure how you get to be an American-Irish author though, as I always understood that when one is born in the United States, they are automatically American and nothing else. I guess, as they say, everyone wants to be Irish. I digress.

Now, much later in the evening, after settling in at the hotel, I was met by a group of other hosts, including Barbara Cody-Burkholder, Nick Bova and his wife Lisa, a fella named Kevin Cooper (who's in charge of directing drivers and participants to golf carts), Kay McGovern, Laura Nelson, Alison LeRoy, Adam Parker, Skip Moersch, and countless more. I found it interesting that Skip would always conceal his identity behind sunglasses but was a straight shooter during any conversations I managed to muster up with him. He seemed like he was an ex-military type of bloke, or perhaps came from a seriously secretive division of the FBI – Free Based Irishmen. I had better remain on his good side if I am to get anywhere in the festival as he seems to have a lot of pull in bringing about drivers, including Mike.

Before I get off-track, as I often do, I must admit it was such an honour to meet so many incredible people. They made me feel as if I were a rock star, although I certainly did not look the part or fit the mold. As it stands, my wee wooden recorder is decades old, collecting dust in an ancient box. Although I remember how to play *Hot Cross Buns* on it, I have been practicing the opening chords of *Riverdance,* as well as *A Gift of a Thistle* from the *Braveheart* soundtrack. However, I do not think this is what the organizers meant on the application form when they said they were seeking a solo performance on the Celtic Rock stage. It is probably the reason why they played it safe by having me come here as an author and not a musician. As the old Irish proverb goes, *"May you get all your wishes but one, so that you will always have something to strive for."*

Moving on. Now, along with the twelve hundred volunteers who make the festival run like clockwork, every one of them took the time to extend the sincerest and warmest of Irish greetings possible to me and said "Céad Míle Fáilte!" In translation, this means "One Hundred Thousand Welcomes!" and awaits every artist who arrives to take part in this prestigious, yearly celebration. I could not believe this included little old me! My ma always did say miracles never cease.

Within a day of being here, I learned that the Dublin Irish Festival has the largest cream buns one could ever wish for! They are legendary – well, perhaps only in my wee mind, that is. Made by Schmidt's in the German Village of Columbus, I swear they are a meal in themselves and could easily require a knife and fork to eat. Although we have cream buns back home in Ireland – a mouthwatering delicacy of the highest order - they are nowhere near the size of the ones made over here. My da once said during a trip home from sea that everything is big in America. He wasn't kidding!

Since I am now on the topic of puff pastries, it goes without saying that our bakeries back home are famous for producing gorgeous goods and tasty treats. However, the legend behind the Dublin Cream Bun was born in a community far from the green fields and rocky shores of Eire – it was right here in the beautiful City of Dublin, Ohio. Simply said, there is nowhere else in America that celebrates everything Irish and takes as much pride in making sure everyone who comes here has the absolute time of their lives to the extent that the organizers of the Dublin Irish Festival do. Hearts are left bursting with cherished memories of making of lifelong friends after a weekend of celebrations, and a deep yearning to return as soon as possible. I can understand why, as I am already dreading having to leave. The beautiful and welcoming folks here have been second to none!

Yesterday, which just happened to be the opening day of the festival, while I was walking to the authors tent, Schmidt's had already parked their food truck not far from where I and my fellow authors were to be located. Adrenaline aside, my heart literally pounded out of my chest, knowing all too well a tray of cream buns quietly sat, waiting patiently, wanting to be devoured. I know I have quite the imagination, but I swear that I heard them calling my name . . .

"Psst. Mo chara, Belfast Child. Wanna know a secret? We are your gateway to heaven. One bite is all it takes; you will never be the same."

It was as if they were poet whisperers or sugary sirens, pulling my preoccupied thoughts toward their delicate, creamy filling and delightful taste. In all fairness, it honestly doesn't take much to distract me. I swear it was a love affair at first sight! I know we Irish fall in love quite easily, so I can only imagine Gerard Butler telling a cream bun "P.S. I Love You", which would have broken Hillary Swank's wee heart. The temptation was seriously far too much to resist. I would have caved to my cravings, but since I had eaten a hearty breakfast earlier that morning, sadly, there was no room at the inn. My salivating taste buds would have to wait.

Setting up my display, I busied myself by emptying boxes of books onto a table while the flaps of the large, vinyl tent were closed in rapid succession. An intense thunderstorm barreled down on the region, bringing dangerous winds and lightning with it. Announcements made over the loudspeakers asked everyone in the area to evacuate and take shelter immediately.

Making my way to a secure area, I waited out the storm while raindrops the size of marbles fell from the heavens. After the all-clear was granted and everyone was allowed to return to their stations, another fella showed up who I had not seen for at least two years. Many of us who are a part of his circle of friends, or perhaps close comrades, have come to know him as the *International Man of Mystery* since he often disappears in the blink of an eye and without a trace! It was none other than my brother from another mother, straight out of the Inishowen Peninsula, which is the most northern tip of southern Ireland: the one and only, John Patrick Sexton! Along with a few other choice names which I will get to, I call him J.P.

The best way I can describe J.P. is that he must be about eight feet tall, has wavy locks, chiseled looks, and wild, Viking hair that blows around freely as if he was constantly in a commercial for shampoo and conditioner. If he uses conditioning body wash though, it isn't working because he lacks a conditioned body. Legend has it he's so large, he uses an entire bar of Irish Spring for every shower. Ha. I'm one to talk. He has more volume in his hair than I have ever had on my television set. Anyway, the first time I met J.P., I thought he was your man from the cover of those wee romance novel books: Fabio!

Upon taking a second, much longer, extremely noticeable (and might I add what was an uncomfortable stare), I saw the only muscles J.P. has on his body are in his thumbs and fingers. This is most likely from him gripping countless pints for many decades. A six-pack to him means a carry out of a half dozen tins of Guinness. I swear that crazy fella could drink for all of Ireland, so much so that I have taken to calling him the "Striking Viking." In saying that, though, I am so glad this wee diary keeps all my wee thoughts safe. If J.P. only knew what went through my unrestrained mind, aside from what he often hears coming out of my unfiltered gub, he could quite easily make me disappear somewhere in the turf bogs of Malin Head!

J.P. joined me and put a Celtic design tablecloth down so the two of us could make our display booth look befitting of respectable Irish authors. It's not like we had our County Antrim and County Donegal accents, or book displays, or Irish tri-color flag hung up directly behind us to give our identities away or anything like that. The fact that I personally wore a blue golf shirt which prominently displayed the words *Belfast Child* embroidered on the front with brilliant white thread was not a dead giveaway either. How in God's green earth would anyone know who we were or where we came from? Thank goodness for Celtic tablecloths! It saved the day for us.

All messin' about aside, it made our wee table look beautiful. I must say he's a man of good taste! After all, he did plonk his eight-foot seven-inch arse down beside me.

Throughout the day, people came into the tent to talk to us and learn about our books, asking questions about Ireland, sharing histories, knowledge, and their experiences of travelling home. After hearing them incorrectly pronounce the names of several counties throughout our wee homeland, my thoughts kept drifting back to the Dublin Cream Bun with my name on it, still sitting in the Schmidt's food truck. But I had to stay by my table. The most sadistic medieval torture methods had nothing on the lure of those buns.

At this point, a cute, green-eyed maiden came to my rescue. She also goes by the name of Danica Richardson and is quite sarcastic in her commentary; I swear there is no filter to that one! Using my Jedi mind powers, I imposed my darkest thoughts upon her weak mind. Either that, or she overheard me moaning all day about what I would love to have. Ack, as my granny used to say to me over the years, "Bless her wee soul." She ran off to get several cups of tea for a few of us before heading over to suss out the creations by my fellow authors. She was obviously an avid reader, as I had not so secretly watched as she scouted all sorts of books and purchased a small library in the process. In all honesty, I guess I couldn't keep my eyes off her, although she was likely oblivious to this since the books were much more interesting to her.

Danica's inquisitive mind must have guided her to explore other vendors and sights around the festival. My stomach will tell you it was an eternity before she decided to pick up one of those glorious, beautiful, mouthwatering delicacies. The problem, in my most humble opinion, was that a suave, attractive, young-ish fellow had gone off himself to set up an *author signing* banner outside the tent.

Unbeknownst to me, since I was off to the side pulling apart poles and putting together two banner curtains, my fellow authors laid their attentive eyes on that stunning creation when she arrived back at the Irish Authors' Corner. Oh, be still my beating heart. I swear she was gorgeous; a gift from the gods. Never had anyone seen anything so perfect, so pure, and so special. The mold must have been shattered after she was created!

Simply said, she was like no other! She stood among the masses, paying no attention to those who cast penetrating looks in her direction, all the while drooling, wishing, wanting. In all honesty, that included me! No matter how hard I tried to break my deeply obvious stare, my eyes remained captivated and focused. It was as if time itself had stood still while many hearts skipped countless beats, especially my own, since it almost sent me into a state of cardiac arrest. This would have most-definitely required several sessions of mouth-to-mouth resuscitation. It was simply far too much to bear. Nothing else mattered.

The word "glorious" fails to come close to describing what occurred in the next moment. Perhaps I was only imagining this, but I profess herald angels descended upon me while singing choruses of Hallelujah, their heavenly harmonies filling the flaps of the vinyl tent. Maybe I was mistaken, in that it actually existed only within the cavernous space between my ears. Looking around me, I saw that the dark, grey skies had parted ways to blistering streams of heavenly light, which glistened down upon her like a sparkling array of diamonds. Low and behold, in that moment, as we held our collective breaths together, a lifelong dream came true in the Irish Authors' Corner . . .

. . . the Dublin Cream Bun made its debut appearance!

The cute, fun loving, green-eyed, sarcastic fair maiden was quite upset when she heard this. Perhaps she herself was a Jedi, as she found this heartfelt introduction captured within my wee diary was not about her as she had thought it to be, yet probably should have been. It was either that or she overheard me talking about this momentous occasion to Julie Burgess, the store manager at The Book Loft. From that exchange, Danica had called me an arse. An arse, I say! Well, then again, who can blame her? A gift which parted ways with her purse was the last six dollars to her name, funds she could have easily used to buy herself a Guinness Cake or three scones with butter from the lovely folks at the Galway Bakers. As the remainder of Danica's money had already parted from her fingertips for books and Irish jewelry, she was completely starving, the poor thing.

Anyway, where was I? Cradled in her hands, all the while being extremely careful not to disturb this gift from the heavens, especially the delicate, sweet filling which had been so carefully added between the outer layers of puffed pastry, the fair maiden placed the Dublin Cream Bun down at a table where two authors were meant to be seated. However, only one was there in all of his glory - low and behold, it was the International Man of Mystery!

With the ravenous look that wild fella from Donegal gets in his eyes, his stomach let out a growl that made the canvas walls of the tent ripple. Even though I was standing well over fifty feet away from him, I was almost deafened by the noise his innards made, watching as his eyes began to glow with a look of sheer intent. The moment was almost unbearable to take.

Seeing the breathtaking delight before him and unable to hold back his hunger any longer, J.P. made his move. Standing up from his seated position, adjusting his books, checking his forms, and hungrily licking his chops, he suddenly announced his intentions – he was going up to the green room in the festival offices to have a bite to eat and a drink. But who would stay back to both stand guard over and promote his 400+ page memoir in his absence?

In that instant, a dashing hero came to the rescue. It was the Irish lad, the poet, the storyteller, the author known simply as Greg. Who else should I be writing about here? Umm, even though I write these questions for and to myself, it is sometimes best for me to not give any answers. Maybe my mum, Catherine and my sister, Karen, were right about me . . . I need locking up! My head does indeed need to be examined.

Anyhow, since I had previously read his book and could provide a healthy synopsis of J.P.'s story, I offered to look after his wares, let people know when he would be back to sign them, and tell them they could certainly purchase them in advance. This would also provide them with more time to wander around and speak to other authors. To be honest, the greatest outcome of this is that it ensured the Dublin Cream Bun did not find itself in a place it had not originally been intended for - Sexton's stomach!

As J.P. exited the tent, I set about to re-adjust my books. My efforts of placing the wee six-foot banner outside the tent did its job as it caught the attention of many more people who came in and spoke to me about my life story. This afforded me the opportunity of promoting J.P.'s story, although I also took great pleasure in telling enquiring minds about how he is often mistaken as being the lovechild of Fabio and any one of the lovely wee dames from within the romance novels. That, along with having the size and looks of Irish giant, Fionn Mac Cumhaill, sans his muscles. Sorry, J.P. but there is no comparison in that department.

In fact, I was that busy, the glorious, delectable creation which had been so prudently selected sadly sat undevoured, and for the most part, was largely ignored! Seconds turned into minutes, which turned into quarter segments of time. The cream bun which had been so carefully sourced and brought over for me to meet its chosen fate by the cute, now angry-at-me sarcastic fair maiden, along with what was meant to be my moans of pure enjoyment as it was being consumed, did not happen. Well, not during that first hour anyway.

By now, J.P. arrived back at the authors tent from his feast, which consisted of midgets and honey-glazed crickets. He was briefed on the events that had occurred while he was gone. His eyes noticed the delicate delight was *still* sitting where it had been so carefully placed sixty minutes before by Danica. Not one to miss an opportunity for revenge, Mr. Sexton openly shared his stewed thoughts for everyone to hear:

"How the hell does that mad hoor allow that to sit for an hour without taking a nibble out of it? Jesus, at our house in Donegal, that would never have stood a chance. It would have been inhaled, devoured in one bite, and washed down with a mug of hot tea."

What J.P. did not realize is, since I had done so much talking, even on his behalf, I didn't have any time to eat. In true and tested fashion, I've been told I could talk the leg of a stool. A pure measurement in having the gift of the gab! Since I am a very slow eater, possibly because of spending so much time waffling away, the poor cream bun sat for another full hour.

By this time, I too was growing hungry and decided that a wee break was needed away from books and banter. Kindly offering to take on the role of promoting my story along with his own, J.P. even sold a few books on my behalf. That was, however, until I came back to the tent after my own feast and saw he had signed *my* name to *his* book! Suddenly, I was transformed into Greg McVicker: author of The Big Yank!

He must have been consumed by the mouthwatering delicacy sitting in front of him that he himself forgot who he was, or who I was, or simply put, he assumed my very identity. J.P. Sexton: The Belfast Child . . . and here he said I was a mad hoor, the cheeky auld frigger. He needs to be locked up in The Crum, which is known as the Crumlin Road Gaol in Belfast! Even though it is used as a tourist attraction these days, I'm sure they could find him a spot.

Anyhow, upon discovering J.P.'s newly-crowned identity, this led to pandemonium within the Irish Authors' Corner. As a full-out slagging was beginning to unfold, Barbara came over to see what all the chaos was about. From this, a superb photo op was granted in which J.P. declared, "Well, if I'm going to be mistaken for Greg McVicker, the near Belfast Child from Newtownabbey and Irish author of The Big Yank, I may as well get stuck into his food."

He then set about to take a mouthful. Prior to that, the scrumptious morsel had actually sat untouched for over four hours. In reflection, the only time I managed to consume any of it was after we closed the authors tent for the night and started walking throughout the festival grounds, taking in late-night entertainment, which was already well underway, including acts such as Connla, Jiggy, We Banjo Three, and The Willis Clan.

It was at the Wake House that I stopped to ask if this was where the dead man lives, and finally began engaging in what else but another full-fledged conversation while having a few bites to celebrate the life of the stuffed mannequin lying there with coins placed over his eyes, the poor soul. As I stood looking into the coffin, I shared a moment of my deepest respect and muttered infamous words heard at countless Irish wakes throughout Northern Ireland: "Ack, sure he looks just like himself, so he does!"

And with that, my dear Diary, began the birth of an urban legend: Dubh Linn Borróg Uachtar, a grá mo chroí! Loosely translated, it simply means Dublin Cream Bun, love of my heart!

Chapter 3: Embassy . . . Sweets!

Date: Thursday, August 1, 2019.
Entry 2: He moves in mysterious ways!
Location: Room 924 - Embassy Suites - Dublin, Ohio.
Time: Far too early in the day.

Dear Diary . . .

My attempt at keep a wee written log about how things have been pretty much failed, so they did. Since it has been two years since I last wrote in you, perhaps I should write "Dear Brain" for this entry. Choices, choices. Brain? Diary? Ack, but sure, it is all the same when I think about it. A place to leave my mad ideas. One inside my skull, the other within my hands.

In case you're wondering, it's me, the Belfast Child, an Irish lad who pours his heart and soul into you. I wonder why I take such long breaks in between writing these entries. What am I afraid of? My thoughts flow effortlessly through the ballpoint tips of pens, the ink becomes one with the embracing parchment of your pages as it parts ways with its hollow tube, leaving structured paragraphs in its wake. I wander through skillfully-crafted handwriting from decades so long ago, abandoned words that left no eyes welling with tears, no mouths drooling with hunger. No, you are the only one lucky enough to see the thoughts that spilled from my charismatic mind.

Yeah, right! Who am I trying to kid? More like a tormented one at that. The reason no one gets a chance to read through these pages is because my thoughts didn't flow onto these pages, they were dumped here. Now I'm left to sort this mess out, then write books while sitting in front of a computer screen. Ha. Writing with ballpoint pen on rough parchment. My handwriting skills went by the way of the dodo bird years ago. Anyways, what do they call this? Brainstorming? Why not a stormy brain . . . mine! My ma always said I was a bit of a daydreamer. I can't imagine why. My sister openly told stories of my serious childhood misadventures. Sigh. It could be argued that she told them better than I do.

I had to go back and read what I last wrote to you from when I was in Dublin, Ohio two years ago. Has it been that long already? Sheesh, not good. But guess what? Here I am once again! I left at four a.m. this morning from Winnipeg and flew in. How I find the energy to write at the moment is beyond me; perhaps it is the delight at being invited to take part in this years' Irish Festival. The lovely organizers asked me back, although I don't exactly know why. The last time we were here, there were countless shenanigans, rowdy banter, and general madness over at the Irish Authors' Corner. I suppose you could say J.P. Sexton and I were behind much of it. If I do say so myself, he's a bad influence on me. It must be part of his Viking heritage!

Upon my arrival this morning, I was met by Nick Bova at the airport. Mike was not here to drive me over to the hotel, although it would have been fantastic to see him as well. Instead, there was a tour bus waiting for me and a couple of musicians. Did I miss a memo? Was I supposed to bring my recorder and accompany those two on stage? Is this the rock n' roll life I have always dreamed of? I suppose I will get those answers later.

Where was I? Oh, yeah, lost in my memories. I am supposed to be writing a chapter for my next book, but since I get easily distracted, my thoughts get carried away to the world of the faeries. Perhaps I should get back to writing about my childhood, how much of a daydreamer I was. If my mum were here to tell you this herself, she would say I always lived in my own wee world. Or perhaps I should be writing this as a letter to my mum and my sister, Karen. I miss you both dearly. I'm sure you are looking down on me at this very moment and saying, "Aww, look at our poor wee Greg. He was always so special – mad, but special. We did say his head was full of hobby horses' shite, so we did!"

Ma, you would tell me that if my brains were made of dynamite, I couldn't part my hair, especially when it came to me getting my work done. Had I received one penny every time you shared your loving thoughts, such as,

"Gregory! Enough actin' the eejit or you'll get my toe up your hole," I would still be skint. I'm getting carried away with my memories here so that's enough of that. But what I would give to hear you tell me that one more time.

With you being the oldest, Karen, you also kept me in line. Life has not been the same since you were both called away. I believe you hear me talk to you every day in my thoughts. I pray you see every word I write. I love and miss you like there is no tomorrow. As for right now, it is no different. In *Absent Friends*, a song written and recorded by legendary Irish musician, Pat McManus on his album *Blues Train to Irish Town*:

> *So, won't your raise your glass,*
> *and we'll gladly drink to absent friends.*
> *Someday, one day, far away I know,*
> *I know we'll meet again.*

As I was saying, I had flown down quite early this morning to Columbus to try and get a jump start on my fellow authors, especially that Arthur Colaianni lad. I'm still trying to figure him out. I believe he's Italian and lives in Wisconsin, but he writes about Ireland and leprechaun kings. I have yet to make the connection between all three of these descriptions of him, unless there is a secret, Irish mafia residing in the underworld, operating out of Italy, that love cheese curds and are no taller than three feet in height. Picture this: **The Leprechaun Godfather.** Wow, I'm sure that's quite the story to be told.

Regardless of Arthur and his tactics of scoping out the Irish Authors' Corner before anyone else arrives, I wanted to have a quick nap and then freshen up, especially for the cute, green-eyed, sarcastic fair maiden. I heard she is flying in later today. And, since I haven't seen her in a year, I hoped we could all go and have a phenomenal supper and a pint at the Dublin Village Tavern. Their roast beef dinners come trimmed with mashed potatoes, peas, gravy, and two massive Yorkshire puddings and a cup of tea. Couple this with a Dublin Cream Bun, and the perfect feast awaits. I am sure a meal of this size could feed the five thousand!

Afterwards, I am going to sit with the Striking Viking and continue planning our upcoming Dublin Irish Festival demonstration. Mr. Sexton and I have had many a wild conversation in the back of transport vehicles driven by Mike, Skip and Adam. They have been privy to us discussing our own wee presentation called *Belfast Riots on Tour.* As it is still in the works and will likely require several permits and official permission from the City of Dublin, Ohio, it's best if I keep the details to a minimum.

In saying that, though, it does involve large vats of Danny Houton's Inishowen Peninsula Poitín as part of our *Funeral for a Viking* play; that is, providing J.P. doesn't drink the place dry before we even get started. Danny was

J.P.'s grandfather whom I read about in *The Big Yank* and in a book of Irish stories which I wrote with him and Irish Californian author, Mark Rickerby called *Four Green Fields: Wild Irish Banter and Stories, Shenanigans and Poetry*. The stories about Danny are truly beyond measure! As for J.P., unless he has direct access to someone who can make miracles happen, or knows something about instant reincarnation, I question if he realizes we will only get to set him on fire the once? This show will most likely become a one-hit wonder. Ack, but sure, God loves a trier! Hopefully this grants us enough clemency for all of our blasphemy and shenanigans at the Dublin Irish Festival while standing outside the pearly gates with St. Peter. Otherwise, we're doomed!

Now where was I? Oh yes, the fair maiden lass. The aforementioned "Professional Cat Herder" was just one of many endearing labels bestowed upon her due to her talents and strenuous efforts to keep track of people. As much as I would prefer to deny it, that does include me. So much so, coffee mugs were made describing this as being her regular profession. Who knew that a free spirit such as myself could take others just like her on such a wild ride?

I must give her my respect, though, as she holds down the fort when I disappear. I've been told I wander off and engage in random meet-and-greets – repeatedly! I prefer to call it networking. Since I hail from Northern Ireland, or Norn Iron as well call it, unfortunately, I was granted the gift of the gab. Thus, I come by it honestly and may as well make the most of it. On the other hand, Jim McVeigh says I was appointed the Irish Ambassador to a small Venezuelan Island, a title as bestowed upon me from the Irish Consul General to Chicago, Brian O'Brien. This was during one of my many absences, umm, I mean my many networking engagements, although I was meant to be in the Irish Authors' Corner, signing books to those who stopped by to say a wee hello. There may be a hint of validity to his statement. Note: Never look a guitar player from the New Lodge Road in the eye, specifically if his name starts with Jim and ends with McVeigh! I will continue my thoughts on that Belfast bloke in just a while.

Speaking of musicians, when I boarded my flight this morning, I did not realize that the two musicians who accompanied me on that flight in Minneapolis and now here in Dublin are from the Irish folk band, Altan. One plays an instrument, the other tours as a stage manager with the group. Anyhow, as the three of us made our way over to the Embassy Suites, I recall one of them speaking about Ray Fean. He drums for Celtic Woman, Jiggy, along with Horslips – the founding fathers of Celtic rock,. The first and last time I saw Horslips was in 2009 in Belfast. Ray had two cymbals which spiraled down toward the drum riser. It was as if he had a snake on either side of him, almost like St. Patrick. I wonder if he is the second coming of our Patron Saint. I went to the gig with our

Molly Kavanagh. She's been the best of friends with the lads in Horslips since they first formed. Fantastic choice in music, Molly. Rock On! And although you can't hear or see this message, I send you, P.K. and the entire McManus clan all my love! I miss you all dearly!

Anyway, the reason for me penning this entry in the first place is that there was a precious gift left outside of my hotel room shortly after my arrival this morning and once I got settled in. It was a wee Dublin Cream Bun! Yet, the strange thing is there was a note attached to it on the tray simply read, *"To our Belfast Child, with love . . ."*

I wasn't sure if someone was taking the cake or in this case, leaving a bun. There was a knock at my door but when I went to answer it, strangely, there was no one there. Although I am in a spacious hotel and looked in every direction, I still did not see anyone! I honestly feel like I'm walking in the shadows of giants here. Unless our International Man of Mystery is staying here as well, there is absolutely no way anyone could have knocked, then disappeared so quickly. The curtains are wide open. As for me, I am sitting at the table overlooking the vast space of the hotel, no one has passed by my window. What gives?

I don't quite understand why was I picked to get one of these special treats? I noticed since I arrived here, it has been strangely quiet. How did anyone know where I was staying, or which room I was in? I thought the hotel staff kept that information secret. Even though my ma always did say to never look a gift horse in the mouth, this is a wee bit on the ridiculous side.

Oh, hang on a wee sec, there's someone knocking at the door . . .

Okay, Diary, this is getting to be a bit much already. You won't believe what happened just now. I opened my door, and again there was no one about! Yet, a bottle of Five Farms Irish Cream sat on the floor at my feet with a tag attached to it that reads, *"From your friendly neighbourhood, Silly Billy . . ."*

I honestly don't quite know what to make of this. The handwriting on the card exactly matches that of my own childish scrawl when I signed the fourth book in my current series of six. It's called *The Adventures of Silly Billy – Sillogy, Volume 1.* It's a trilogy of silly stories based on my childhood misadventures growing up in Newtownabbey, thus it became a Sillogy. Although I sign each book with this inscription, the ink on the wee card is fresh. Whoever is behind this has disappeared without a trace . . .

I have an ominous, sinking feeling about this. My shamrock senses are tingling. Something is seriously afoot. I am racking my brains - well, whatever brains I have according to my parents' loving commentary on the space between my ears. Greg, come on, man. Concentrate. Think about it! The first time you sunk your teeth into a Dublin Cream Bun was when Danica picked up that magnificent puff pastry from Schmidt's and brought it into the author's tent. In turn, it created the urban legend. She's not here right now, so that rules her out.

Who's behind this? What's the reasoning? Am I overthinking this? Who would have left me such an awesome treat, knowing my love of those glorious dainties? But to also leave me a bottle of Five Farms Irish Cream as well? Maybe this is part of the new welcoming gift from the beautiful committee members who make the Dublin Irish Festival what it is. Perhaps I should ignore my thoughts, listen to my gut, and take a bite to satisfy my cravings before washing it all down with a shot or two. Oh, what harm would it do if I did . . .

No, follow your instincts! As much as I appreciate the sentiment, what was it that the two wee cards said again?

"To our Belfast Child, with love . . ." "From your friendly neighbourhood, Silly Billy . . ."

To sign both items – one in my book name, the other as my childhood self? This does not make sense. I wonder if it is the eight-foot plus Fabio look-alike getting me back for my never-ending hooliganisms and shenaniganism's. If so, he's doing a good job of it for it is sending a serious case of the heebee-jeebies straight up my spine!

I had better keep writing my thoughts down here all the same. What about you, Karen? What do you think? Call the Ghostbusters? I enjoy having a bit of craic like the rest of them, but this is unnerving. As soon as I know, I'll write a wee update in here and give you an update. Give mum my best and please keep me safe on this journey. I'm sure you already know this – I love and miss you both . . .

Hey, wait a minute. When I was in the hallway after that last knock at my door, I saw that the bus driver who transported myself and the Altan folks to the Embassy Suites was resting down in the lobby. He was quite a nice fellow, extremely helpful to us all. Frig, I totally forgot to leave him a tip for his service. That's not like me!

The best tip I could offer him right now would be, *"Keep your friends close; keep your enemies closer"*, although my ma used to say one good deed deserves another! I bet he'd love a wee Dublin Cream Bun from Schmidt's along with the bottle of Five Farms Irish Cream. Awesome idea! I'll call the hotel staff and ask them to make him a hot mug of tea. With them running a distraction, and since he likes to talk just as much as I do, I'll be able to sneak on to his bus and leave both of these items as a wee gift for him. Maybe that will give me the clues I need to figure out who is behind this, and why!

Chapter 5: Well, That's Pure Crummy

The ominous dark clouds stretched like fingers of death from the curse announced by Moses in *The Ten Commandments*. Arthur stood at the window of his Embassy Suites room watching spires of brilliant August sunshine breaking through the clouds to reveal the turquoise morning sky beyond.

A knock on the door startled him. No one would be up and ready before him, he thought. He checked his Mickey Mouse watch, which confirmed that there was plenty of time to meet his fellow authors for breakfast before heading out to the Dublin Irish Fest grounds. They would all be housed in a tent located on a little hill overlooking the vast expanse of the festival plain which once was a corn field. For this Dublin was in the heartland of America, in a place called Ohio. He turned away from the half-day and half-night scene hanging over the city of Dublin and made his way to the door, grabbing his backpack from the desk chair, though he couldn't tell you as to why he did that. In the end it didn't matter. The only thing important was that he would arrive at the tent before any of the other authors, as was his custom.

Placing the backpack on the carpeted floor, he slowly opened the door and found no one on the other side. As he began to shut it again with a curse on his lips for having been startled, the glistening of the sugary frosting of what turned out to be a cream bun caught his eye. Stooping down, he gently folded the ends of the napkin on which it lay and lifted it to his nose for a quick sniff followed by a sigh of joy when inhaling the delightful sweet smell. Just as he brought it to his lips to taste the renowned treat of the fest, something made him stop.

"Why the hell would I eat something found on the floor of a hotel?" he asked himself. He thought better of it and left it on the bathroom counter.

Swinging the backpack over his shoulder, he left for the elevator only to find the entire third floor oddly devoid of people. He looked over the railing and down onto the cavernous lobby. It too was without people save for a staff person near the waterfall. He looked at Mickey once again and thought he was still on Central time, but that wouldn't have made any difference as it would be an hour later in Ohio and therefore there should be people about.

Looking out the elevator window, which was really its back wall, he noticed a figure in black. It appeared almost as a shadow streaking across the lobby but with clothes on. By the time he ran to the entrance door to catch that person, he found only the shuttle bus waiting and no one in sight except the driver, who was useless in providing any information as he was sitting in the bus and listening to, what else, Irish music. Arthur rather enjoyed hearing the tune *Fiddler's Green* as it was featured in his newest novel.

Jumping onto the bus as a leprechaun might do from land to his pot o' gold, he decided to get to the fest and be there first, as usual. He would be the only passenger going to the festival grounds. That sweet smell of the cream bun lingered and was making him wish he had eaten the treat. Looking up from his unsuccessful foraging through his backpack for a Snickers bar, he noticed that the driver was eating a duplicate of what had been left for him. If one were to watch him at that point, they would have gotten a glimpse of a plump little man just opening his sack on Christmas Eve and not that of a slightly taller version of the magical leprechaun he thought himself to resemble.

When he disembarked, the winds were picking up speed. He tugged down on his beige cap with the Irish Harp embroidered on it, lest it blow into the darkening sky. He turned to thank the driver but was too late. The shuttle driver's seat was empty. Only the remains of the cream bun lay on the seat.

Thinking that he was destined to starve that morning, Arthur made his way to the mound on which the ***Irish Authors' Corner*** tent was located. Within it would soon be a collection of writers coming from sea to shining sea, from across the fruited plains and as far away as the Emerald Isle itself. Here they would flock with their tales of legends, magic, history, fantasies, poetry, Irish Dance, thrillers, love, and bloody murders. The wind whipped around him as he stood looking at the discolored canvas of the tent wrapped around poles to present on that morning of cream bun joy found and rejected. To his historical nature, it appeared like an ancient tomb of stone found near the Cliffs of Moher rather than a tent lined with tables for each author to display creative efforts that flocks of visitors would hopefully seek.

Lifting up a flap of overlapping canvas, he peeked in. An eerie green glow permeated the interior. He scanned the tables looking for his. Stepping inside, he realized the green light was not some mysterious extraterrestrial phenomena but came from a string of green Shamrock lights someone had forgotten to disconnect from the previous night. Standing in the middle of the tent he thought, "What a perfect scene this would be for a murder mystery. All that would be needed is for some green creature to appear and attack him."

He shuddered and smiled at his cleverness as he turned right to walk over to his table across from The Book Loft's checkout station. He stopped in his tracks as the purple plastic bin containing his books sat upon his assigned table like a coffin upon a bier. Its translucent sides picked up the eerie light and reflected it in a purplish green glow. Just as he was appreciating the spookiness of the appearance of his bin, he noticed something was lying on top of it.

The wind was now howling as the sides of the tent billowed in and out. Arthur was frightening himself with all his thoughts of murder scenes and missing shuttle drivers. Nevertheless, he approached his table to inspect that which lay upon the bin. On a napkin with Embassy Suites embossed at the corner were the remains of yet another cream bun. It was fresh, thus couldn't have been left from the previous night.

Deciding to check out each author's table to see if cream bun remains were located on them, he wrapped the bun in the napkin and brought it with him on his light investigation. His efforts brought him little success save finding a few crumbs, undoubtedly from a cream bun. They did however create a trail of sorts which led him to that of the sponsor of the Author's Tent, The Book Loft. There he found a white bakery box tied with a green ribbon in the place of the cash register.

As he hesitated over whether he should open the box or call for security, he realized that the scent coming from it was the same as that which came from the treat left at his door and that of which the shuttle driver munched on coming over from the hotel. He felt safe in revealing the contents of the box. Slithering behind the very row of tables on which he found the trail of crumbs was the same shadowy figure he had spotted streaking across the lobby from the elevator. Perhaps it was that Old-Fashioned he drank the previous night, the first in his life, which made his senses a bit numb. He never heard a sound of the approaching shadow. His hands were busily untying the ribbon as the black-gloved hands of the shadow grabbed him across his mouth and about his chest. In what seemed to be an instant, he was dragged from the tent and into the dark morning, now breaking once again into sunlight.

When the authors began to file into the tent later that morning, they were amazed not to find the elder statesman of their band of writers there to greet them. Only the box with the untied ribbon, and a backpack lying in front of the checkout station, gave any clue that he or someone had been in the tent.

Chapter 7: Investigation or Interrogation

Ann and I were cruising southbound on Interstate 71 at a comfortable speed of sixty-five miles-per-hour in the seventy mile-per-hour zone, enjoying the soothing music of Enya, when my cell phone cut our enjoyment of *Only Time.*

"Hello," I answered.

"Mike, this is Greg McVicker. We have a problem at the festival. Arthur is missing and something is amiss. We need your investigative experience right away. Can you hurry here?"

"Greg, we're about ten miles out," I said. "I'll step on it."

After clicking off, I told Ann, "There's an emergency at the Dublin Irish Festival and they need me now."

"Let's hustle," Ann replied.

I stepped on the accelerator and jettisoned up to sixty-eight miles-per-hour, then reached over to activate the four-way flashers. Now in emergency mode, the other cars opened up a pathway for us to move forward, and off we went, still staying under the seventy-mile-per hour limit, of course.

"Ya know," Ann observed. "I always thought there was something odd about Arthur. He frequently disappears and goes off somewhere. I wonder where he goes."

"This is a big one, Ann," I said. "No time to think bad things about Arthur. Everyone's concerned."

Taking the exit ramp off Route 71 onto Route 270 West, an Ohio State patrol car rolled up next to me. I was able to roll down the window and shout, "Retired Investigator, now re-activated! We need to get to the Dublin Irish Festival." He gave me the thumbs up, turned on his emergency lights, and pulled in front of me to initiate the escort. The familiar sound of the siren brought back memories of daring, superhuman exploits of my earlier days. Oh, how I miss those exciting calls and the voice of the dispatcher saying, "You got it, Mike, go take care of it." My heart was pounding as thoughts of good triumphing over evil filled my memory.

We approached exit 17 and my mind snapped back to the current emergency as I focused on my surroundings, making mental notes of people, their movements, vehicles with sketchy drivers avoiding my trained inspection, along with the smells and sounds of any devious deeds. We pulled off onto Emerald Parkway, where the state patrol officer let me advance onto the festival grounds. I gave him a thank you salute and zipped down to the maintenance garage where a golf cart awaited. The four B.F. Goodrich's that served me so well screeched to a halt as a cloud of dust and pebbles bounced and vaulted out of the way. I jumped out, taking my trusted sleuth's bag with me, as Ann and I hustled to the cart.

"Oh no, Ann," I said. "You can't go in the cart. This is top investigative business. You need to go in a different cart."

"Yes, I understand," Ann said knowingly, having been an investigator's wife for thirty-seven years.

Arriving at the Irish Authors' Corner, I was greeted by Greg.

"Still no Arthur," *h*e said anxiously. "His books are here but he's gone as if some supernatural power lifted him away."

"Supernatural power?" I said. "How could that be? We need to think of some suspicious person or occurrence caused Arthur's absence, not a supernatural phenomenon."

"Get on it right away, Mr. Investigator," said Greg before muttering, "Magnum P.I., eat your heart out!"

"Let's start with a roll of yellow caution tape and protect the scene of his disappearance. There could be valuable evidence hiding from our unsuspecting eyes. Next, we'll set up a search team and do a crisscross pattern throughout the grounds."

"It's not like he's a small diamond ring concealed in the grass," said Sinead. "A straight linear pattern should be sufficient."

"He is a small diamond in the rough, that guy is," said Greg.

"Enough of the small talk," I said. "We'll start with the linear search like Sinead suggested, while always watching for clues like footprints or dropped breadcrumbs from Arthur. Then, if needed, we'll change our pattern to fit our clothes."

"Cloth," said Brenna from the background.

"What?" said I. "Do you have something with cloth?"

"*Pattern to fit your cloth,* is the saying," said Brenna.

"Right, like a herringbone pattern, which clothes are made of," I said.

Brenna raised her eyebrows and looked skyward in exasperation.

"What's this?" I said, pointing to a hole covered by caution tape in the pattern of an "X" in front of the cash register.

"Just a warning of the hole so no one twists their ankle," said Julie from The Book Loft.

Suddenly, Patricia Hopper Patteson, one of the authors, said, "Mike, Laura the festival's Assistant Director is here."

"What do you have?" said Laura.

"One of our authors is missing," I said. "It's unusual that nobody knows where he is."

"Who is missing?" said Laura.

"Arthur Colaianni," I said.

Laura had a puzzled look on her face, "Who's that? We don't have an Arthur Colaianni in the Irish Authors' Corner."

"It's Arthur, Arthur Cola," I said. Then it hit me like a ton of Cream Buns falling off the back of the Schmidt's delivery truck. Arthur had an alias; the little Italian Irish author had an assumed identity. He infiltrated our close Irish network to spy for the Mafioso. I decided to tuck that investigative lead into my retentive memory bank. That void had been purged since I retired.

"We can call the police in to assist," said Laura.

"Right now, he is only missing," I said. "Let's check further, and if we need the police, I'll let you know. We have secured his table where he was last seen, just in case."

"Keep me informed," said Laura.

"I will. Also, can we have a few of the volunteers to do a methodical search of the grounds? We'll be done within the hour before the gates open."

Laura nodded and said, "I will send ten people down to help."

"Perfect," I said. "What was Arthur wearing?"

Sinead spoke up, "He had on a lime green, short-sleeve, collared shirt and green shorts with white socks pulled up taut over his ankles."

"Like a professional over-sixty, Italian Bocce player?" I asked.

"Well, I guess like that," said Sinead.

"Okay," I said. "Now the rest you, go to your stations. I have to check on something first, but then I'll come around and interview each of you separately."

I left the tent area in my official investigator's golf cart - unmarked, of course, as all investigators' vehicles are. I zipped down to the Community Center and went into the green room. "I need a nice, cold Gatorade."

The volunteer helper spoke up, "Aren't you . . . haven't I seen you on TV before? No, I think it was YouTube. You look so familiar. I know! You sing *Irish* songs!"

"Nice guess for a green room volunteer," I said. "But no, I'm a crack investigator. What I mean is, I crack mysterious crimes and bring people to justice." I stopped to think about her question and then said, "I was in the newspaper once, directing traffic at a fire scene, maybe that story went across the Associated Press network. Sorry, I didn't smile for the picture."

"Oh, I must have mixed you up with a banjo player I was thinking of," she said.

"Ah, a banjo player, *Deliverance* is one of my favorite movies. However, I must get to work on another mystery. I'll be just outside the door if any calls come in for me."

I went outside and caught each shuttle driver as they made their stops. They all got the same question, "Did you transport any short, Italian-looking, grey-haired men slightly taller than a leprechaun back to the hotel today?

He calls himself Arthur but I'm not sure that's his real name."

The answers were very similar. "An Italian-looking leprechaun? I think I would've notice that, or even slightly tall leprechauns." They each had something to add when I asked about the authors riding in the vans. I made note of the peculiar habits as they reported them. One driver noted, "Inquisitive people, always wanting to know about the festival, the people we transport, even my working hours and habits. Nosy people, them authors. Why do you ask?"

"I'm an investigator and an author," I said.

"Oh, it figures, you're twice as bad as the rest of them."

"Good compliment, my dear man, and thank you for your time."

I returned to the tent with a notebook full of odd author behavior. Oh, the things you learn about your friends when you dig into their past. I was now ready to interview each author knowing that if Arthur was just missing or wandered off, someone would find him. But my investigative intuition said, "Foul play!" I sensed that some author's jealousy, distorted reality, or skewed fantasy had led them astray to kidnap or eliminate poor pint-sized author Arthur.

"I'm back," I announced to the group. "I'll be around to each of you shortly."

Starting left to right, I first approached Sinead Tyrone, author of *Crossing the Lough Between*. "So, you're from Buffalo, home of the McKinley assassination." I needed to put her off guard from the start.

"Yes, I am, and President McKinley was killed there one hundred and eighteen years ago," she said, trying to distance herself from the murderous nature of the city. "You know, I work for an attorney; actually, a whole law firm."

I ignored the statement and said, "I learned that the shuttle driver dropped you off at the Crowne Plaza. What where you doing there?"

"Oh, I forgot that we changed hotels and he just said 'okay' when I asked, so I got off, and the lobby was familiar so I didn't think anything of it. I went to my room."

"But you didn't have a key for any rooms in the Crowne Plaza."

"Oddly, the key fit."

"No, no, no, keys don't fit anymore. The keys today are proximity cards done by electronic waves floating through the air."

"My key card worked."

"Let me see it."

"Why?"

"Because, I said so."

"Oh, alright, if I have to," said Sinead as she reached into her handbag and produced a key card.

"This is a Crowne Plaza card," said I. "Are you registered there?"

"I don't think so." Sinead thought for a moment. "Maybe it's last year's card," she happily blurted.

"Not if it opened the door," I said, boxing her story in. "I'm going to keep this card, and when I'm finished here, you and I are going to the Crowne Plaza. What will I find?"

"I keep more books over there," Sinead admitted.

"*Your* books or Arthur's books?"

"Maybe there's some of each. I like Arthur's writing."

"I see. And why did you tell me that you worked for a law firm? Do you need a lawyer with regards to this missing man?" I asked.

"Oh no, no, no, not at all," she said confidently. However, there was a nervous edge to her demeanor, so I asked, "Who would you suspect if anything devious happened to Arthur?"

Sinead explained, "I don't think anyone would do anything to hurt poor Arthur. To think one of our fellow authors had done him harm is unthinkable."

With that, I moved on to the next suspect - I mean author. I approached Mary Carter who was in the process of describing one of her books to an early prospective reader. She had written *Murder in an Irish Village* and other murder mysteries in Irish settings. *She seems a little too comfortable in the ways of deception,* I thought.

Once finished with her spiel, the potential reader said, "I'll stop back later. I don't want to carry books all day." With that, the reader left the Irish Authors' Corner carrying her bags of Irish trinkets, tee-shirts, and an early morning cold Guinness.

"I see you're very crafty with your art," I said. "How did you learn so much about the evil ways of heartless perpetrators?"

"I have a past you don't want to know about," she said.

"Oh, on the contrary! I do want to know about," I said.

"Let's just say I followed a murder case in a Cook County courtroom several years ago. It was intriguing."

"I'm sure it was," I said. "What do you know about Arthur being missing?"

"Not much," said Mary. "I saw him last night after we returned from the festival and he said he had to go to bed soon because he had to get up early."

"What for?"

"He didn't say."

"And you haven't seen him since last night?"

"No," she said. "Not after we were in Room 429 together. You know - you were there. He was drinking, singing, laughing and having a fun time."

"Yes, I remember. Now, who would you suspect if anything happened to Arthur?"

"Anyone is capable, and we all have a reason to eliminate a competitor - including you, Mr. McCarthy." No reaction from me. She continued, "My guess is Greg's tour manager, Danica. She runs his interference, and by eliminating Arthur, Greg would be one of the high-sellers. Of course, Ben needs to be cautious. He may be next."

"What are you saying?" I said.

Mary said, "Ben is a high-seller, and Danica will knock him off so Greg takes the limelight."

"I see. Now don't you go leaving town before this is finished, ya hear?" I said with great authority.

"Why? I haven't done anything."

I moved on to James McVeigh, an author who was born and raised in Northern Ireland, and for some reason thought cold, damp Wisconsin offered a better future. After living there, he wrote children's books about gastrointestinal melees that produce bodily noises titled *The Adventures of Farty McFee.*

"Not a laughing matter for children to read," I thought. "Sick sense of humor, this one!"

"What do you know about this affair?" I started.

He replied, "Did you know that Arthur downed an alcoholic Old-Fashioned last night?"

"I actually saw it happen," I said to make the kinship with the foul-penned author who just sidestepped my question. "What bearing does that have on his disappearance?"

"He's a changed man, having tasted the devil in the bottle," said James.

"Tell me more," I said.

"Don't you see? He's off sneaking behind some tree taking a few nips of the bottle."

"Not so fast, McVeigh," I said. "Arthur is a good man. One drink does not make a fallen derelict."

"Oh, you Americans," said McVeigh. "Not only did he take a drink, a photo was taken and posted on Facebook. He's on the slippery slope."

"Enough of this degradation. The search of the grounds will prove your theory wrong. He will not be hiding behind a tree with a bottle in hand and the smell of cheap whiskey on his breath. I know you were taught by the Jesuits and learned to twist and turn facts around to fit your worldview. Yes, I am going to keep my eyes on you."

"The Jesuits taught me how to think. You should have obtained a Catholic education. It would have helped you in your work."

"I was taught by priests and nuns too. You can't upstage me," I said. I have heard James laugh before but this time he roared with laughter; a complete affront to the investigative process.

I moved to the next author. Speaking of nuns, next was Cindy Thomson, a pious, kindly soul who has always helped any of the authors in need. Her work is *Brigid of Ireland* about another kind soul. The tension of Arthur's disappearance had rattled her to the core, and she lashed out with, "Why are you asking me about Arthur? I don't know anything."

"Easy, Cindy," I said. "You may have knowledge I am unaware of."

"Well if you ask me, I think Danica is behind this. She knows the cream bun and where to get one. She probably took him there for one."

"Cream bun? What is that exactly?"

"It's a delicacy - one bite and you're hooked," said Cindy.

"What's with you people?" I shouted. "First, it's alcohol and now it's a cream bun? You're all imaging that we are going to find Arthur drunk with powdered sugar all over his face. You guys are making him into a regular Hemingway."

I regretted saying that as soon as it left my lips. "My apologies to Mr. Hemingway," I whispered to myself. He's a saint, a glorified one, a most valuable player, a Hall-of-Famer of writers. Oh my, I needed to focus so I could move on and find some credible leads to find our dear Arthur. But Cindy was not through with me yet.

"Maybe J.P. wasn't detained in Dublin after all," she continued.

"J.P. Sexton, the other missing author, you mean? The one denied exit from Ireland? You raise an interesting thought, but it's easy to check. Wait a minute - why did you say that? Have you seen him?"

"No, but I have my doubts," she said.

"I thought you were as pure as a nun, and now I see how devious you are," I said.

"Just a thought," said Cindy flippantly.

I moved toward Laura Treacy Bentley, next in line for an interview, but first I needed a timeout. I reached for my career-saving sleuth's bag in my golf cart, opened it, pushed aside my magnifying glass, and took out a half-empty bottle. I raised the bottle to my lips, took a swig of Gatorade, and let out a satisfied "Ahh." As the liquid flowed into my system, I received my reward in a rush of clarity, energy, and focus. Replacing the cap to save future benefits, I returned to my duty.

"Laura Treacy Bentley," I started. "You came in a little late for the party, didn't you?"

"Whatever do you mean, Mr. McCarthy?" said Laura, taking a swig of her own Gatorade.

"I mean, you arrived late for the festival, or should I say you arrived late to the Irish Authors' Corner."

"Oh, I had other business to tend to before coming to the festival, so I know nothing about Arthur."

"But you know all about disappearing people and criminal activity in your story, such as *The Silver Tattoo.*"

"That's fantasy, not reality," said Laura.

"Small leap from one to another," I said.

"I have credentials, you know," she said.

"I do know," I said. "So did Nancy Crampton Brophy, the Chinese writer Liu Yongbiao, Blake Leibel, Richard Klinkhamer, Juliet Hulme AKA Anne Perry, and Krystian Bala, just to name a few authors-turned-criminals. Krystian Bala wrote the novel *Amok,* where he foolishly described his crime, which led to solving the murder he committed. So you see, authors can have a convoluted approach to reality."

"I have an alibi, and my husband can verify my whereabouts," said Laura.

"I have no doubt of your innocence in Arthur's case. I was merely pointing out any member of society can fall to the misdeeds of life, or should I say . . . death."

"Thank you for pointing that out," said Laura clearly annoyed.

"No offense intended," I said. "But I understand you had a bit to drink last night."

"I was dehydrated and light-headed," she said.

"The shuttle driver thought you were a little tipsy."

"He must have mixed me up with some band member or someone else," she deflected.

"I see," I said. "Those shuttle drivers are pretty smart and observant. On another note, what should happen to someone who abducts Arthur?"

"She should be buried alive in the sand sculpture during a bagpipe serenade," said Laura.

"Whoa, that's a pretty specific punishment. Have you thought about this before, planned something?"

"I like Arthur. He's sweet, and those cheesecake ladies at the Schmidt's truck are sweet on him, too. Gave him a freebie, they did."

"Oh, so you think *they're* behind this?"

"Just sayin'."

"I have nothing further at this time." I said. "Thank you, and certainly feel free to contact me with any thoughts on the matter."

"Sure thing," said Laura.

I moved on and thought, *That didn't go so well; maybe too much Gatorade. I also wondered who was hanging out at the cream bun truck. Is that where everyone goes on their break?*

Next I spoke to Patricia Hopper Patteson, author of *Aunjel,* another look at the world's underbelly. But like Laura, Cindy, Mary, and Sinead before her, Patricia has an untaintedness about her. This interview was short, with little detail until she questioned Arthur's family.

"Who is his family and where are they?" she questioned.

"Why do you bring up his family?" I asked.

"His wife isn't here," she said.

"Ah, yes, a person's absence always is a cause of suspicion," I said sarcastically.

"Well," she said, "there is talk going around that Arthur took a drink last night. Maybe his wife came along with some other family members and swooped him away from all these bad influences."

"Noble thought," I said. "My family would have cheered my social imbibing."

"Exactly. Not a normal reaction, even though it could be this simple answer."

Onward I went, looking for that one clue to tip the scales to Arthur's whereabouts. Greg McVicker was next and the hardest from which to extract information. Not that he wouldn't talk or cooperate, he wouldn't stop talking, and he went on and on about his yearning for a cream bun. I had enough when he said, "I wasn't paying any attention to what you were talking about, "Magnum". Ack, sure I have many squirrel moments, so I do. I was using my Jedi mind power on that sarcastic, cute, wee fair maiden standing over there - The Guke Slinger. You know her as Danica. I'm hoping to make her get a wee Dublin Cream Bun for me from the Schmidt's food truck, so I am."

"Stop!" I finally shouted, "No more cream buns! No more Gatorade for anybody! Or sweets, or caffeine, or Old-Fashioneds!"

"It's an uncontrollable urge, you know," said Greg.

"Let's get this on track," I said. "What do you think happened to Arthur?"

"I think he went into that hole in front of The Book Loft cash register. Do you see it over there? The one with the big orange X marking the spot, so it is. I think it was a leprechaun trap."

Now I know why I retired. Even though I miss the excitement of the flashing lights and sirens, I didn't miss the crazy things people said. "Yes, I see the hole, and you're telling me Arthur stepped in that hole and down he went?"

"No, you got it wrong," said Greg. "Without a doubt, yer woman Julie Burgess, the Book Loft worker - she kidnapped Arthur and pushed him down the hole to use him as part of her Celtic display within the Irish Authors section at The Book Loft. Room 13. It's haunted, so it is. Arthur will be wailing like a banshee. The sound effects will be dead brilliant, so they will."

"And you think *I* got it wrong," I said. "Well, thanks for explaining that to me. Now, what do you think should happen to this person, our Julie from The Book Loft who abducted Arthur and dragged him down that gopher hole?"

"Easy answer. She should be made to drink foreign whiskey from County Antrim, Norn Iron. I think they call it Wee Millie's Bush. You can only imagine what that stuff does to an Irish author. One drop of it against their lips and look out . . . they start playing Lambeg drums!"

"Okay, I have one more question for you, Greg. Have you ever thought about eliminating Arthur from the Irish Authors' Corner?"

Greg's answer: "To be honest, which is my biggest downfall, I thought about eliminating everyone from the tent, so I did. That way, when all the people from the festival came to the Irish Authors' Corner, they would only see me. Since my books will be sold out so quickly, the New York Times will have to list me as THE bestseller, so they will. Say, can you give me a hand with this?"

"Eliminating authors? Well it looks like you already started. Are you working with Julie to eliminate the other authors?"

"No, I didn't help Julie, but I hope she cleans out the tent soon before more customers come in."

I learned early in my career not to dismiss crazy talk because somewhere in all that banter is an element of truth. But what did Greg say that was accurate? Certainly not falling into a rabbit hole or whatever it was. Was there an effort to eliminate competing authors? I moved on.

Next was another fantasy writer, Ben Anderson. His victims, I mean, characters are children in the novel series The McGunnegal Chronicles.

Ben explained his thoughts on Arthur's disappearance, "I last saw Arthur last night going to the elevator at the hotel. After he got off, there was a straw and the smell of lemon. I wondered what Arthur could be up to?"

"Ben, are you saying that Arthur had a kiddie cocktail in the elevator?"

"Um, well, maybe, or an adult cocktail."

"How unlike Arthur to imbibe in such intoxicating beverages," I said. "By the way, did you go to Mass this morning at the festival?"

"Yes, I did," said Ben, avoiding eye contact.

"Was Arthur there?"

"No, I didn't see him."

"Crowded?

"No, not crowded but they were playing hip music with guitars and all. I was distracted."

Now his left eye was twitching.

"I see," said I. Just then, another thought came to me. "Ben, you're knowledgeable about the Otherworld in Celtic mythology. You know, things or beings that live or travel below the surface. I'm not one to believe such ridiculous things, but we are in a Celtic world here. What are your thoughts of that hole over there by the cash register?

"That hole with the tape?" Ben said, "That's just an old gopher hole, like in Caddyshack where that little vermin kept poking his head up. I'm sure the grounds crew put the tape there to keep him down until after the festival.

"Never mind," I said. "Next!

Eddie Price was next, the award-winning author of *Widder's Landing, Life on the Kentucky Frontier* as well as children's books like *Little Miss Grubby Toes Steps on a Bee.* It's hard to interview a person with a life-size Elmo sitting on his lap. Each question I asked Eddie was answered by Elmo.

"Next!" I said. "No, wait a minute. I need a break." I stepped outside the tent and looked skyward. "No rain. Good!

After a moment's rest, I sat down with my long-time friend Jeanne Crane, who I knew had logical and even-tempered thoughts. The question was short and simple: "What do you know?

"Really, nothing," she said. "I haven't seen Arthur since yesterday at the tent here.

"Thank you," I said and moved on.

Brenna Briggs was next. She was waiting for me with her alibi all ready. I could tell by the look on her face that it would be impossible for her to participate in any deed. Poor Mrs. Briggs, but I'll get to that. First, I took the excuse right away. "I know you can't move very well, but you just may be the mastermind behind this."

"Oh, I know you think I'm behind this, but how could I ever orchestrate such a devious deed?"

Just then her son, Shannon, came running into the tent. "Anything I can do for you, mother?"

I just looked at her.

"Okay, okay, I have help but I would never knowingly harm anyone."

"I understand," I said. "But Shannon, do you have a moment?"

He looked at his mother to see whether anything was pressing. "No problem," he said after getting the nod from mom.

"What do you know about Arthur?" I said.

"Who is Arthur? An author?" said Shannon.

"Yes, and he is missing."

"I don't know the man. I only make sure Mom gets what she needs."

"Yes, I know," I said. "Thank you for your time."

Shannon left the tent as I moved to Therese Gilardi, author of *Narvla's Celtic New Year*. "Anything you can add to Arthur's disappearance? Any unusual happenings over the last couple of days while sitting next to his table?"

"Nothing that I noticed," said Therese.

"I see," said I.

I conducted a visual examination of Arthur's table with his books stored in boxes overnight. He had a few receipts of his sales tucked into one of the boxes. I left everything intact and untouched just in case it turned into a criminal case.

Terence O'Leary, the only remaining author, came into the tent. He was unaware of Arthur's disappearance, had no knowledge of him, and hadn't seen him.

That left two non-authors to interview, Julie Burgess, The Book Loft employee who enjoyed being the unofficial coordinator of the Irish Authors' Corner, and Danica, Greg's unofficial coordinator of activities, lovingly referred to as his Professional Cat Herder.

I started with Danica. "Just so I can clarify how you ended up in the Irish Authors' Corner, your connection is with Greg McVicker, the Belfast Child?"

"That's right."

"You monitor his activities so he doesn't stay in one place too long, and you herd him to his next responsibility. In other words, you watch out for him, right?"

"Right!"

"You even once said that you were in *his indentured servitude*?"

"Yes, I said that," said Danica. "I am there for cheap labor - for set up, tear down and paperwork, while he dazzles the patrons with his witty, mesmerizing banter."

"Got it. And you watch his table when he wanders off or has a speaking engagement, takes a lunch break, and so forth?"

"Not exactly, I go to lunch with him, sometimes," Danica said.

"Understood," I said. "Not only that but you watch or sell J.P.'s books too?"

"Yeah, J.P. couldn't make it here. You know the story."

"Yes, he's missing, too. I know," I said.

"He's not missing, he's in Dublin. In Ireland."

"He's supposed to be here but he's not. Arthur is supposed to be here but he's not. Somewhere there's supposed to be a cream bun, but there's not one here. And you promote, coordinate, sell, and handle Greg's book business, right?"

"Well, I . . ."

"I what?" I inquired. "This little charade can stop here before it gets too ugly. Where's Arthur? You know, the high-selling, non-Irish author - while you sit there with an authentic, full-blooded Irishman - make that two Irishmen including J.P. Or have you eliminated J.P. too?"

"I have done no such thing, Mr. Investigator!"

I think I had her on the edge of tears, but I wasn't in the mood for a sobbing marshmallow during this intense investigation so I said, "Just checking." I smiled before moving on. "By the way, where were you this morning?"

"I had breakfast with Mad Dog McVicker. We joined other fellow authors in the hotel breakfast area. I can't honestly say I remember Arthur being there or not. A bit of Guke the night before had left my brain a bit foggy. I know I saw Arthur at breakfast that weekend, but to say Sunday was one, I'm honestly not sure.

I did notice he wasn't at the tent right away in the morning when we arrived, but didn't really think anything of it, as I thought he may have been at the mass. Not knowing exactly when mass was, as I'm not always so inclined, and not Catholic, I didn't really think another thought about it."

"Pretty detailed account," I said. "You know what Sherlock Holmes said - *The lady doth protest too much, methinks.* Maybe you're hiding something."

"It was Shakespeare, Hamlet, Act III, Scene III," said Greg's fair young maiden.

"Right, whatever," I said. "And you are blaming the Guke, the Guckenheimer cheap whiskey you use for the Old-Fashioneds, for your failure to remember the important details."

"I think you are overlooking the festivals *little people,*" said the Professional Cat Herder.

"You mean the children?" I asked.

"No, the wee people, the fairies and leprechauns. Maybe they thought he was one of their own."

"Maybe," I said. "So, I'll ask again – where's Arthur?"

"I don't know. I personally have never thought about eliminating Arthur from the Irish Authors' Corner. I enjoy his books and am anxiously awaiting the new mysteries! Plus, he's a fellow Wisconsinite, living in Burlington, about twenty minutes from my house. I will add that Jim McVeigh is also now a fellow Wisconsinite, a mere half hour beyond Arthur."

"Yes, the wonderful state of Wisconsin, home of the Cheeseheads."

That left Julie. I walked over to her station. Brian, her assistant, volunteered to take over while I had a little chat with Julie.

"What can you tell me about Arthur's disappearance?"

Julie said, "I am simply *shocked* by Arthur's disappearance. However, I'm just a simple bookseller. I know nothing, aside from the business dealings of the festival."

"But you were here early this morning, weren't you?" I said.

"I was," said Julie. "I was in the Irish Authors' Corner as per usual, where Arthur is usually my first author to be set up and ready to sell."

"Do you believe Arthur is really missing?" I asked.

"I would have said abducted in years past," she said. "I recently learned that Arthur Cola was in fact, Arthur

Colaianni, a name I may have known when I was younger, but I can no longer state anything definite.

"The Italian connection, I presume.

"Yes, but I prefer not to speak of it further, you know," said Julie.

"Oh yes, I know what happens to those who rat them out. I prefer to call them witnesses."

"My thought is," started Julie, "he was telling me he was beginning to dabble in murder mysteries. I believe you should ask Mary Carter, and also Mrs. Laura Treacy Bentley. I can see both taking issue. Then again, I suspect the obvious, those we never see - you know, J.P. and Mark Rickerby."

I asked, "Have you ever thought about eliminating Arthur from the Irish Authors' Corner?"

Julie said, "I have never eliminated anyone from the Irish Authors' Corner, except the Circus guy, oh, and the Fairy, and that one donkey guy. I would never eliminate a Colaianni. I know better."

"I see," I said. "Thank you."

I felt depleted as I turned away from my colleagues whom I had questioned so pointedly and put them on the spot regarding their thoughts and whereabouts, even questioning their integrity. In one sense, I was happy no one immediately surfaced as suspicious, but I was confident someone was holding out. If so, the cream bun was an important aspect. It had surfaced too many times.

"Mike," said Sinead. "One of the volunteers is here and wants to talk to you."

"How can I help you?" I asked an older gentleman in a golf cart.

"The search of the grounds is complete. We didn't find your friend Arthur."

"Thank you, and my compliments to the team for their efforts."

Time had ticked on and no Arthur appeared. I needed to process my thoughts: what's next, who is most likely to have the missing links, and who done it.

The interviews brought to light various theories but no hard evidence. There were a few jealousies, a few were threatened by competing genres, some who had felt the wee people intervened, and then my own prejudices. However, two people stood out in my mind as potential suspects – Greg McVicker and Danica Richardson - should this case become more serious. Indeed, it was Greg that called me on the road, thereby taking the initiative to deflect suspicion from himself, but in all his crazy talk he let out his desire to knock off the other authors one by one. It was his way to the New York Times Bestsellers list. Such an act of treachery is clearly a motive, but he would have to knock off a lot more authors than us to make it onto that list – impractical as it is. He is aided by Danica, and has clearly soured her mind. She hangs on like a cult-follower or a rock star groupie cheerleading his efforts. Hopefully, she hasn't been led into that dark hole of debauchery. Those two need my special attention.

I was going over my notes, when a young festival volunteer came running up. "Mr. McCarthy," he said, breathing heavily. "They just pulled a body out of the pond behind the Community Center. It looks like a wee one."

A chorus of moans could be heard across the Irish Authors' Corner, except for one lone voice – Danica's. "I'm glad it wasn't J.P."

I turned and looked her way. I studied her face, looking for a nervous relief or a tinge of a smile, but she remained stoic. Greg just gave a slow nod.

I turned back to the volunteer and said, "I'll be right there."

Solemnly, I gathered my notes and went to the golf cart. I immediately responded to the pond and found Lieutenant Kavanaugh in charge of the dragging operation.

"Lieutenant," I said. "I am Michael McCarthy, looking into the disappearance of Arthur Cola."

"Yes, I heard. What do you have for me?"

"Before I fill you in on the details, I have one request - that you continue dragging the pond. There may be a second body in there."

He looked puzzled.

"They call him The Big Yank," I said.

Who can say where the road goes
Where the day flows, only time.
~ Enya

Chapter 9: A Recreational Body

Sunday morning. Usually a peaceful time, when gentle daybreak and the soft trills of birdsongs add to the quiet sense of worship and reflection.

This morning, I'd gone for an early swim in our hotel's luxurious pool, then enjoyed a leisurely breakfast with my fellow authors before taking the shuttle over to Irish Festival grounds.

I liked to arrive early enough each morning to reorganize my table setup, say a prayer for a successful day for myself and each of the authors at the Irish Authors' Corner who had become like family to me over the past few years, and then ease my way into the day.

This Sunday, however, the Irish Authors' Corner I stepped into was far from peaceful.

"Arthur's missing!" was the buzz that ran through the tent. "Has anyone seen Arthur?"

Now you have to know, Arthur Cola was the quietest of any of us. A devoted family man. A peaceable man, short in stature but hugely kind, always greeting people with a warm smile. The thought that he could have met with foul play unnerved me. Of all the authors in our circle, Arthur was the last one any of us would expect harm to come to. Sure, Jim McVeigh, whose children's fart stories had no doubt driven many a parent up the wall, could have his detractors among the festival crowd. Ben Anderson, whose massive tomes had certainly broken many a family's budget, could be a target. Brenna Briggs' Irish dancer series most assuredly had become an expensive obsession with young dancers, who would have pleaded and wheeled their way into ownership of the books at their parents' expense, turning many a mother to thoughts of destruction. In fact, as I eyed my colleagues around the tent, I could imagine each one, except me of course, being the recipient of some nasty turn of events, some hateful happenstance.

But not Arthur. Not ever Arthur.

On the other hand, what did I really know about the man? We met once a year at the festival. He always seemed pleasant enough. He had surprised us, though, the night before when we all met at "party central", AKA Room 429 of our hotel, where he'd imbibed one of Danica's (AKA the Guke Slinger's) alcoholic concoctions. We'd never seen that side of Arthur before. He'd turned into quite a funny man after that drink - teasing, cajoling, calling each of us out on various things until tears ran down our cheeks and our sides ached from the laughter.

Thinking back on it now, might he have pushed something a bit too far? Might he have cut someone too deep? In the wee hours of the morning, when I thought we'd all tucked ourselves safely into our beds, might someone have stayed up, coaxed wee Arthur out "for one more nightcap", and done poor Arthur bodily harm?

I eyed my companions with suspicion now. What if the unthinkable had happened? What if, God forbid, Arthur Cola was not merely missing, but, horror of horrors, dead? Could there be a murderer amongst us?

We had no weapons among us, as far as I knew. Certainly, those who had flown to Dublin Ohio could not have concealed a killing tool. Our weapons were pens, our victims characters on paper, not flesh and blood.

On the other hand, Danica had made sure I brought a knife to the party - "to cut the oranges for our drinks" she had said, and I had complied, bringing my sharpest kitchen knife with me. And what of that knife now? My God! If it were found to be a murder weapon, could I possibly be implicated in a murder? I traveled alone! I had no witnesses to back up any alibi I might produce! That was it! I'd been framed! I was going down river! Headed for the big house! Life as I knew it was over!

Get a hold of yourself! I thought. *Put your imagination to rest! Think clearly!*

I thought back to our party scene. Maybe the knife wasn't the murder weapon. That would be too obvious. Surely, in a room full of authors, something more clever would be utilized.

Jim had a guitar, but he would surely not break his beloved instrument for something as silly as murder. His son, Pierce, though, had a washtub bass with a heavy rope. Could that have been the tool by which poor Arthur might have met his demise?

Mary had a shoe that had tried to kill her the first day of the festival! Might she have realized what a powerful weapon it was, and bludgeoned poor Arthur with it?

Danica had a "muddler", a wooden utensil she used in preparing our drinks. Was the red on the end of that muddler really from maraschino cherries?

As I pondered suspects and weapons, Michael McCarthy, fellow author and retired investigator, asked me questions. I answered as best I could, but something struck while I talked with him. A cold shiver ran up my arms, along my neck, and down my back. Something didn't seem right. He was a fine investigator, but perhaps a little too refined in his questioning. After all, a murderer would know just what inquiries would lead the investigation away from a suspect as well as to one.

And what of Ann, his beautiful, and rather quiet, wife - always at his side, until now. Where had she suddenly swanned off to?

I needed time to clear my head of the ugly thoughts now crowding it. A few festival patrons were entering the tent, most of whom were attending one of the various church services on the festival grounds. Lisa and Wendy just dropped Theresa off at the Author's tent. "Could you give me a ride back to the green room?" I asked.

Being the wonderful, accommodating people they are, they replied, "Of course."

They offered to wait while I selected a pastry and tea at the green room commissary, but I declined. I needed longer to think.

As I walked back, I came upon the wishing tree, where people's handwritten notes were affixed with colorful ribbons, all expressing prayers, hopes and dreams. I came across one from fellow author Cindy, expressing wishes for a safe, successful, blessed festival for all.

Then, to the right of that, I spotted something very suspicious. It was written in Irish. When translated, it meant "There will be one less author today".

Even more suspicious, the note had been typed onto a clear label, then affixed to the wishing tree card.

Upon closer examination, I spotted something else. A clue, perhaps. Smudged on the side of the note was something a bit greasy. Oh, wait. I recalled seeing that substance before. Why, it looked like a wee bit of cream from a Dublin Cream Bun.

My shaking became uncontrollable now. Not only was I sure Arthur had fallen victim to some crime, now the entire festival population was suspect.

The only one I could clear in my mind was J.P., our beloved fellow author stranded in the wrong Dublin - Ireland instead of Ohio.

Or was he?

The *International Man of Mystery* we had dubbed him, *"IMOM"* for short. We'd even concocted a song about his being stuck on the wrong side of the big pond. But now I wondered. He was, after all, well versed in espionage, knew how to camouflage himself, how to hide himself away safe from danger, how to appear invisible.

Perhaps his passport mix-up had been a clever ruse, shielding himself from suspicion in the event of any criminal occurrence at the festival.

And he spoke Irish fluently.

And he had a penchant for cream buns.

On the other hand, he could not hate Arthur so much as to want to have the man disappear.

Although Arthur's book sales were increasing while J.P.'s own, due to his supposed absence, declined.

And Arthur last night had drunk J.P.'s share of the Guke concoction.

Should I report my findings and suspicions to Michael, I wondered, or wait until Michael and Ann were more fully cleared in my mind.

I returned to the Irish Authors' Corner with my questions unresolved, only to find a new wrinkle. A body had been found in the pond by the recreation center.

I passed out.

Chapter 11: Elementary, My Dear Arthur

Date:	Sunday, August 4, 2019.
Entry 3:	Social Worker Suspicions!
Location:	Irish Authors' Corner.
Time:	Two hours before gates open.

Dear Diary . . .

I am going to start this entry by saying I am using my social work training to capture what will look like a contact note, so it will. But this is necessary! Never mind what happened to me on Thursday morning at the Embassy Suites with the whole Dublin Cream Bun incident, followed by the bottle of Five Farms Irish Cream. I *still* have not figured out what that was all about. But don't worry, I am not done with that just yet, so I'm not.

There is some serious stuff going down here in Dublin, Ohio. I don't know what to do right now. I am supposed to stay here right through 'til Monday afternoon before catching my flight back to Winnipeg, but I have a feeling I might not be getting out of here then, either.

If you recall, I hoped to beat Arthur Colaianni, Italian Godfather-turned-Irish Leprechaun King, to the Irish Authors' Corner just for a bit of craic. Since he is such an early riser, that idea quickly subsided. I swear he must go there during the witching hour, so he must. I honestly don't know how he does it. Not only that, I've been engaging with a lot of amazing people coming into the Corner who picked up an assortment of books from me. Of course, every one of them has been carefully scribed with a personal note both in Gaeilge and English. That is, with the exception of the *Silly Billy* books, as I scrawl in those with my childish handwriting. But, as I have been exceptionally busy with my usual escapades of networking with as many professionals as humanly possible, I haven't paid much attention to what's been going around me. My mum was right when she said I live in my own wee world.

I am sitting here at my table within the Irish Authors' Corner and need to get these thoughts captured. Looking at the faces of my fellow authors who are gathered, several have looks of shock drawn all over their poor wee gubs. I let them know I would call Michael McCarthy. It was the least I could do at that point. Although I do not know much about him other than seeing him here at the Dublin Irish Festival, as well as joining him the previous year in Buffalo with his wife, Ann, along with Sinead Tyrone and J.P. Sexton, I didn't have much to go on. It was the fair maiden who pointed out he is a **N**ew **Y**ork **S**pecial **P**olice **O**perations **I**nvestigations **L**ead. I guess that makes him a NY SPOIL. She learned this on one of her many rendezvous' while sourcing more books to read. Some days I swear she herself is a walking library, with a head full of information on my fellow writers. I'd be best to keep that information to myself as it might come in handy later on, depending on how everything comes together here, or on the other hand, falls apart.

Although, having said that, there are days like this when I am grateful for my photographic memory in observing and later capturing details. As an example, would you believe that before I came here for the festival, a fellow supervisor, Rosco, from another agency who I also do contract work for had the nerve to say this to me:

"Your contact notes on that intake you investigated are far too detailed. You need to learn how to condense. Nine pages? Six thousand words? You wrote from 10:30 pm to 2:00 am? There were details in there I didn't need to know. It was as if I was reading a book. I don't have time to be going through all this information. Just give me the facts."

Are you kidding? You *"don't have time."* Just *"give you the facts?"* Well, pardon my ignorance, Mr. Man of Self-Importance. Would you believe he laughed at me when I said I am an author of six published books? His response? *"That explains it!"* I told him that as a supervisor myself, I ask my staff to personally ensure they capture every small detail for their benefit. In our line of work, unfortunately, we refer to this as the CYA approach.

Simply stated, **C**over **Y**our **Ar**se!

That really got under my skin, so it did. From that conversation, I tried "condensing" my contact notes for him but remembered these are for the people I work with, my colleagues and collaterals, and anyone else who requires access to them. Plus, if I ever leave my career, go into a different line of work, and am called back to court, say in five years from now, I'd better know the who, what, where, why and when from all my dates of engagement. Otherwise, it won't be his arse being condensed on the firing line, it'll be mine! Condense? I condemn it, Rosco! *"Innocence lost a long time ago, now karma has control."* Ha!

Anyway, enough of that, as I am sure there must be steam piping out of my ears here right now. When I rang Michael, something did not add up about the call. So, to cover my arse (make a memo of that, Rosco), I made explicit mental notes of every detail that was shared.

"Hello, Michael?" I began. "This is Greg, so it is. What about ye? I hope you're well."

Although I sounded a bit rushed in my initial engagement with him over the telephone, which is definitely not my normal approach, there were obvious hints of private panic in my voice. Whether or not anyone in the crowd standing beside me was aware of this, I didn't know or care. All I knew is that we had a situation - a grave situation. Whenever we had a situation in Belfast, it was always grave, so it was. I tried my best to continue with the knowledge I had of the situation.

"We have a problem at the festival. Yer wee man, Arthur Colaianni, has disappeared, so he has. Something is amiss. - - - Yes, Danica. You told me that. I will pass that on. - - - Here, hang on a second, you talk to him. Tell him what your brother, Rusty, said to me. No, silly, not the first time I met him when he woke me out of a dead sleep and said, "I'm sorry to wake you; have a good night." I swear by Almighty God that when that skyscraper of a brother of yours walked through the door of his home, upon opening my weary eyes to see him standing there in his gear, that along with his booming voice, it was none other than the cybernetically enhanced Detroit Police Department Officer, Alexander J. Murphy. Yes, Rusty "RoboCop" Richardson. He scared the bejesus out of me that night, so he did.

Anyways, he was a Presidential Guard, so he would know! - - - What do you mean, no? - - - It sounds like he's driving and needs to concentrate on the road. It's better if you talk to him. - - - Ack, here, never mind. Sorry, Michael. You can probably appreciate there's a lot of panic going on. The fair maiden says that we need your investigative experience right away. Can you hurry up and get down here immediately? It's not good, so it's not."

He responded with, "Greg, we're about ten miles out. I'll step on it."

After Michael hung up the phone, without realizing it, words blurted out of me, "Jesus Murphy. He is a man of few words, so he is. Here I thought he was an author.

What kind of a response is that? I can count his ten words on my two hands. Rosco must have had him condensed!"

After putting my phone away, I figured Michael was going to need some help to make his rounds and try to locate our fellow author, Arthur. I excused myself from the crowd and immediately made my way over to a few gentlemen standing nearby: Kevin Cooper (the keeper of golf carts), Nick Bova, and Skip Moerch. They were taking a break from their duties and discussing the day ahead of them. It was Nick who saw me first.

"Hey, Greg," said Nick. "How are things going for you today? Sorry we've been so busy. None of us has had a chance to come and see all of you guys. Perhaps we can catch up and have a chat tonight at the wind-up party."

"Nick, it's all good; not to worry," I replied, before lowering my voice to barely a whisper. "Actually, it's not so good, if I am to be honest with you three lads. I'm going to need your help here. Is there somewhere private we can meet to talk for a moment or two?"

Kevin spoke up. "Why don't we go to the maintenance shed where we keep all of the golf carts? No one goes in there but us. We won't be interrupted, and we won't have to speak in hushed tones. Come on. Let's go."

Following their lead, I climbed onto a six-person golf cart but chose to stand at the back so I could hopefully sort my thoughts. My good intentions suddenly became a bad idea when I realized there were two yellow hand and ankle straps attached to the frame! That cart was not an ordinary one used to transport people around the grounds. I solemnly swear it moved at the speed of light, so it did. I blinked my eyes in rapid succession to shed the tears that kept welling up in them. Barreling our way down the road at breakneck speeds, I strained to look at the others who were all peacefully seated. They didn't seem at all phased that our lips and cheeks were flapping in the wind as if we had simply gone for a day of skydiving from twelve-thousand feet using a golf cart. That, along with the fact that my drooling slobbers were flying in all directions. I guess it was a good thing I had a place all to myself!

Reaching what must feel like Mach 5, a serious thought dawned upon my unassuming mind. "Wait a wee minute - why is it that they are the only ones wearing safety goggles? Hello. Cranium cavity to Greg, come in. Do you read me? That thought is a bit of a stretch, so it is – those are not safety goggles – they are shamrock-shaped party glasses! Maybe they were left over from their St. Patrick's Day celebration. Regardless, where is your pair? And why is there a small camera pointed directly at you?"

Who knew I would be in for the ride of my life, driving six times faster than any posted speed limit outside on Interstate 270? A strange feeling then washed over me that this was their way of initiating rookie riders to see who made the best and worst facial displays, but more so, to get back at those who create havoc and madness in the back of their transport vehicles while going to and from the festival grounds. If so, J.P. Sexton and Jim McVeigh have no idea what lies ahead for them.

My thoughts didn't get much of a chance to sink in since we were at the maintenance shed in mere seconds flat. It was there that they revealed their secret – although I think my face and the contents of my stomach were still a few miles back near the Irish Authors' Corner.

"Greg," said Kevin. "In case you were wondering, we call this our **P**addy **O**nly **W**agon, or **P.O.W.** for short. After removing its governor, Nick and Skip secretly installed a D.H. Holy Frig Nitro Boost under the pedal after we stumbled across a shipment of the stuff, although it was not initially intended for our use. We had it tested here locally. Would you believe it is sextuple-distilled, which is unheard of in every part of the world. It is the purest form of rocket fuel. The label on the box said, "Handle with Immense Caution and Care, Extremely Combustible." What was also interesting is it said, "For Human Consumption - only if born of Irish or Viking blood!"

My thoughts and suspicions did not need to be aroused much after that disclosure as two key terms made where this had originated blatantly obvious – 1: Sextuple. 2: Viking blood! I had noticed there was a shot glass-sized bottle emblazoned with a skull and crossbones logo, and the skull was wearing a four-leaf clover as a bowtie. Beneath it was a card which read, "Consume at your own peril, unless you are of Irish or Viking heritage – if so, take a trip using Donegal's *Holiest Water!* D.H." I later learned they were placed in three rooms at the Embassy Suites to welcome participants taking part, and that the festival organizers were not involved in this gesture. Since I was so tired after two flights, I did not pay any further attention to it. Now, I wonder what the meaning behind it is?

Seeing that I was distracted for a moment, Kevin cleared his throat and then continued with his statement. "As for us, it serves two distinct purposes – one, to speed up our golf game, and two, just for a wee bit of craic. You Belfast and Donegal lads aren't the only ones who delve into shenanigans. We thought you and J.P. may want to use this during your *Belfast Riots on Tour* presentation:

How to get a P.O.W. from The Crum to The Kesh Without Support from Armoured Personnel!"

Hearing this, I was onto these three like Kerrygold butter on mashed potatoes. The Kesh, previously called the Long Kesh Detention Centre and known colloquially as 'The Maze' or 'The H-Blocks' in Norn Iron, was used to house Irish prisoners during 'The Troubles.' It seems they pay extra attention to the craic, banter and all shenanigan planning that goes on in the back of the transport vehicles, especially when the Striking Viking or myself happen to be onboard. Perhaps they're planning on locking us both up!

Upon exiting the cart, I shook my head back and forth rapidly, my lips flapping and exerting sounds which are normally heard in Warner Bros. cartoons, or from the character known as Roger Rabbit. By the way, did anyone figure out who killed him? Anyhow, putting that thought aside, once my mouth had settled back into a somewhat normal shape, I spoke up, emphasizing two key elements.

"Fella's, there's no time to waste. A lot of strange things have happened since Thursday. There was a Dublin Cream Bun left outside of my room at the Embassy Suites, yet the delivery person vanished. Next, I got a bottle of Five Farms Irish Cream delivered to my door; the same thing – they knocked and split. I didn't know who was behind it, so I snuck onto the Fun Bus and left those as a gift to thank the driver, Nick, the same one Mike directed me to at the airport, with Irish folk music band, Altan."

Skip looked at me sideways as if I had just blessed myself with Danny Houton's holy water, and had perhaps baptized myself by way of osmosis or guzzled a pint. The purest of the pure – Inishowen Peninsula Poitín – it was to be used cautiously! I continued with my hurried thoughts.

"Listen, I can't explain it. One of the authors vanished into thin air. Arthur Colaianni. He's gone, without so much as a trace, other than a few cream bun crumbs!"

Nick cast the same sidelong glance as Skip, whispered that Altan were also from Donegal, and then spoke up.

"Lisa and I know most of the authors, Greg. I can pretty much guarantee we don't have an Arthur Colaianni in the Irish Authors' Corner. That is an Italian surname.

Perhaps you are mistaking him for our sopranist? Our Executive Director, Alison LeRoy, received an application from his tour manager for him to perform on our Celtic Rock stage with The Irish Tenors during the grand finale."

I was not prepared to hear this information. Maybe they thought I was having them on.

"Honest to . . . Jesus Murphy. What going on? Nick, you know I love to have a bit of banter, but I haven't lost my mind. Skip, you've seen how I get on with J.P. in the back of the transport vehicles, but I'm not saying this just for the craic. Can you and Nick run me back to the tent? Michael McCarthy is on his way here to the festival grounds and is probably going to need a dedicated cart, so he is. He's a New York Rochester . . . an invest . . . I think he's a NY SPOIL working undercover as an author, wait, a claims adjuster, or perhaps an investigative librarian. He is going to help lead this thing, whatever it is he needs to lead. I have to get back and make an urgent phone call."

Kevin handed me his shamrock safety glasses and wished me the luck of the Irish. With that, along with my co-pilots Skip and Nick, my mouth was again throwing slobbers out to the festival grounds as we flew back toward the Irish Authors' Corner. The mystery, which was deepening further each second, was now as thick as a pint of Guinness, so it was. It was here I eventually met up with our intrepid author, the one who moonlights as a claims adjusting police officer or something to that effect. I really have no clue which way it goes other than to say that his not so undercover golf cart moved at about the same pace as a turtle goes for a casual stroll when it's not in a hurry to get anywhere.

Even though the others hadn't noticed I was gone for a while, my thoughts were still rattled. Knowing about the events at my hotel room, how I was provided with two extra gifts without seeing or hearing anyone other than a knock at the door each time, a mystery greater than any of us could have possibly realized was unfolding before our eyes. Perhaps I should have indeed drank the contents within the shot-sized bottle. Maybe things would have made much more sense to me as nothing is adding up whatsoever, so it's not. At least the trip might be cool!

When Michael finally arrived at the tent and gathered up his belongings, I was already anxiously waiting to tell him what I knew. I figured I may as well put it all out there on the line, even before he asked me.

"Michael, there is still no sign of Arthur Colaianni. His books are sitting over there, but he's gone, as if some supernatural power lifted him away. He has vanished without a trace. I know this sounds like a shot in the dark, but would you happen to know the secret number for Agents Fox Mulder and Dana Scully? I seriously think this has something to do with The X-Files."

"Supernatural power?" he said. "How could that be? We need to think of some suspicious person or occurrence that may have caused Arthur's absence, not a supernatural phenomenon."

"Seriously?", I said. "I'm not so sure about that, but okay, no worries. Get on it right away, Mr. Investigator." I then muttered, "Magnum P.I., eat your heart out!"

It was his initial engagement that really made me begin to think something was amiss with his approach to me as his colleague, or perhaps more so with the events surrounding us. Was this his way of creating a diversion to conceal something much bigger than any of us could possibly know of? I think I'm going to keep my wee eyes on him, just as much as he will most likely be doing to me, along with anyone else he chooses to interrogate. So much for him being a NY SPOIL. He is a NY SPOIL SPORT:

A **N**ew **Y**ork **S**pecial **P**olice **O**perations **I**nvestigations **L**ead **S**acrificing **P**ersons **O**f **R**ighteous **T**estimony.

He's the SPOIL and I'm the SPORT! Ha! Take that to the bank and cash it, "Magnum". Who knew that sarcasm would become the name of the game?

When asking questions, I noticed Magnum McCarthy selectively captured my answers, in partial format. What I have written here is what I said to him and what his responses were to me, in explicit and intimate detail, though I don't think he took my full answers very seriously. Why was that? What was he hiding?

The weekend had been a lot of fun in the Irish Authors' Corner. A group of us had gotten together the night before for some laughter and music. As he began conducting his search for Arthur, I found his methodology to be strikingly sharp in its approach. We were no longer his colleagues. In my opinion, each one of us was suddenly deemed to be a suspect when Arthur vanished. We were all hurting, wondering, fearful of the unknown. For whatever reason, I took issue with this, especially when Magnum McCarthy said, "Let's start with a roll of yellow caution tape and protect the scene of his disappearance. There could be valuable evidence hiding from our unsuspecting eyes. Next, we'll set up a search team and do a crisscross pattern throughout the grounds." Time for me to shake things up!

We followed that direction and after we were done, I decided to wrap myself up in some of the yellow tape and shouted toward Michael, "Hey, just in case. You never can be too cautious, so you can't!" all the while making myself into a partial mummy. I went on to say, "You never know who your friends and enemies are."

I am not sure if anyone realized my intent, although this statement brought me back to the initial tip I was going to give to the tour bus driver: "Keep your friends close; keep your enemies closer."

As the relaxed chatter and witty banter cleared from the whole Irish Authors' Corner, I tried to interject partial moments of humour into the mix, even if this was just for my own sanity. I often find when the chips are down, laughter can be a valuable coping mechanism. Thus, I paused for a second after Michael said, "Enough of the small talk; we'll start with the linear search like Sinead suggested but keep watching for clues like footprints or dropped breadcrumbs from Arthur."

"But sure, how did you know he was eating a loaf of bread? Are we looking for whole wheat, rye, white or sourdough breadcrumbs?" I asked with great sincerity. My question was met with a deadpan expression. That moment, or so it seemed, was lost on everyone but me.

At that, Brenna Briggs started to speak to Michael about cloth. To be honest, I never saw her arrive. I didn't even know she was there. It also took me a few seconds to realize she had been accompanied by her son, Shannon. I am sure Michael believes he too is as much of a suspect as the rest of us are because he is always there to help his mum out. I will bet that Michael probably thinks they are like Bonnie and Clyde, Thelma and Louise - or better yet, Brenna and Shannon! It couldn't have been more obvious!

I thought this could be another appropriate moment to provide some light-hearted humour, and ease everyone's mounting tensions and rapidly rising temperatures. An Irish intervention was in order. I watched as their next exchange unfolded, all the while trying to get a handle on what they were talking about.

"Cloth," said Brenna.

"What?" replied Michael. He then asked Brenna, "Do you have something with cloth?"

"Pattern to fit your cloth, is the saying," was Brenna's response, only for Michael to then reply with, "Right, like a herringbone pattern, which clothes are made of."

Say what? At this point, I became wholeheartedly lost in their back-and-forth dialogue. Right after Michael made his last comment, I'm sure he witnessed, as I did, that Brenna raised her eyebrows and looked skyward in exasperation. Pouncing on this opportunity, I looked at Brenna, then looked skyward before deciding to speak to the heavens, although my mouth was partially covered with yellow caution tape. I am sure in the minds of some, if not all, it didn't stay on long enough as I continued to say whatever fell out of my unfiltered brain.

"Hey. You. Up there. Our fellow author sounds biblical to me, so he does. I didn't know he was one of yours and walked around with loaves of bread wrapped in cloth. Are we going to get a storm? Locusts? A plague? Is this a second coming of the twelve disciples? According to the scriptures, there's Matthew, Mark, Luke, and John. Congrats - now you have King Arthur."

I got a weird feeling that everyone was now busy watching me talking to the skies (they were), all of them with an even greater look of wild exasperation on their faces than Brenna had. I kept staring, waiting for an answer from the heavens. It was Michael who broke the unnerving silence that had fallen upon the tent. If this had of been nightfall, crickets would've been doing the same.

He shifted his attention to an area in front of The Book Loft and spoke to Julie Burgess, who was also the keeper of the authors tent. I was thankful this would finally take some of his attention off me.

I returned to my station and began furiously documenting some notes in my laptop computer about the events which were occurring live, second by crucial second. Even by entering only a few bullet points, I knew from my own training that this ensured that I would capture every intricate detail, just in case. I was not going to take any chances or miss anything.

Within a few moments, I noticed that Laura Nelson, the Assistant Director, had made her way to the Irish Authors' Corner. I made a mental note of this, thinking Nick Bova had most likely gone over to see her to make mention of what I shared with him back at the maintenance shed. I am sure things were not adding up for him either and he wanted to make sure all of the entertainers and artists were spoken for. He had become friends with many of us. In the grand scheme of things, he wants to ensure our safety, as does the organizational crew of the Dublin Irish Festival. What was quite interesting, though, is that Michael had given the exact same name to Laura as I did to Nick about our fellow author. Laura looked just as confused.

I carefully listened to the exchange between Laura and Michael. Seeing they had decided to call in a handful of volunteers, I made my way to the Spoken Word tent. Upon my arrival, I saw Melissa Stacy there with the sound board engineer, rehearsing her lines. Melissa is the one who was responsible for introducing each author before they got up and spoke. I thought she could help us out as well by making announcements at the beginning and end of each presentation. That way, audience participation thereafter would hopefully help us further in trying to locate Mr. Arthur Colaianni, even if there was widescale belief he would be singing later that day.

Wait a minute. How did I not realize this sooner? Arthur is Italian. Lives in Wisconsin. Writes books about Irish Leprechaun Kings. He assumes three different cultural identities and seamlessly blends into each one of them without anyone blinking an eye. Sneaky! Who knew that a chameleon lives and writes amongst us. A master of his craft. The work of a Godfather.

This afternoon, when the grand finale is getting close, I will need to make a trip over to the Celtic Rock stage and pay The Irish Tenors a wee visit.

But first, I must make that pressing phone call . . .

Chapter 13: One Unlucky Viking

Our apologies, ladies and gentlemen. J.P. penned this chapter. Being an International Man of Mystery, we have no clue what he wanted to say. We believe he wrote this using his Secret Spy Last Jedi ink. If you wish, you could use this page to collect autographs from those authors who contributed to this book. Or draw a wee Viking lightsaber!

Chapter 15: Revenge is a Dish . . .

Date:	Sunday, August 4, 2019.
Entry 4:	Inhibiting the Investigator!
Location:	Irish Authors' Corner.
Time:	Ninety minutes before opening time.

Dear Diary . . .

Since this place is a beehive of activity, I am going to go deep into my thoughts and continue writing my contact notes. You must think this is strange – my writing so much within these pages. Believe me, it is just as strange for me as well. But there is nothing more I can do right now other than keep my shamrock senses at the highest level of alert – four leaves.

I will start by capturing my observations. If we hope to solve this mystery, I am going to need to be a sleuth as much as anyone else. It has become readily apparent that everyone here is not only a suspect since that body was pulled from the pond, they are targets too . . . including me! Poor Sinead fainted as soon as she realized what was going on. Cindy is jotting something down on paper but the only thing I could make out was the heading *"Wishful Thinking"* - although she seems seriously deep in thought as she writes. I remembered something my son Ciaran learned from playing hockey as a goalie: "Keep your head on a swivel when going into the corners, for you do not know who is behind you."

Now to get down to some intense business here.

Observation One: Michael "Magnum" McCarthy met with Laura Nelson. She is the Assistant Director to the Executive Director, Alison LeRoy. Laura offered to call the local police service in, but Michael refused her offer to do so. I ask, why wouldn't a claims adjusting, investigating, librarian, author turned NY SPOIL SPORT wish to have the support of local law enforcement? It doesn't add up.

Observation Two: I overheard Magnum tell Laura he had "secured Arthur's table." How exactly did he do that other than to put caution tape up around the area? Did he also happen to tell her that he used other authors as his associates to do so, and that any evidence could have been planted or removed? His best lead, to my knowledge, is cloth and breadcrumbs. He may as well be looking for a needle in a haystack.

Observation Three: Moments ago, Magnum climbed onto his unmarked golf cart and headed for parts unknown. I had to laugh at this, though. Compared to my 'to infinity and beyond' rocket ride with Nick and Skip, seeing Michael drive was like watching an oversized child playing on a stationary machine which requires a quarter to make it rock backward and forward for two-minutes. Vroom, vroom. Bon voyage, mon ami!

While penning my thoughts down, I was interrupted by Kevin, who popped in at the tent and headed straight for me. I instinctively initiated a distraction as to not have him draw any attention to himself.

"Nice to see you, sir," I said. "Here's your copy of my third book, *One Cross to Bear: Humanity through Narrative Prose.* By the way, I'll be presenting my own take on Celtic folklore and mythology over at the Spoken Word Tent this evening. I think you will most certainly enjoy my second presentation from this book, which is called *The Banshee of Dunluce Castle.* If you've never had a chance to experience what this hauntingly beautiful place on the North Antrim coast offers to its unsuspecting guests, specifically tourists, you're in for a real treat, so you are."

"Awesome! That's great to hear," he said. "I love delving into paranormal phenomenon, especially anything associated with The X-Files. I am sure you are familiar with Agents Fox Mulder and Dana Scully. Thank you for this. I can't wait."

Taking a quick look around, I saw that everyone else was wrapped up in conversations with fellow authors. A few were separated from the rest of us, sitting at their stations with their heads down in silent prayer, while others were wanting nothing to do with stories of ghosts, faeries, and The X-Files. Kevin whispered his next set of instructions to me. I helped by opening the book to a random page, pretending to walk him through the pieces I was to be reading.

"Greg, I need my safety goggles. I am going up to the green room to get ready for the volunteers who are about to start transporting musicians to their various stages in time for the gates to open. Everyone is at the morning mass right now. Prayer services should be wrapped up in about twenty minutes or so."

Looking around to make sure no one was watching, I whispered, "Here you go, Kevin. Thank you for the use of these. I need to make my way over to the Celtic Rock stage and speak to the lads in The Irish Tenors. I have a sneaking suspicion I am going to find some more clues over there. The only thing I am missing is some Scooby Snacks."

"Well," said Kevin, "you may wish to sort yourself out before you go. From that last cart ride with the lads, I must admit you do resemble Shaggy a bit. Your head looks like an explosion at a mattress factory. Or maybe you're moonlighting as a mad scientist. You do suit the part quite well. No offense intended, of course. But I suggest you don't go up there right now. That Michael fellow began asking questions about you as soon as he got to the maintenance shed. He never asked for or spoke about anyone else."

Looking around again and being careful to ensure no one picked up on us talking, I said, "No offense taken, Kevin. Thanks all the same. What is that all about, I wonder? Why is he choosing to go after me? Can Magnum not see I was the one who alerted him to what is unfolding out here on the grounds? I even came over to tell you guys he would need a golf cart, so I did."

Kevin responded, "That's just it, Greg. We saw you didn't hesitate to jump into action to help in trying to find your missing friend, Arthur. You informed us about the events outside your hotel room at the Embassy Suites, yet you immediately became Michael's suspect. So why do you think we decided to give you some help from behind the scenes. Look at him go!"

I turned my head to see that Magnum's unmarked golf cart had pulled a few feet away from the tent. He was as happy as can be with his bag of supplies, and completely oblivious to the fact that he was barely moving. I turned back to my colleague and again spoke in a hushed tone.

"Kevin, I could watch paint dry faster than that thing moves, so I could. I swear it's almost as stationary as when he first parked it. Good grief. What is wrong with it? Does it have a dead battery? Perhaps it wasn't charged in time to be used? Are there problems with the wiring? I hate to point out the obvious and help my adversary, but I could crawl faster to wherever he is planning to go right now."

Kevin looked me squarely in the eyes, and with a deadpan tone, said, "You can thank me later for the help. Do you remember I was saying Nick and Skip had taken the governor out of the cart we used to help transform the Paddy Only Wagon? Well, seeing that Michael put a target squarely on your back, Skip installed it directly beside the other one already in his cart before allowing him to leave the maintenance shed. He sharply questioned us about it, so Skip told him our policy is to keep our environmental footprint as small as possible. Skip then said to Michael, "Each ride you take will feel brisk, and since it will be smooth and quiet, your cart is environmentally friendly for official Free Based Irishmen business. He bought it!"

I chuckled at this statement because it made sense as to why the performance of Michael's mode of transportation was beyond lackluster. I looked at Kevin and said, "And here my ma would tell me I am full of the divilment. You guys are no better, or worse really for that matter. What more can I say other than brilliant? As they say, revenge is a dish best served cold, so it is. I appreciate the help!"

"No worries, my friend," he said. "We watch the madness you guys create while you are here all weekend. We also like to have fun. It keeps us on our toes and keeps our colleagues laughing when they hear the stories after the weekend wraps up at our wind-up party. It's a time when we all go through withdrawal while waiting to start planning the next one. Now listen, I remember you said you had an urgent errand to get sorted, thus why you needed to get back here so quick. I don't want to keep you from doing that. I see you are busy working at your laptop, likely writing another book as we saw you do here last year. What was that called again? I remember you showed me the cover for it and said it was a difficult story to write. The cover was quite striking as I recall."

"That it was," I replied. "It's called *At Least He Wasn't Hitting You*. It's the personal memoir of an amazing lady who fought to overcome the unimaginable experiences she faced over ten, grueling years in a marriage fraught with emotional, psychological, verbal and financial abuse. I wrote it over eighteen days as she told me the story about her experiences – 37,500 words. Talk about challenging! Yet, my goal is to continue networking with colleagues as far and wide as possible to hopefully have it adapted into a screenplay. There are countless others who have walked in her shoes and unfortunately, never get the chance to tell their stories. Hopefully, they can through this one. It's a heartbreaking read. Some refer to it 'gaslighting'."

Shaking his head in disbelief, he said, "Man, I don't know how you do it, but I'm glad you do! That is a lot of writing in a short period of time. Didn't you say last year you were working both a full-time and a part-time job and were writing that book all at the same time?"

My reply was probably the shortest one I have ever given. "Yes. It was exhausting. But the story needed to be told. And here the book is now, making its debut launch right here in Dublin, Ohio!"

As Kevin shook my hand, he said, "Congratulations on that accomplishment, Greg. Your energy is boundless. We see it when you are here and that's only over four or five days. Listen, good luck with everything you're doing and continue to set your mind to. Whenever you get a chance, before five o'clock this afternoon, make sure you chat with Johnny Harte. He is the representative for the company sponsoring the main performer on the Celtic Rock stage. It's on the other side of the grounds from where we are so leave early if you're in a hurry."

Before he could turn away, I put my hand on his wrist and said, "Kevin, speaking of getting somewhere in a hurry, can you run me back down to the maintenance shed in the Paddy Only Wagon? I'm going to need to break away from the group here to make more notes as I too suspect some people, but I also must make a phone call. My shamrock senses are telling me other authors around the tent here are pointing their fingers squarely at me in being the culprit behind the disappearance of the Italian Leprechaun King Godfather from Wisconsin. How they came to that conclusion is beyond me, but I am not about to take any chances. I am going to expand my investigative thoughts and take a closer look at a few more of them."

"Keep your friends close; keep your enemies closer" perforated my racing thoughts once more.

Kevin paused and then cautioned me. "Greg, do you not think you might become even more suspect amongst your peers if you take off again?"

My reply was not in hushed or whispered tones this time, but in my normal voice. I wanted to ensure some of them would hear what I had to say in my own defense.

"Mo chara, which is Gaeilge for "my friend", if they already have deemed me as a suspect, prime or otherwise, what is the point of me waiting around here for them to gossip, whether in front of me or behind my back. It's all the same at this moment. I may as well be seen in the eyes of a few as out networking yet again, which I do on a regular basis. They should be used to it by now. If not, then a suspect I am, a suspect I will remain. There is nothing I can do to change their thoughts if they're determined to deflect attention away from themselves, is there? Especially with Magnum McCarthy on the loose!"

Kevin gave me an all-knowing nod in agreement with what I meant by that. We then took our leave toward the maintenance shed, arriving in seconds flat. Before zooming away to his next stop, he directed me to an office, as this was the best location to start putting my thoughts together. I thanked him, took out my laptop, and realized a second clue was already waiting within it for me to help me figure out the mystery behind Arthur Colaianni's disappearance.

Chapter 17: Ground Control to Malin Head

Date:	Sunday, August 4, 2019.
Entry 5:	Breaker, Breaker: Mad Dog to Mad Hoor!
Location:	Maintenance Shed – Dublin Irish Festival.
Time:	Sixty minutes before gates open.

Dear Diary . . .

I am sitting here lost in thought, with headphones on, listening to an interview with Mama's Boys from 1985. I need to settle my nerves so I can focus on the task at hand. I'm fed up having to enter so many notes, so I have to keep reminding myself how critical it is to get these captured in case something happens to me. I have begun to analyze how Michael "Magnum" McCarthy has been speaking to - well, more so *at* me. He did not capture my full responses but was extremely selective in what he wrote down. I can't help wondering if he's trying to frame me. I only know of one person who will be able to provide the answers to this.

Suddenly, I heard someone speak, which startled me so much, I nearly jumped out of my skin.

"Bear with me a wee second. Once I get these last few entries in, I have to make that urgent phone call once and for all."

My thoughts had gone from my mind to the pages of my diary to being spoken out loud, almost as a way for me to reassure myself since there was no one else around for me to talk to. Perhaps my mind had gone rogue and was trying to provide me with a bit of comfort or support while I continued wrapping up what I needed to get done. My nerves were beyond frazzled. I didn't realize it was me who was the one doing the talking.

I left my laptop to tap out the numbers on the keypad of my phone screen. My fingers trembled while trying to enter the pin code to get access to it, failing on the first three attempts. Why was this happening to me? I had nothing to hide. It was obvious my nerves were frazzled.

"C'mon, Greg. Would you hurry up for God's sakes!"

My methods of self-reassurance were failing miserably. I knew how important it was for me to get this call made and hurry back to the Irish Authors' Corner, especially for the guests who would be arriving after the morning mass was done. Everything would have to be normal for their arrival, whatever that was. Nothing had been normal this past few days.

I continued to speak my thoughts out loud. These included those as spoken by Tommy McManus, the drummer for Mama's Boys, when asked what it is he does when his brothers, Pat McManus and John McManus, are off doing their own guitar and bass solos all the while running about the stage, leaving fans to stare at him:

"Well, I just like after every second beat, I stand up and wave me hands around again."

Our voices echoed in harmony – Tommy's within my headphones and mine reverberating around the empty maintenance shed. In that exact instant, I realized how desperately I needed these few seconds of distraction to try and calm myself. Regardless of the thousands of times I have listened to this very interview and could almost speak it as if it were I who was being interviewed, simply hearing the voices of my childhood idols seemed to ease my stresses, even if only a little.

After the interview ended, the music app on my phone began playing, although I was not paying much attention to anything in that moment. So much so, in fact, that I began dialing the numbers, unaware of the shift occurring within my disturbed brain and the subliminal messaging it was now receiving:

". . . eight six seven, five three oh nine – eight six seven, five three oh nine . . ."

What am I doing? The person I need to speak to is J.P. Sexton. How on God's green earth did I get Jenny's number? Who the hell is she? Why am I phoning her? I then realized this was in no thanks to the song by Tommy Tutone, which had now found its way from my playlist and into my thoughts. I took a deep breath and prayed for strength.

Pulling up my contact list, I scrolled down until I finally found the entry I had been looking for. It had been added under the listing of the Malin Head Mad Hoor. A second entry in my phone referred to him as the Striking Viking, which was the number I was to ring him at if I was ever in Ireland and required his assistance. Dialing the first number, I could hear the long-distance pips, which meant he was still overseas and had not yet made it back to the shores of America. "That is not a good sign," I muttered.

Upon hearing his voice and trying to sound somewhat cheery, I said, "Hiya. Is that John Patrick Sexton, the fellow who steals cream buns from wains, the International Man of Mystery, and the lovechild of Fionn Mac Cumhaill?"

"It is indeed," replied J.P. "Mad Dog McVicker. Do you ever realize half the shite that comes out of your mouth, mucker? What's the craic with ya, you crazy bastard?"

"John," I responded, "why you are still in Ireland? What is going on? I thought you were getting a flight over and heading down to catch the last of the festival. I've got thirty-eight copies of your bestselling novel *The Big Yank* here. It is not selling so well right now, so it's not. It's quite hard to do when the prodigy of lunacy is not here to sign copies of his own book."

"Greg, listen up," he began. "I flew home on my Irish passport because my U.S. passport is in for renewal. I didn't realize I had to fly out on my American passport and return on it as well, even though I'm a dual citizen. They denied me my entry back into the country until I met with the U.S. Consulate. Although I have my clearances, I can't get a flight now. Everything is in chaos. I'm up in Malin Head having a pint at Farren's Bar with Hugh, the owner. My grandfather, Danny Houton, well, he and I were patrons when Hugh's grandparents owned this bar."

"Wait a minute?" I replied. "What was that you said about being a jewel citizen. What are ya, the bloody emerald of the Irish isle? Jesus, you live with horseshoes firmly embedded, so you do. Someone over there finally realized you are indeed the lovechild of Fabio and one of the damsels from the front cover of the romance novels he posed for, and they granted you clemency for your sins. Oh, Johnny Boy, the pipes, the pipes are calling . . ."

"*Dual* citizen, you head the ball," he retorted, cutting me off before I could butcher one of our more valued possessions, that being the lyrics to *Danny Boy*. "I said dual, not jewel likes yous'uns say in Northern Ireland. I'm more like a diamond in the rough."

"Ah, right," I responded. "Sorry, your Donegal accent is a bit like what my ma told me I was all those years growing up . . . thick! If you ask me, John, you're a rough version of Neil Diamond is what you are. Give us a tune, will ye? I could use something to brighten me up just a bit. Something other than your diddly dee music."

John laughed at this before breaking into his own lyrical version of *I Am I Said*.

"Well, I'm New York City born and raised. But nowadays, I'm lost between two shores. Ireland's fine, but it ain't home, New York's home but it ain't mine no more."

Immediately regretting my referring to J.P. as being anything close to the musical legend since his version of the song was beyond decrepit both in its conception and presentation, I made a mental note to never do that again and pressed on with my initial thoughts.

"You had to meet with the U.S. Consulate? See if you had of done what I did with respect to networking with Brian O'Brien, you would've become one of his esteemed associates and been appointed as the Irish Ambassador to some nation – perhaps Malin Head as it is in the middle of nowhere. Did you know the last thing to land there beside your wee Donegal arse was the Millennium Falcon? Here, tell me this, will ye . . . are you, J.P. Sexton, *The Last Jedi?*"

His response was swifter than Darth Vader swinging about his lightsaber with its sinister, crimson hue.

"Greg, you friggin' eejit, you. I went down to Dublin to plead for them to get me back in to America and told them the circumstances behind the Dublin Irish Festival. They didn't budge and said I should never have left the country in the first place. I had come back here for some inspiration to write my latest novel. Had I have known this was going to happen, I would have been back sooner to make sure I got to the festival. Sure, I'm missing out on all the craic."

"Listen to me a wee minute, Skywalker," I said. "I am sure you got more than enough inspiration for your next novel with all you experienced back home. But here, you are missing out on more than craic. There's some serious stuff going down right now. As it stands, lightsaber's are being pointed in all directions, but more so at me. I can't imagine why. One of the author's disappeared. He has basically vanished into thin air. Personally, I think this has something to do with The X-Files, so I do. But since I can't get access to Agent Mulder or Agent Scully, and because you are well-versed in the art of making people blend into the background without ever being seen again, would an International Man of Mystery such as yourself happen to know anything about his disappearance?"

Hearing this, John immediately shifted the focus of my direct line of questioning and directed all attention away from himself. He had mastered the art of stealth.

"Ack, you're not talking about The Orangutan, are you, Greg?" he said. "Sure, yer man, Colin Broderick only joined us for the one year at the festival. The last I heard, he was filming his latest movie in Country Tyrone. I wouldn't have expected to see him there. Either that or he is busy hanging out with Josh Brolin on the set of some movie. You do know they are the best of friends, right?"

I responded with an exasperated, almost defiant tone. "Aye, but sure I'm well aware of that, so I am, John! No, I am talking about your wee Leprechaun Godfather fella from Wisconsin; his name is Arthur Colaianni."

J.P. went quiet for a second before coming back at me with, "What name did you say? Colaianni? Are you wise? That's an Italian surname. Isn't he a famous soprano?"

I couldn't believe I was hearing this reference yet again. "John, no, listen. He sits at the end of the tables and his spot is always tastefully decorated. Directly across from Julie Burgess, the store manager with The Book Loft. As you know, they are the ones who sponsor the authors tent each year. He is always the first one to arrive. I swear he must sleep there overnight and uses his hotel room to shower whenever none of us are paying any attention, which is pretty much all the time. A lady sat beside him, Therese Gilardi, although I don't know who she is. She's either a new author to the festival, one who missed the last few years, or was planted by Michael Magnum McCarthy as she also has a name which may be a mixture of French and Italian. I am not sure if she has any Irish heritage."

It was painfully obvious to me that J. P. Sexton, the Mad Hoor from Malin Head, and now quite possibly The Last Jedi, had absolutely no idea what had been going on. His own plate was likely overflowing from the events that had kept him away from the Dublin Irish Festival for a second year in a row. At the time of the first, in 2018, he had been out riding his bicycle in Florida. A woman from Las Vegas, who was driving a rental car, crashed into him and ended up breaking his collar bone in the process. She later told him she didn't see him. How anyone could not see one of the last remaining Irish giants is totally beyond me. Perhaps his finely-chiseled looks and locks of flowing hair distracted her; perhaps she had a motive and hit him on purpose, wanted to take him home, and ravish the Fabio look-alike back to full health only to fall in love like they do in the movies. Perhaps I need to go and get my head examined for thinking and writing this shite down.

"John," I said. "Listen to me carefully. I need your help with this. The New York SPOIL is taking serious issue with everyone and has deemed them as being a suspect. Especially me! What else is new, though? I'm always the scapegoat. I became the easiest target for him, so I did."

"Greg, what in under God's name is a New York SPOIL?" he asked.

"New York Special Police Officer Investigations Lead. It's yer man, Michael E. McCarthy," I replied before continuing with my thoughts. "Don't you remember? He retired from the claims investigations unit within the Rochester police force, and has since pursued a lifelong dream in becoming a librarian? Or something like that. I really have no clue what he did before. This is what I am taking from what I've heard. The Guke Slinger knows much more, so she does. I call him Magnum McCarthy."

"Aye, I remember who he is," said John. "Other than being a police detective, what's so special about him?"

"Well," I said, "he has taken it upon himself to become an investigator for the mystery unravelling right now, so he has. To be honest, the only thing truly unravelling are my nerves, as he is getting on them, so he is. Aye, him along with everyone else if I'm to be honest, John. I have a grave suspicion they all think I'm responsible for the disappearance of Arthur Colaianni."

John's response was not what I wanted to hear.

"Let me guess. You knocked him off for nicking a bite of your Dublin Cream Bun? I know your quare protective of those things. It's like trying to remove a mother bear from her cub. You let the pastry sit for four hours and then sneak away to have them in private, albeit the last time I heard you went to the Wake House with your fair maiden Guke Slinger to offer deepest condolences. You had your feast while you were staring at the dead mannequin lying there. You needed a wee Irish wake fix. She told me about it, saying she had never seen such madness!"

My reaction was swift. "John, quit actin' an eejit or I'll shove my boot down the phone and you'll get my toe square up yer hole, so you will. Sweet Jesus, I sounded just like me ma there."

John burst into a fit of laughter upon hearing this. I continued with my thoughts.

"Listen, yer man, the NY SPOIL – Magnum. I have been watching him closely, so I have, especially when he was writing down his contact notes from our discussions. Why do you think that is?"

"Why do I think that is? It sounds like he's being set up for a take-down, that's what that is. It shouldn't take a rocket scientist to figure that out," said John. "But sure, you are far from that criteria or level of understanding. I swear if NASA were to hire you, their first experiment should be to ship you up to the moon as a permanent resident for the love and peace of all mankind."

"John, you're dead wrong about that, so you are. My ma always said I was wired up to a Mars Bar but not plugged in, so she did. She never said anything about the moon. That is exactly the reason why I'm ringing you, Mr. Brainiac. Listen, I'm going to have a look through some of my carefully detailed notes here. As you will see, I will first tell you what he asked, followed by how I responded. Let me pull those from my diary. Hang on a second. Bear with me a wee moment. I'm trying to cover my arse."

John continued speaking to me while I was in the process of trying to find the information I had been writing down, including my first engagement with Michael after he arrived back at the festival grounds with his wife, Ann.

"John, listen to this very carefully. When Magnum McCarthy approached me - and keep in mind that I am the one who had placed the initial phone call to him letting him know what was going down - I said to him, 'Michael. There is still no sign of Arthur. His books are sitting over there, but he's gone as if some supernatural power lifted him away. He has vanished without a trace. I know this is a shot in the dark, so it is, but would you happen to know the secret telephone number for Agents Fox Mulder and Dana Scully? I seriously think this has something to do with The X-Files.'"

After clearing his throat, John said, "Greg McVicker. In the name of Jesus, and for the love of Ireland, are you bleedin' wise in the head? Did you actually say that to him? You *are* nuts!"

"John, I did indeed say that to him," I replied before continuing with, "What's wrong with that?" I could feel my forehead furrow forward, my eyebrows pull together, my skin tighten, and my face go flushed.

"Greg, sweet Mother of God. You seriously asked a retired Rochester, New York Police Detective if he had the phone number to Agents Fox Mulder and Dana Scully? Do you know who they are? They're actors, you buck eejit! David Duchovny and Gillian Anderson! Who the frig would plant that seed in your mind? You are seriously the daftest bugger I have ever known!"

"John, you're so dead wrong, so you are," I said. "Y'see when I called Magnum, well, right before that, the fair maiden called her brother, Rusty 'RoboCop' Richardson. As you know, he worked as a Presidential Guard, so he did. My shamrock senses were tingling at that moment, so they were. Since Danica would not let me speak to him directly, I phoned him and had a three-way call so she could hear my questions. Do you know what RoboCop said when I told him there may be extraterrestrial activity surrounding Arthur's disappearance because he vanished without a trace? He asked if I had ever watched *National Treasure* 2. Rusty said when Nicholas Cage looked at page forty-seven in the *Book of Secrets* after its location in the Library of Congress was divulged, he found the private phone numbers to Agents Fox Mulder and Dana Scully. That book contains documents collected for presidents by presidents, and are meant to be for presidents' eyes only. Page forty-seven is connected to The X-Files, so it is. And that's why I asked him for Mulder and Scully's phone numbers. Being a cybernetically enhanced Detroit Police Department Officer, Robocop would be able to access all of their databases and would have first-hand knowledge!"

"Mad Dog," he began. "I know you are not wise in the head, but are you that gullible to believe what Rusty told you? I think he was winding you up, just for the craic. And what was the name you said? Nicholas Cage? What are you playing at? Who's that?"

John's voice got higher when he asked me that question. My suspicion was he was trying to deflect attention again.

"Wise up, will ye?", I said. "Why would Rusty be having a wind? He's dead on, so he is. A good bloke. Although I suspect you likely corrupted him that time you were hanging out with him at the other Irish festival. As for Nicholas Cage, he acted in several movies, so he did. His uncle is the famous director, Francis Ford Coppola. And The X-Files are real, so they are!"

Not one to filter his thoughts, John said, "Honest to frig, I think your head's in the clouds. I am going to ring Purdysburn to ask if they have an escaped patient by the name of Greg McVicker who also goes by the name of the Belfast Child, and to tell them that you have been seen running wild at an Irish Festival in Dublin, Ohio."

I blurted out, "Hawlon to your knickers a wee second, will ye? And here I thought I was ringing you for support and sage advice. Perhaps I do need my head examined."

John snickered at this comment. He loved nothing more than to crawl under my skin and drive me up the bend. Going back into my laptop, I maximized the screen where I had captured the questions Michael had asked and how I had responded to him in explicit detail. Perhaps I was being far too honest with the claims investigating librarian, although from what I could see of what he had written, simply put, the discrepancies were glaring.

"Okay, John, are you ready for this? 'What do you think happened to Arthur?' This was one of Magnum McCarthy's questions to me."

J.P. paused for a second before telling me he thought there was simply nothing wrong whatsoever with Michael asking me that. He then asked how I responded to him.

"John, he wrote the following from my answer, so he did. 'I think he went into that hole in front of The Book Loft cash register. Do you see it over there? The one with the big orange X marking the spot. I think it was a leprechaun trap.'"

"Okay, Greg," said John. "Tell me, what exactly is it you think is wrong with that, aside from the obvious?"

"John, take note of this carefully," I said. "That is exactly the problem right there. What I just read to you is what Magnum wrote down. He did not document my answer in full, so he didn't. He is being selective about what he wants to hear."

"Okay, then," said J.P. "If that is the case, what exactly did you say to him then, Greg?"

My response was obviously agitated. "I said this to him, verbatim. You tell me what is wrong with it. Ready? Okay, here goes. I will go slowly so you can get every word down. Wait, better yet, while you and I are on the phone, I am going to copy and paste my answer from my diary and send it to you in an email to save us some time here. Check your computer. I've just sent it."

Opening the message that appeared on his computer, J.P. read it aloud: "I think he went into that hole in front of The Book Loft cash register. Did you see it? They had a big orange X marking the spot. The first thing I thought was someone nicked the Sash that J.P. Sexton smuggled out during Operation Derry in preparation for our upcoming show which is called *Belfast Riots In Tourist Season – Opinionated! Underappreciated! Totalitarianism!"*

Before he managed to finish reading the rest of the email, John pointed out a simple fact to me which I had completely missed.

"Greg," he said. "Not only did he *not* capture your thoughts in full, there may have been a *valid* reason for that. In case you haven't figured this out, the upcoming show which you told Michael the two of us are presenting – and although I doubt this, are you the slightest bit aware what the acronym for that spells?"

He emphasized the last part of his comment to me to ensure I heard it in full and then slowly repeated himself, deliberately pausing between each letter.

B R I T S O U T

A miracle must have occurred as I went silent before coming back with, "Did you say BRITS OUT? Wow, who knew we were such masterminds? I had no clue. It must be a wee sign from the heavens in bringing about historical awareness in Northern Ireland. Here, will you remind me to make a sacrificial offering of a Dublin Cream Bun to the big guy in the sky the next time I go in for confession, although I will likely be in there for an eternity, so I will. The priest might not ever let me out!"

John cut me off before I could go any further, likely part of his efforts to run damage control, but probably for himself as he still needed to get a flight out of Ireland and back into the USA. This was all the more likely if our phone call was being monitored by Free Based Irishmen.

"You delirious hoor! Do you honestly think the folks at the Dublin Irish Festival are going to allow either of us to present a show with a name like that attached to it? You need to get your head examined twice as much as I previously thought if you think we are going to be able to pull something like that off. One of the committee members is bound to pick up on that. They'll ban us both from the grounds before we ever get a chance to step foot onto it again. You are going to get us done, you bleedin' culchie. D'ya see if you had brains, you'd be dangerous!"

"But, John," I protested, "you are missing the boat. Our show is all about culture and flags, so it is. We are simply bringing the true, lived experiences of growing up in Norn Iron to America, and making it a family event. Using pyro, we will have burned out double-decker buses still on fire, overturned cars, create your very own balaclava using baklava, colour your shield by numbers, stone throwing distance contests, and water cannon wars. For the children, five rides in a paddy wagon comes with a nutritious meal of a bap and crisps with a tin of coke. Adults can purchase chip butty sandwiches paired with an alcoholic drink – we can play the part and call them Molotov cocktails!"

John responded by saying, "You know what, Greg. As much as you are not wise in the head and should be relocated to another planet, you have a good point there. Actually, we could do some great work with this show. I can't wait to get stuck into it. What else did he happen to ask you? Anything about the other suspects amongst our crowd in the authors tent?"

It was as if J.P. had suddenly forgotten how he had called me a delirious hoor and a bleedin' culchie a few moments earlier, all the while trying to gracefully save his own overgrown arse in the process.

I replied, "Here, c'mere 'til I tell you this. Wait 'til you hear. He says this to me, so he did. He says, 'What do you think happened to Arthur?' But what he wrote down was only a wee bit of it. Here, go back and finish reading what I sent to you. Read it out to me, will ye?"

Following my direction, John read, "I then thought it was a trap for a leprechaun. Ack, but sure for all the size of him, Arthur could have easily disappeared down that wee hole like Yoda and no one would have even noticed."

"John," I said. "As you can now see, Magnum never properly captured what I had said to him, so he didn't. He only took out the pieces he felt were necessary to him."

I could almost hear J.P. tapping out Morse Code to have me hauled off by the wee men in the white coats, or off to the land of the faeries so I could undergo a full lobotomy since I considered Arthur had possibly been lifted by the leprechauns. That was, until I filled him in on what was actually said.

"Check your email again, mo chara. There's much more to it than that."

As soon as the window popped up on his screen advising he had again received mail, John began reading out loud once more.

"After providing my response, Michael continued his sharp line of questioning and said to me, 'Yes, I see the hole, and you're telling me Arthur stepped in that hole and down he went?'"

I informed J.P. that Magnum's eyes were glazing over while listening to my answers, and said I'm sure he likely thought I was as rabid as a dog with rabies. Regardless, I had responded to him with the following statement:

"No, you got it wrong, Michael. Without a doubt, it was yer woman, Julie Burgess, along with her security detail. Let me think a wee second here. Yes! Gary Lovely, Bryan Boylan and Sean Boley! They kidnapped Arthur and pushed him down the hole to use him as part of their Celtic display within the Irish Authors section at The Book Loft. Room 13. It's haunted, so it is. Julie told us all about it when we were there for the advance book signing on Thursday night. They have a few ghosts living in there, including one who likes to help, one who is mischievous, and another who is the ghost of the man who originally created the store. I think there are seven spirits in total. As for Arthur Colaianni, he will be wailing like a banshee. The sound effects will be dead brilliant, so they will. They can have Arthur all they want. But I won't let them take the sash my father *never* wore, so I won't; it's the very same one J.P. knicked from County Derry. It plays a wee role in our *Belfast Riots In Tourist Season – Opinionated! Underappreciated! Totalitarianism!* presentation. The driver in our paddy wagon gets to wear it, along with a bowler hat, blue jeans, a balaclava, a camouflaged jacket, and a pair of Doc Martin boots. That way, no one can say we're not representing both sides! It is a presentation of equal opportunity, so it is!"

By this time, I had to ask if J.P. was still on the phone. The silence was deafening. The International Man of Mystery finally spoke up:

"Greg, after hearing and reading all of this, tell me one thing. Do you reside in the land of the living? Or is your head planted firmly up your arse?"

Shocked by this statement, which I should not have been because his unfiltered mind and gub are just as bad or worse than my own, I replied, "What would make you say something like that?"

J.P. drew a deep breath as he knew his response was going to be rather detailed.

"Do you think Michael is going to take you seriously? Because you waffled on so much, he probably thinks *you* are the suspect for using diversion tactics. People who work in the business of investigations look to find nuggets of truth, even in the most outlandish of statements. You're not far off, although I believe from having hung out with you as long as I have, you probably think everything you've told him is gospel! What else, pray tell, did he ask? To be honest, I have to give Michael credit for putting up with all of your shenanigans. You'd drive a saint to drink!"

"Magnum McCarthy took partial statements from my answers. He seemed to make up his questions as he went along," I responded. "He didn't follow his own notes, as I never mentioned anything about a gopher. Although he did ask me this, 'What do you think should happen to this person, or Julie from The Book Loft, who abducted Arthur and dragged him down that gopher hole?'"

"And then what?" asked J.P. "Did you call him out on that? Did you notice he never made any reference to Gary, Bryan, or Sean? Does Michael have an immunity deal with those lads directly?"

My response to John was almost as full as his previous statement had been to me.

"No, I did not. I wanted to see where his line of questioning went, and made mental notes that he ignored those three fellows. What I did say was this. 'Easy answer, so it is. They should all be made to drink foreign whiskey from County Antrim. I think they call it Wee Millie's Bush. You can imagine what that stuff does to an Irish author. Or better yet, those who are true followers and attend Kafflick mass once a year at Christmas time. One brush of that liquid poison against their lips and look out . . . they'll start marching while bashing Lambeg drums!'"

I heard muffled laughter in John's voice as he tried to contain himself, but he coughed a few times and returned to his previous serious tone as I continued telling him about how the interview went down. After a moment, he asked me if Michael wanted to throttle me because of how I was presenting my answers.

"I didn't stop to ask him what his thoughts were, John," I said. "When he asked about my plans to eliminate authors in the tent, since I said this would be a great way of getting on the New York Times Bestseller list, he felt the interview was over and he had the information he needed. Not in my mind, it wasn't."

"You're not just a mad hoor, you seriously need locking up and for the key to be thrown away," said John, sounding very sincere, as if this could indeed happen. It was as if he had read my own thoughts, which were a mirror image of how I felt about him more often than not.

"John," I said. "Listen to this. Before he could terrorize his next victim as he did me, I paused, lowered my voice to a whisper, and said I had some important information to share with him."

"Greg," he responded. "You mean to say you gave him an Irish goodbye? When people think you're done, you speak for another forty-five minutes straight. How did you manage to keep him engaged? Did you talk a lot more auld shite in the process? I am sure the poor man was mortified with the fact he'd even asked for you to speak to him in the first place. His head must have been melted. See you, Mad Dog McVicker? You could talk the leg off a stool or the hind leg off a donkey!"

I replied, "John, this is what I did. Since Magnum was looking for a suspect, and as I ended up being squarely in his sightlines, I thought I may as well give him much more than he could have possibly bargained for. Stall the ball for a wee moment again, will ye?"

I turned back to my laptop and sent him another copy-and-paste of what Michael had asked me before advising J.P. to check his email. It was again John who read this out. As he was doing so, I prepared yet another email message for him so he could see the two responses together.

"You never asked me about the Guke Slinger . . . Danica is her name! Or Dah-Nee-Tza. Ooh, it sounds so sexy, so it does. It derives from Slavic mythology and means *Morning Star*. I looked it up yesterday, so I did. A guardian goddess, she is the younger sister to the big ball of flame in the universe, the Sun. It all makes perfect sense. With her split-second sarcasm, she could roast the arse clean off ya! Even though she'd drive a saint to drink, just as she has done to me, can I interest you in joining me for a singalong, Michael? You'll know this one as soon as you hear me start. It's world famous. Ready? One, two, three and GO. Her eyes, they shone like the diamonds . . . ack, sure they're more like emeralds, so they are."

Hearing this, J.P. was surprised Michael didn't call in police reinforcement or have me hauled off to the nearest detention facility for not being of sound mind. I told him Magnum had tried to walk away from me at this point, but wouldn't you know, the further he walked, the louder my voice became.

"Michael! Last night, in the hotel! Room six, six, six. . . the Number of the Beast. I never told you this but the rock band, Iron Maiden, reminds me of Dah-Nee-Tza, so they do. Have you ever been on the receiving end of her sarcasm? There's no winning with that one. She invited us all up to her room - four, two, nine - screaming heard at Garden Stein! We all recorded *The Ballad of J.P. Sexton*, so we did. Jim and I said that mad hoor should be locked up in The Crum."

"In the name of Jesus," blurted John. "You said he took partial notes compared to what you were telling him. Is it any wonder? You are seriously one conversation from getting yourself put away permanently in an asylum, but even they would turn you loose for their own safety and sanity! Did Michael have duct tape on him? I know I would have taped you to a chair! Speaking of taping, I am surprised he did not use an audio recording device since he knows how much you like to talk. Is it any wonder you get called *Mad Dog*? I thought insanity flowed only through my family. But, as I have learned, you aren't wise whatsoever. You don't even drink like us Viking fishermen – we get marinated on several jars of D.H. Poitín before heading out on the boats. It doesn't only put hairs on your chest, but muscles on your body like you've never seen."

"John," I replied. "You may as well start drinking a lot more if that's the case, because the only muscles you have are mixed in with a bag of cockles you purchased down by the seashore. Now here, I am telling you, I was watching exactly what Michael was writing down. Not once did any of it match up to everything I was saying. But listen - Nick Bova, Skip Moersch and Kevin Cooper are all onto him. They realized he was only speaking about me specifically when he went to get his ride on the back of a turtle."

"Do I want to know what you mean by that, Greg?" John asked, all the while throwing caution to the wind.

Checking the time on my phone, I said, "John, listen. I had better go and make my way back to the tent before people start piling in there. I have yet to get set up. But quickly, Magnum is using an unmarked golf cart with two governors installed in its engine. Basically, the cart barely goes but because of the tires on it and how silent it runs, the driver is lulled into the false sense that each ride is brisk, while meeting environmental standards. As for us, on the other hand, we're using a cart which runs on D.H. Holy Frig Nitro Boost. I swear it travels at the speed of light, so it does."

"What did you say, Greg?" said John, cutting me off at blistering speed, just like the Paddy Only Wagon travels. "D.H. Holy Frig Nitro Boost? Is that what they called our secret family recipe? You only need one jar of that because it's so flammable, it burns for days. If you drink one shot of the stuff, it causes what some think are hallucinations. However, I can tell you from my own experimentation, it places you into a deep trance, your spirit travels, and you end up conversing with some dead Irish legend from decades gone by.

It is different for everyone, though, based on your deepest desires of who you would most love to meet but never had the opportunity. There are a few qualifications, however. You MUST have Irish or Viking blood in you to do so. Otherwise, you get severely blootered! Secondly, the dead come back in your thoughts without any advance warning and call you out to meet with them, but only you can see them. It has been said many a person was seen speaking into darkness and were put away for reasons of insanity. Meanwhile, they were conversing with the one they brought back from the spirit world. This is not something folks should take lightly."

I could not believe what I was hearing. J.P. was calling me out for telling him about mentioning The X-Files' agents Scully and Mulder, yet here he was telling me about the use of his grandfather's extremely potent Poitín, a recipe of such measured pureness, if mixed incorrectly, had driven many a maker mad and straight to his death over the cliffs of Donegal where it was secretly crafted away from the watchful eyes of An Garda Síochána na hÉireann – also more commonly referred to as the Irish police service.

If J.P. believes we can summon and chat to some dead Irish legend, I should give this a try! To dispel my doubts, he also promised to show me the exact location on my next trip home in November. That ought to be an experience in itself! He continued with his thoughts.

"I didn't ship you any extra of that other than what was strictly for our Funeral for a Viking presentation. Or perhaps I did send you a wee bit more. Yes, I sent you that, copies of my memoir, *The Big Yank* and *The Sash My Father Never Wore* from County Derry for the *Belfast Riots on Tour* show, or whatever you've now renamed it. How did you happen to get your hands on that? I was supposed to pick it up once I arrived in Dublin, Ohio for the Irish festival."

"I didn't," I responded. "But I know who did. Don't go anywhere. I'll ring you back shortly."

Chapter 19: Wishful Thinking

I'm the only local author in the Irish Authors' Corner. That makes me an outlander. I'm the Claire of the Dublin Irish Festival. Well, not exactly, maybe in a Barney Fife kind of way, but an outlander nonetheless. The other authors, sweet friends though they have become, all party without me at the hotel and then treat me as though I'm a saint. Because I write about saints, maybe; I don't know.

Only three people in the tent, so far as I know, have read my book *Brigid of Ireland*: Jeanne Crane, Brenna Briggs, and possibly Danica, Greg's fair maiden. I say possibly because she just purchased that book from me yesterday and I hear she's a speed reader. She's always reading when she's not procuring cream buns, which, when you think about it, makes Danica a lovely person to have around. At least I had always thought so. Now, due to the circumstances in the Irish Authors' Corner, it's hard to know what to believe

Funny how the cream bun has become such an icon with the authors. In Ohio, we don't even call them that. They are cream puffs from Schmidt's—world famous even before everyone here in the tent started talking about them and the Irish guys started calling them that. J.P. Sexton tried to steal one once from Greg. He said Greg was acting like the big man and talking to all the readers without taking a breath so if he wasn't going to eat the thing, J.P. would. I think there's some kind of rivalry between them to tell you the truth. Something about who looks more like Fabio.

Jim McVeigh with his long locks would be part of it too except he's a children's author and that would be weird. Against his brand as an author, to say the least. J.P. didn't come this year. Or they said he didn't. Danica made a point of telling everyone about some passport issue J.P. had. More likely, the two of them are plotting some kind of revenge to get back at Greg for allowing that pricey cream puff to sit uneaten and melting in the August heat. I mean, J.P.'s books *were* there. I mentioned my theory to Mike, the so-called investigator, but he dismissed me. I'm an outlander, after all.

I really wish I had gone to church that morning before the tent opened. Divine intervention was sorely needed, something more than Greg McVicker wrapping himself in caution tape and mumbling some Northern Irish lingo skyward, which honest to God was what he was doing. The chaos of someone missing and Mike McCarthy questioning everyone as though he had some official status, was more than unnerving.

I must have had some inkling about what would be needed because before going to the tent, I paused at the Wishing Tree to write down a wish. I felt led to do this, as if someone was praying me to it. Sinead Tyrone, probably. She was always doing sweet things like that. It was definitely something supernatural that caused me to pause at the tree because ordinarily I would be rushing to try to beat Arthur Cola to the tent. I don't know how in the world he always got there before everyone else, but it was a type of challenge now to get there first. But instead, I was writing something down on a sticky note to be hung on the tree:

A Prayer for the Lost

He who sings without a note
He who drinks without a cup
He who writes without a pen
May he find what is lost
And lose what is found.

Lame, I know. I don't even know what it means. And I signed my name! Who in the world will ever think of me, Cindy Thomson, as a creative writer? An outlander, yes. A writer? Hmm. All I can say in my defense is the words seemed not to come from me. I had intended a prayer but had those words actually come from a more sinister force?

Before I left the Wishing Tree, I noticed a batch of torn cloth ribbons tied all over the branches. While cloth is used on fairy trees in Ireland, here we have sticky notes. Why would anyone use cloth?

Someone sighed over my shoulder. I turned to see Brenna. "Lovely, isn't it?"

"Yes. Gotta go." I wanted to beat both her and Arthur to the tent, and Brenna had an escort, her son, to help her so I knew I better hurry. I hoped she wouldn't see my wish. She liked my book *Brigid of Ireland* and I didn't want her to think less of me by reading the terrible poetry I had penned. I paused, backed up while facing her, and attempted to rip that sticky note from the branch but it wouldn't budge. With a nervous giggle, I rushed away. There were about a thousand wishes there. No one would notice mine.

But when I arrived, there was a lot of confusion, with Mike asking questions, and no Arthur. Everyone beat him there so they all thought someone had abducted him. How ridiculous. His books were already there so he'd probably just gone off for a cream bun. But then . . . lots of shouting about a body being found in the pond just beyond the Wishing Tree. I knew nothing about it, of course, but decided it would be better not to mention the fact that I'd just been down there. They'd find out soon enough. That Brenna or her son didn't mention seeing me there was my lame wish bearing my signature.

Perhaps I could redirect Mike's investigation away from the Wishing Tree.

Chapter 21: Feast of the Gods

Date:	Sunday, August 4, 2019.
Entry 6:	A Wish, A Tree, A Lad Named Flatley!
Location:	Irish Authors' Corner.
Time:	Fifteen minutes before the gates opened.

Dear Diary . . .

After I ended my telephone call with the International Man of Mystery, I stretched and took a deep breath, trying to collect my thoughts and process everything that had been going on since my arrival a few days prior on Thursday morning. Although the festival always brings me to the brink of exhaustion and collapse, this one took things to a whole new level.

I noticed a shadowy figure out of the corner of my eye making a move toward me, which startled me to no end. My nerves were now on heightened alert. As quick as it was there, it disappeared out of sight. Nick Bova walked into the maintenance shed at Kevin's request. He said I would need a transport so that others who normally monitored my time while networking wouldn't start asking questions as to my whereabouts. Since the shadow had sent shivers up my spine, I felt it was time I made like a banana and split! I took him up on the opportunity.

"Are you okay, Greg?", Nick asked. "You look startled, as if you saw a ghost or something. Are you now being chased by your own shadow? Come on. Climb in and let's get moving." He wasn't aware of what had just happened.

I saw that Nick was not using the P.O.W. cart to come and get me this time, so I asked him about it. He explained that Kevin decided to hold onto it to allow others to see me talking to or driving with different staff. This would avoid drawing any more unwanted attention to myself or, for that matter, to them. Nick went on to say the festival was about to open so I should get back over to my station at the Authors' Corner. He then set about helping me get there.

"I'll be fine, Nick", I responded. "They all know I look for every opportunity to network and often disappear for short periods of time to do so. It should not be anything new to them. Say, do you have anyone living in the maintenance shed? Or any *thing*, for that matter?"

Nick cautioned me that although this might be the case with my fellow authors, his wife, Lisa, was at this morning's mass and had privately radioed Nick, telling him there was going to be an onslaught of eager readers coming to the Irish Authors' Corner. He didn't answer my question about the shed.

"They've heard about you, your missing author, and your love, Greg. Are you not aware of what is going on?"

"My love?", I responded. "Who, pray tell, might they be talking about, Nick? Oh, are they perhaps referring to

"She Who Shall Not Be Named"? The one who unleashes the Cruciatus Curse upon my soul through her unrelenting sarcasm? She has several different aliases around here! I have a new one for her. Wait until you hear what it is . . ."

Before I could blurt the rest of the words out, Nick cut me off.

"What was that you said? Lady Voldemo . . . No, not whatsoever! She's your manager from what the planning committee understands. Well, at least that's what's listed on her festival credentials. If my memory services me correctly, the actual name which was given to us for her on the application form is 'Professional Cat Herder.' Do you know anything about that?"

"Yeah, it's a long story, Nick," I replied sheepishly. "Talk to Jim McVeigh, Sinead Tyrone or to her wee friend, Angie Bertetto Swagger, who was responsible for getting the coffee cup made in honour of her efforts. However, Angie's comments are totally biased; the Imperius Curse was cast upon her!"

Shifting all attention away from this lighthearted engagement, as it would take me an eternity to explain to Nick how she came by this name, I then said, "Jesus, my mouth is dry from all of this talking and the lengthy phone call I had with J.P. Are we able to stop somewhere and get a wee drop? And what was that about my love? You never did get to finish your thoughts." Nick paused for a second, then chose to not immediately address my question, instead shifting the dialogue once more. It was as if we were playing a game of conversational chess.

"Funny enough, Greg," he said, "Lisa told me you could probably use a cup of tea right about now. She is going to bring you some cheesecake, although I understand that is not what you prefer. Anyways, Kay McGovern briefed us this morning before mass and said people saw you running around the grounds yesterday with your hands in the air, standing in front of the Celtic Cross, making an offering like it was a sacrificial lamb, all the while chanting in tongues of Gaelic. Many observers thought you were doing a traditional blessing for an Irish Claddagh ring. You know this better than any of us, Greg - they are used as wedding bands in Ireland. Wendy Bell was curiously watching you; she asked if one of the Irish speakers hosting a workshop could come over and provide the translation for us as she thought from her research you were performing a ritual based on Celtic paganism."

The truth is, this was a fairly normal moment for me, since chaos, madness and pure shenanigans are freely distributed into every moment of the festival. I waited for an opportunity to explain to Nick what I had been doing and saying, but he continued his thoughts without taking a breath. As much as Nick has become a good friend, it was as if he needed to get everything shared with me in case he couldn't get a chance later in the day, especially being the last full celebration of the festival, which always required an all hands-on deck approach; all 1,200 volunteers, that is. Either that, or Magnum McCarthy tried to interrogate him.

"Here - you may find this interesting," said Nick. "The female volunteer you talked to earlier this morning at the Spoken Word tent, you might know her - Melissa Stacy - well, she sought permission from Alison LeRoy and Laura Nelson to speak to the clergy before the ceremony started and asked that they let people know to keep an eye out for that Arthur Colaianni fellow you told her about. She is serious about her job and said you were deeply concerned for his wellbeing. Since there were quite the few thousand people in attendance at mass this morning, it will help us get the word out that much further. She distributed printed copies of a photo which was given to her by that overly-enthusiastic fellow who is parading around here playing detective. Here, have a look at it yourself."

I took one look at the photo and groaned. The picture Michael had shared was taken back in 2017 and included all the authors in attendance that year. We had all gathered in front of the Irish Authors' Corner and posed for a photo as a wonderful memory. As great of an idea as this was at the time, Michael had now drawn red circles around a few faces, each of whom were familiar to me, and included Jim McVeigh, J.P. Sexton and Colin Broderick. The Ulster lads!

Coincidentally, or not, neither J.P nor Colin were at this year's festival. On top of that, using a green felt marker, he drew an arrow pointing directly at my head, but provided no obvious explanation as to why it was there. My suspicions about Magnum's intent grew to another level.

"What is he playing at? He's up to no good," I thought.

Arthur did not resemble anyone from Wisconsin or Italy whatsoever, nor a Leprechaun King either, for that matter. His name was not even given as the one between us all who was reported as missing! However, upon a second, much more thoughtful look at the photograph, which was now out there amongst the festival participants and in full circulation, I noticed something even more peculiar. A lady who was not there in 2017 was suddenly at the festival this year, but was very much keeping her distance from most of us. What was her name again? Therese Gilardi! That's it. Another author with an Italian last name and a French first name. What it is about these Italians and their chameleon identities? She was the one who was sitting right beside Arthur. If anyone might know where he had disappeared to, it could very well be her.

I shook my head in disbelief before handing the photo back to Nick, and explained the issue I had with it.

"So much for him being a detective, Nick," I said. "What use is this to anyone? Folks are going to be asking others in the crowd if anyone has seen them, all the while pointing to the faces of J.P. and Colin. Just so you and Lisa know, J.P. is currently back home in County Donegal – and he told me he will not be able to make it in time for the festival. Colin is scouting locations in County Tyrone for his latest production. Since neither of them are here, it is going to add more chaos to an already overflowing mix. And what about that green arrow? What do you think? Is Michael "Magnum" McCarthy up to something? Is he trying to undermine my own efforts to find Arthur?"

Nick quietly took in what I said, along with my constant questions, and continued to drive me along in the golf cart, taking us in a direction we did not normally go. Lost in my thoughts, I finally lifted my head as Nick began slowing down and tapped me on the shoulder, only to see the Wishing Tree was now in front of me. He paused and said I should get a look at what is written on the wishes on the tree - there were thousands of the same message. I turned to Nick with a bewildered look on my face, asking why we were here. He finally answered that one question.

"Do you see what you have created? This is what I meant by 'your love', Greg. Look what you've done!"

Staring back at me, scrawled in a variety of handwriting styles, attached to the Wishing Tree, was the message *"Dubh Linn borróg uachtar, a grá mo chroí!"* Nick looked at me and said Laura had informed him that the Schmidt's Food Truck had a run on Dublin Cream Buns, so much so it was like watching the feeding of the five thousand. John Schmidt told her himself that they could not keep up with the outrageous demand for them and had to bring in extra staff! John then asked Laura if a meeting could be arranged so that he and I could take a photo together – he wanted to feature one of my co-authored books with J.P. Sexton and Mark Rickerby in the Schmidt's Sausage Haus und Restaurant as is located in Columbus, Ohio. Oh my. Such an honour!

"I've since learned the truth about this. Folks intently watched as you held a puff pastry above your head, offering it up to the Celtic Cross, all the while saying, "Dubh Linn borróg uachtar, a grá mo chroí!" Murry Drury, who was learning the Gaelic language, came out from the workshop and repeated what you were saying. Wendy asked Murry to say it again, then translate it to English, before jumping up to a microphone and told those watching in awe you were saying "Dublin Cream Bun, love of my heart." They all thought the moment was so magical, festival attendees all lined up for hours and even began to whisper, 'P.S. I love You' after making their purchase and before taking their first bite – simply said, Greg, it was love at first sight. They figured this was some mystical Irish way of finding and falling in love, like getting the gift of the gab from kissing the Blarney Stone in County Cork. You can now add the title of 'Matchmaker' to your résumé. The one sad part, though, Hillary Swank's heart is indeed going to be broken after all!"

My response was not so swift, but rather detailed. What else is new?

"Oh, Jesus Murphy, have mercy on my poor wee Irish soul. Wait until Fabio Fionn, the Love Child from Malin

Head hears about this. I swear he will have me certified, committed, crucified, and locked away in Purdysburn in Belfast. The men in the white coats will be locking me up for the goodness of all mankind, so they will. And they won't be bakers, I can promise you that."

Nick looked at me, smiled, and said, "To be honest, I don't think it's Purdysburn you will need to worry about, Greg. Wait until your *manager*, Dah-Nee-Tza, hears about this one. Does she have Jedi mind powers?"

I lowered my head for a moment, only to look back up. Using the sign of the cross from my childhood days growing up Roman Catholic, I blessed myself three times while saying "Lord have mercy, Christ have mercy, Lord have mercy" in succession. God only knows what fate lies ahead for me once Danica hears this. After all, it was she who brought the first Dublin Cream Bun into the Irish Authors' Corner. And, well, from my first diary entry back on page 19, I suppose the rest is history. I don't think she'll be calling me an arse this time, but something much worse and not worth writing in these pages!

Out of the corner of my eye, I noticed one wish on the tree had a different message on it. However, Nick had already pressed the pedal on his golf cart and started moving slowly forward.

"Nick, hang on a second. Do you see this? Look." I had startled Nick since I not only asked him to wait, I also threw my left arm in front of him.

Getting off the golf cart, I focused on one card in particular and read the inscription on it. What was peculiar is it had been typed onto a clear label and affixed to a card before being placed on to the Wishing Tree.

"What exactly does that read, Greg?", Nick asked.

I responded by simply saying, "Beidh údar amháin níos lú ann inniu."

Nick stared inquisitively before I finally looked back at him and broke the awkward moment of silence which had descended on the two of us. It was as if I expected Nick to also be somewhat fluent in the Irish language and was awaiting his response to it.

"Strangely enough and when translated from our traditional voice of Gaeilge, it means, 'Today there will be one less author.' And wouldn't you know it, Arthur Colaianni went missing just this morning, which happens to be the final day of the festival. What are the chances this would be placed here along with all these other cards? Who else knew about this, I wonder? Did anyone else take notice that this card didn't match the other wishes?"

It was then that I realized one of the lovely folks in amongst our family circle of authors had been practicing Gaelic. This was only after they had asked both J.P. and I two years prior at this same festival for a few words, which they could then scribe into the books they were signing, or say as a greeting when meeting prospective buyers who approached their table. They wanted to learn from the best wordsmiths around – the wild fella's from County Antrim and County Donegal. One was a charmer. The other, as J.P. mentioned previously, is a mad hoor of the highest order. During a wee trip by a bunch of us over to LaZenia, Spain for a three-day rock concert at Paddy's Point, one or the both of us decided our colleagues should perhaps inscribe this into their books, just for the craic: "Póg mo thóin, por favor."

Looking back at the tree, I saw a second wish, which seemed to perhaps be completely out of place, or perhaps it had been placed there expressly for the salvation of my soul. It was called *A Prayer for the Lost,* and although I thought I knew who the author might be based on the signature, the moment was what I truly needed. Even though I should be considered a heathen from many of my diary entries, I genuflected, then blessed myself in Gaelic before reading the prayer loudly enough for myself and anyone within my immediate vicinity to hear:

In ainm an Athar,
Agus an Mhic,
Agus an spioraid Naoimh,
Amen.

He who sings without a note
He who drinks without a cup
He who writes without a pen

May he find what is lost
And lose what is found.

After placing my hand to my lips and returning a kiss to the note on which the prayer was written, I paused for a second before taking my seat beside Nick once again.

"Nick, I had better get back to the Irish Authors' Corner," I said. "I need to start entering this engagement with you into my diary, and begin flushing out my suspicions as to who may indeed be behind this whole mystery. Although, in saying that, there is much work ahead of me today. I am going to need help from a few musicians, authors, and most likely some of the other festival representatives here who celebrate home, namely a fast-footed lad by the name of Michael Flatley."

Aghast at my comment, Nick looked at me sternly and said, "Michael Flatley? Do you mean the creator of *Riverdance, Lord of the Dance* and *Feet of Flames*? A native of South Side Chicago? Greg, if you look at the schedule, you will see he is not here. He's gone into retirement. Sure, he has hung up his dancing shoes – his last performance was on St. Patrick's Day in 2016 at a show in Las Vegas."

"Aye, Nick. He may have indeed done just that for now, but wait and see . . ."

Nick continued with his thoughts. "Greg, he holds the Guinness World Record for the fastest tap dancing, at thirty-five taps per second. Did you know his feet were also insured for 57.6 million dollars U.S.?"

Looking straight ahead of me and without blinking an eye, I said, "Aye, I know that Nick. Sure, I understand J.P. Sexton has already taken that much insurance out on me. Although, as soon as he finds out the Professional Cat Herder is probably going to send me to meet my maker once she learns about my pagan ritual yesterday at the Celtic Cross, he will likely double down and take bets."

Smiling like a Cheshire Cat and readjusting himself in the driver's seat of the golf cart, Nick pressed down the pedal and drove toward the Irish Authors' Corner without another word.

Chapter 23: From Screenplay Writer to Production Manager

After arriving back at the Irish Authors' Corner with Nick, I immediately took inventory of my surroundings. I noticed my book display area had mostly remained untouched – that is, except for the yellow caution tape that had since been placed around it, almost segregating me from everyone else stationed on either side of me and around the tent in a U shape. I laughed out loud and shook my head in disbelief. My fellow authors had taken the time to get me back with my own form of 'shenaniganism's' while I was away making my phone call to Fabio Fionn MacSexton, or so I thought.

"Greg, you've finally come back," said a gentle, familiar voice from behind me. I turned around to see Lisa Bova and went to give her a warm, friendly Irish hug. However, because she was holding a small tray of cheesecake, I placed my arms over one another and onto my own shoulders, telling her this was a virtual hug to say thank you for the thoughtful gift. As I had interrupted her, she continued speaking.

"I thought you could use this treat, although I know you would prefer a Dublin Cream Bun. Wendy Bell told me about your offering at the Celtic Cross yesterday and how pandemonium broke out thereafter. You have elevated puff pastry to a new level here. All of the festival attendees, including the City of Dublin staff, are wanting to get their hands on it. The belief is . . ."

Clearing my throat, I finished her thought for her, as I sometimes do: "Aye, it is steeped in Celtic mythology, so it is. Folks are under the impression that if they first whisper, 'P.S. I Love You' after making their purchase and before taking their first bite, they will fall in love."

Without missing a beat, and in perfect unison, we finished the sentence together. "It's like getting the gift of the gab from kissing the Blarney Stone in County Cork." We looked at each other and burst into a fit of laughter, sharing a much-needed moment of comic relief due to everything else that was going on.

I apologized to Lisa as there was no place for her to put the tray of cheesecake down since my table was in disarray. I had come back to set up my display of books on top of the tablecloth featuring Irish designs and patterns which the fair maiden purchased and had her wee mum, Danielle, sew together for me, but the yellow caution tape took precedence as if to somehow warn people to avoid me like the plague. I asked if Lisa knew anything about this. Lowering her voice to a whisper, she replied, "Greg, I do know who is responsible for this, but you have to first understand the young lad is extremely overprotective of his mother, who is stationed a few seats from you. His name is Shannon."

Startled, I looked over to where he was standing, which was right next to my fellow author, Brenna Briggs. Taller than his miniscule mum, Shannon stooped down to whisper into her ear. Brenna was looking directly at myself and Lisa, trying not to be obvious about what he was sharing. Lisa already knew.

"Greg, along with everyone else here, Shannon was interviewed by Michael McCarthy. As he was taking the notes down, Shannon was intently looking at Michael's notebook rather than focusing on the task at hand. I don't believe Michael knew he was doing this. However, Shannon noticed you had said your biggest downfall is honesty, and that you thought about eliminating everyone from the Irish Authors' Corner so the New York Times would list you as the bestseller. He noted you had asked Michael to give you a hand with it, although he in turn asked you if Julie Burgess was working with you on completing this. He started asking a lot of questions."

She went on to say, "Since Michael was a former police detective stationed in Rochester, New York, Shannon thinks the two of you are in cahoots. He put up the yellow caution tape around your table. If you can, take a quick look, but do so without being too obvious. You will see he has also moved Brenna's table an additional six feet away from yours and stacked boxes in between as to give the illusion that they needed the space."

I looked to see that Shannon had built a cardboard wall between our tables. I shook my head, chagrined. "Lisa, these folks don't understand the Irish banter, craic and wit. We are all about having a bit of a laugh, making light of everything that we can. It is our coping mechanism, a strategy I suppose any of us who was born during The Troubles in Norn Iron learned in the womb. Otherwise, we would have all ended up being complete lunatics."

Lisa glanced at me with raised eyebrows, knowing I was stating the obvious. I continued.

"Alright, Lisa. I know where you are going with that look. But it is true. We poke fun at anything and everything. We do have our serious conversations, but when trouble descends upon us, as they say, laughter is the best medicine. Obviously, they don't know who I am or how much I love to share in a bit of craic. Sure, even my fellow author, Mark Rickerby would tell you that. Along with J.P. Sexton and I, Mark joined us in collaborating to write a book called *Four Green Fields* about growing up either in the Republic of Ireland as J.P. did, in Northern Ireland as I did, but more so, in Belfast as Mark's beloved father, John Sidney Rickerby did. John and Mark are from the opposite side of the community compared to J.P. and I – they were raised as Protestants. However, from that book and the stories we shared, I can tell you we share the same irreverent sense of humour. One of John Rickerby's stories in that book is called *Fenians and Milk Bottles*, about an experience he had in the 1940's. Even with a title such as that and its derogative reference toward Irish Roman Catholics, it was brilliant in that John showed that no matter what side of the community in Belfast we came from, we're all pretty much one and the same, and that humour was and still is our saving grace."

Precariously, Lisa placed the cheesecake tray onto the nearest table which gave up a little bit of space as Shannon had begun stacking boxes there as well. It was previously occupied by Laura Bentley. I would go on to learn that she and her husband, Ralph, took leave shortly after the chaos started surrounding the disappearance of our fellow author. Since we had all been informed well in advance that they were double booked for festivals, we knew Laura would be leaving earlier, effectively eliminating her from my pool of suspects.

Lisa continued with her thoughts. "Speaking of Mark Rickerby, before I forget, our Assistant Director, Laura Nelson – she received a package from Always A Day Late Express this morning from California, but it is addressed to yourself. Mark called moments after it arrived and said it was urgent you got it as soon as possible. You might want take a look at this." She then handed me the package.

As I started to remove the tab from the envelope, Lisa went on to say, "I know all about your Irish humour, Greg.

Barbara Burkholder-Cody told me about you and J.P. a few years ago when the two of you made your debut appearance at the festival, and how you both roped Jim McVeigh and Colin Broderick into it as well. Poor Ben Anderson was stuck in between the lot of you. He said he has never laughed so hard in his life! It was said you and J.P. did an impromptu, yet never-ending show for the folks who were coming in to buy your books and had gathered an audience. Not to forget, that is the time and birthplace of your Dublin Cream Bun story! Say, did Danica ever forgive you for that one? She must have been so annoyed with you! I can only imagine what she said."

"No, forgiveness with that one doesn't come easy, Lisa," I replied. "I am still on the end of her perpetual sarcasm and jokes. You have no idea how much torture comes with that!"

"Awww. Poor Geggy," said Lisa in an extremely sardonic voice, one which was all too familiar to my ears!

The words, "Sweet Jesus, have mercy on my poor wee soul," burst out of me. "Please tell me you are not taking lessons from her, for that is *exactly* what Danica does to me every time I point out I am taking more of her playful abuse. Oh, the torture I must endure."

Looking back at me, Lisa said, "As the old saying goes, if opportunity knocks, take it, even if it means it is at your expense. Did you not read the super-small, barely noticeable to the naked eye, fine print written in invisible ink on her initial email before signing up for this? What was it that attracted you to her? It must have been her majestic personality!"

Startled by her unadulterated impersonation of Danica, I almost jumped out of my skin. "Majestic? Are you kidding me? She has multiple personalities, so she does, but since there are so many, I never know which one is going to respond first! I have blushed that much at what comes out of her unfiltered mouth, I honestly should be granted Sainthood!"

Lisa began giggling at my comment as she had enjoyed watching Danica do this to me at the festival throughout the past few years and decided to give it a try herself. Relishing in this moment, she then said, "Answer this for me, Greg. Has she ever asked how one might say "I love you" in Gaelic?

Sheepishly, I looked at her and responded, "Actually, I think she has, Lisa, countless times but her translation of it is a bit off if you ask me, so it is."

"Oh, really?" said Lisa, pushing the tray of cheesecake further onto the table to ensure it was safe. She then asked, "What exactly does she say to you, pray tell?

Lowering both my head and my voice, I simply said, "Shut up, Greg!"

Lisa brought her hand to her mouth to try and stifle a giggle, which proved frugal. She erupted into a fit of uncontrollable laughter and collapsed into Wendy who had just arrived to catch the tail end of our conversation. Within seconds, Lisa and Wendy were doubled over, recollecting the madness of J.P. and myself along with Colin and Jim; the birth and development of what has now become the legendary Dublin Cream Bun story, as well as the Professional Cat Herding, Guke slinging fair maiden taking every opportunity to enact evil revenge upon me.

"Sláinte mhaith," I said with a chuckle while raising a bottle of lemonade. "Laughter is indeed the spice of life."

Turning my attention back to the envelope, I removed its contents and started unfolding the pages. There were a few extra items in the bottom of the package, although I did not immediately look to see what those were. I took myself off to the side and began reading the letter.

"Greg, my dear friend and fellow Belfast author," it began. *"As you are probably already aware, it is me, Mark. I was not able to make it to the festival as I am working on bringing my latest screenplay to full production. It is a parody. We already filmed a test trailer for it. Now it is a matter of trying to secure the funding to bring it from infancy to the big screen. I can tell you I am working around the clock. I am blessed to have it in my corner as it helps keeps track of time. Since every spare second I have is being fully invested into making this dream come true, I was unable to make the festival. The title of my latest screenplay is Ben Hoor 2. As it is being filmed in the most northern point of southern Ireland, I bet you will not be able to guess who the lead*

actor is going to be. He has the looks, height and charisma, but he lacks muscles. We had to order a deluxe bodysuit for him!"

I knew Mark was working on a screenplay since I had visited him and his family a year before while down in the sunny sands and surf of Malibu, California. I had gone to Palm Springs for a social work conference and decided to stay a few extra days as to not miss the opportunity of meeting my fellow writer for the first time. Completely surrounded by Hollywood legends, sound studios, talk shows, and star-studded footpaths filled with residents and tourists, Mark was in the prime location for film and television production.

His letter continued, *"Just so you know, I was speaking with J.P just this morning about his lines, which are more or less simple grunting noises, he let me know about the Funeral for a Viking presentation the two of you are planning for the Dublin Irish Festival. We had a very lengthy chat about this, although he did say it was much shorter than every telephone and in-person conversation he has ever had with you. I think the idea is certainly out of this world, but does J.P. realize this will likely be a one-time show if you are planning on placing him on top of a ship, setting it on fire and pushing him out to sea? Also, I did research on the grounds of the Dublin Irish Festival. Since there is no water nearby and I hate to point out the obvious, I wonder how the two of you planned to accomplish this colossal feat?"*

Mark made a tremendous point. Although J.P. and I had planned everything else out and were now ready to move the production from the development stage to live design, even though we had not secured permits from the City of Dublin to do so just yet, let alone received their explicit and unfettered permission, we were very much enthused about having this happen. I wondered about what Mark had said; that is, if J.P. knew he and I were not able to push him out to sea. I returned to his letter.

"I was reviewing the River Access portion of website for the city of Dublin, Ohio. Quoting this directly from there, it states, "The City of Dublin is committed to providing residents access to waterways." I could not find any mention about two mad Irishmen who had been invited out to their yearly celebratory festival and have since gone rogue! Anyway, just to make you both aware, there are currently four formal access points along the Scioto River for canoes and kayaks in Dublin:

1. *Amberleigh Community Park*
2. *Dublin Spring Park*
3. *Emerald Parkway Bridge Parking Lot (beneath I-270 on Riverside Drive)*
4. *Scioto Park*

Now, do you see there is nothing listed about launching Viking ships along the river or having a funeral in same? This *could be somewhat problematic for the two of you. As such, I did some additional research. There is a website in the United Kingdom that creates wooden model size replicas of Viking ships which can be set on fire and launched. The problem with this is that they cost £430.00, or approximately $550.00. In saying so, with each presentation, unless you are planning to charge gate fees for this production and are able to recreate pint size versions of J.P., which will likely still be taller than most Irish people, you will need a sponsor to cover your costs. Otherwise, as hellacious as it is, the two of you will go bankrupt in no time flat."*

The other issue with this is when Vikings have funerals, there are other warriors who are trained in the art of bow and arrow. They dip their arrows in vats of oil, place them into a fire and launch them into the ship to start the process. J.P. told me he is trained in this art form but, since you are planning on having a Viking funeral featuring him, he is not able to do this himself. I hope you clearly understand what I am getting at here. The task now comes down to you. If my memory serves me correctly, a story which you wrote and shared in our collaborative effort was called ***"Murphy's Law: My Friend of Misery"*** *in that if something could go wrong for you, it did several times over. What was there? At least fourteen occurrences? No pun intended here, Greg, but I am sure you get my drift. This is not a good idea. Whatsoever! Not only do I fear for the safety of yourself, but for J.P. and everyone else involved."*

"Wonderful of Mark to think about my safety and wellbeing," I thought to myself. I am sure he was even more worried about everyone else around me since he was familiar with how clumsy I was as a child after reading my fourth book based on my real-life childhood adventures, *"The Adventures of Silly Billy – Sillogy: Volume 1."* For a second, I recalled when Mark had asked me how the name of the book came about. I explained that since it is a trilogy of silly stories, it became a *Sillogy*!

Clearing my thoughts and taking a quick look around to see everyone else was busy at their tables, I once again went back to his letter.

"Not to worry, though - all is not lost here. I thought of another way the two of you could pull this off. You could build what is called a Viking Pyre and incorporate it as part of your Belfast Riots on Tour presentation. However, I must inform you this involves a Protestant element and most likely not what you had in mind.

Whilst speaking to J.P., I told him about this. At first, he thought I was out of my mind, but after explaining the issue of the river access, and since you are already stationed on several acres of land at the festival, you have much more room for the audience and their participation. Bear in mind that safety should be your first and foremost concern. Being the International Man of Mystery that he is, I told J.P. to contact my uncle, who is employed with the Belfast City Council. He is the fellow who helps to source wooden pallets which are delivered to bonefire sites all around Belfast and in surrounding areas. These are subsequently used for eleventh night preparations.

In order to make this happen, I sent J.P. the instructions required to secure a score of pallets. I made him an identification tag using one of his secretive names and sent it over for his review. He must now get a photograph of himself wearing a sash (I heard he secured one in County Derry), go to the council and present himself. The title on his badge must say POC FADA."

I lifted my head from intently reading this letter, wondering what Mark was up to using a Gaelic word to secure pallets from the Belfast City Council in support of our *Funeral for a Viking* presentation. In translation, the term *Poc Fada* means "long puck." Every year, an All-Ireland Poc Fada championship is held, testing the skills of the top players within the Irish sports of Camogie (played by women) and Hurling (played by men). He has no hope with this, I thought. Regardless of this, I kept reading.

"Now Greg, I am sure you are currently wondering why I am using a Gaelic word. In this case, POC FADA stands for ***P****allet* ***O****fficial* ***C****ollector –* ***F****or* ***A****merica's* ***D****ebut* ***A****ppearance. However, the explanation J.P. must give is he is replicating a bonefire at a festival in the U.S. to showcase what the yearly fuss is all about each July, although we ourselves know that he is going to be using this to create his Viking Pyre.*

I have been thinking further about this. Are you able to get your hands onto an effigy by chance? If this show is indeed successful, the two of you will be able to replicate it as a Broadway play, although I personally believe it will be a one-time event even without sending J.P. off on his otherworldly journey. With that, I would like to take a break from my screenplay writing and become the official production manager of this travesty. It'll be like a modern-day Macbeth, though with very little Shakespeare and a whole lot of tragedy. Since I live in California, I will be able to get a camera crew to come and record this train wreck, perhaps for a future documentary!

Best wishes to you, brother."

The letter ended but that was not the end of Mark's messaging to me. There was a sheet taped inside the envelope on paper which matched the colour of the envelope itself. If I had just turned it upside down to empty out the loose contents which remained within it, I would have completely missed the secondary message intended strictly for my eyes only. For some reason, I had peered into the envelope and discovered the extra warning within. It was like an Irish goodbye, only in written form!

"P.S: Be safe and look after yourself, Greg. I understand one of your fellow author's disappeared. I hope he turns up safely. Don't tell anyone this, but would you believe I ran into two actors – or they ran into me - as I was in the process of sending

this package to you – you may happen to have heard of them – David Duchovny and Gillian Anderson. They are here in Burbank. I was on my way to mail this letter when they blocked my path. I asked if they were making preparations to go back onto the set of The X-Files and start filming all over again – they told me this was not the case but that they were working on an active file. I was gub smacked when they brought up your name and the name of a fellow named Arthur Colaianni. Do you know who he is?

They did not say to me who he was but asked I mention his name in my letter to you. Of course, they had to spell out that last name. It doesn't make any sense to me personally, but something big is going down. Why would a man with an Italian surname be associated with an Irish lad such as yourself? Is he possibly the one behind the disappearance of the author who went missing? I also ask how is it that they were at the same location as I and ran an interference to prevent me from sending this package to you until they apprised me of what was going on. Am I now an accessory to this?

By the way, they said notable Irish characters from the past are reaching out to a few of the authors up there who are not directly from Ireland. They are giving them precise messages to help locate the missing person. David said that you personally must be cautious, as there are those who are going to try to undermine your work to get to the bottom of this. Gillian asked me to give you this personal message:

– Keep your friends close, and your enemies closer! ~ Mark."

Since that last word of caution brought Mark's urgent letter to an end, I looked into the envelope to see he had indeed sent me a copy of J.P.'s official badge credentials, along with another set for me, and one for himself. "Wow, he certainly has put a lot of planning into this," I thought. On the back of each one was this: *From Viking to Valhalla – A Mark Rickerby Production. In association with Malin Head's Striking Viking and Belfast Child Publications.*

Taking a moment to reflect on everything Mark said, there were key elements that he referenced which are required if we are to proceed further with our presentation - the first being Broadway, and the second - getting a hold of an effigy. I made a mental note to myself that a trip would be needed a little later in the day to ask if Alison or Laura would have one that I may be able to borrow from their annual St. Patrick's Day parade. The biggest and more obvious of this entire mystery though, was that both David Duchovny and Gillian Anderson found Mark in California but were not working on a set production of The X-Files, yet they knew about the disappearance of Arthur.

At that, I heard a voice which broke my concentration.

"Greg. Perhaps the fine folks at the Wake House might be able to provide you with some much-needed assistance. Stop there. I am sure there you will find a clue or two . . ."

Chapter 25: My Shamrock Senses are Tingling

Date: Sunday, August 4, 2019.
Entry 7: From Authors to Suspects!
Location: Irish Authors' Tent – Dublin Irish Festival.
Time: Ten minutes after opening time.

Dear Diary . . .

Would you believe it's me again? Yeah, well. I leave such an everlasting and unforgettable impression – in my own mind, that is. I hope you managed to read my previous entries from early Thursday morning and the others since then. Wait, what am I writing? I must keep my head down as there is a lot of suspicious activity going on.

Get low, Greg. Lower. There you go. Someone left behind their sunglasses. Put them on.

I honestly have to stop whispering to myself. I think I have a healthy understanding as to why the others have taken to calling me Mad Dog McVicker. It's because what my ma said all those years is true. I am *not* wise in the head. I miss her loving terms of endearment. Nevertheless, I think I have lost my mind; that is if I hadn't already done so previously. This mystery surrounding Arthur vanishing without much to go on has pushed me over the edge.

Anyway, do you remember I was saying my shamrock senses were tingling? If my wee ma were here, she would know exactly what's going on. As kids, we affectionately referred to her as *Katie the Spud Lady* as she always knew everything my siblings and I were up to. She told us she had eyes on the back of her head! Perhaps I have inherited her potato like abilities.

After mass ended, the gates opened and visitors gathered within the author's tent. A rumor was floating around that the remnants of a Dublin Cream Bun and a box were discovered at The Book Loft table where Julie does her transactions for us, yet there was still no sign of the Leprechaun Godfather. I had personally hoped Arthur would have surfaced during my time at the maintenance shed while I was speaking with The Last Jedi, but no such luck. Not one of my fellow authors had seen him in that time – if they did, they weren't saying. Everyone was succinct, enigmatic, concealing more than they revealed.

As for the body that was supposedly pulled from the pond near the recreation centre – some thought it was J.P., but as I have spoken to him, I know he is alive and well albeit not wise in the head like me. That phone call helped me discover another clue, but I am going to keep that information to myself. For some nagging reason, I have a suspicious feeling I'll learn more once I head over to the Celtic Rock stage this afternoon. It's going to take some stealthy work to expose those answers, though.

Before I sauntered back in here, I saw Melissa Stacy again. She filled me in on everything that has transpired since we first spoke, including many more volunteers who are now hanging around our immediate area. Melissa said she spoke to Mike Herriott, my original greeter at the airport, who also helps run us back and forth from the hotel to the festival. Although I have not seen much of Mike, he told Melissa that the fella who transported me from the Columbus airport when I arrived on Thursday stayed back at the hotel that morning as he wasn't on shift and wanted to relax. That's the same driver whose tour bus I snuck onto and left a wee cream bun for. He seemed so unassuming, although Mike found out he had hoped to get autographs from the Red Hot Chili Pipers and a selfie with the boyos in We Banjo 3, which is why he stayed back. Is he somehow connected to all of this? I wonder if he told Mike he received two gifts that morning or if it would make him a suspect as well? I guess it is best to steer clear of everyone's radar at this time, especially as a result of the interrogation tactics being deployed by the New York Spoil. I am sure people are talking about that.

Although sitting at my table, I must force myself to explore the disaster inside my head. Since the plethora of events this morning, Michael is now sitting very quietly (I am one to talk. Miracles never cease, as my wee ma would say) to my left in the author's tent on the other side of Jeanne Crane. His golf cart, which is parked directly behind him, is guarded by something that looks similar to the mannequin at the Wake House. How he managed to pull that off is beyond me. Michael is writing notes to himself, listening to Sinead while waiting to speak to guests about his books. I wonder if he is interrogating those guests by way of slipping specific instructions into their books but is pretending these are his inscriptions.

Wait a second, where is Ann? It's not like her to be missing in action. I had better make a note of that.

Beside Jeannie sits her best friend, Priscilla Richter, who is busy reading one of the books she purchased. I notice Therese Gilardi has left her table – again! Is Michael keeping track of this? She has been extremely distant from us throughout the weekend, and although she keeps to herself, she is quite careless in trying to keep her actions secretive. Therese reaches into her purse and then pulls out what appears to be a small glass bottle; maybe perfume. Holding it in her hand for a moment, she looks around to ensure no one is watching before raising it toward her neck, then she turns her back. Is she drinking it? If so, what exactly is it? She then leaves.

Damn. Just when I thought I was going to catch her in the act, a lady is approaching my display. She is coming at me directly from Michael's table, pointing her finger and smiling. What is that all about? Hang on a second - why did she stop to browse through a copy of *The Big Yank*? Is she possibly looking for something specific for Michael such as an email address for him? I should put up a sign saying "J.P. is missing in action", although it might cause further panic, and we have enough of that going on! Then again, it might be lovely to see Magnum McCarthy go frantic and leave the rest of us alone.

Okay, I'm back. I was privileged to have met that lovely lady a time or two before. It was brilliant to see her again, although not under these circumstances. At first, I did not recognize who she was because I was trying to keep my head down while taking notes about my surroundings. This is the worst feeling yet, as everyone around here has since become a suspect. The lady's name is Anastasia Sebourn. She has an incredible smile, a beautiful personality, and is a wonderful soul. Since she picked up a copy of *Four Green Fields* from me, and as she was over at Michael's table before coming over here, is it fair to say the interrogator is now in the process of corrupting her? Is he going to use my signed book to conduct a handwriting analysis and psychological assessment? Did he buy her the book to ensnare me? And could the reason she asked me not to inscribe the inner message to her be to prevent becoming a suspect herself by virtue of previous association with me? My thoughts are on edge since I am now questioning her intentions, as good as they may be. I shouldn't do that. I need to offer her an apology. I'm sure she realized I was not my usual jovial self.

I walked around from my table and went out to where my banners are. I stopped her, gave her a hug and thanked her for coming back to see me again. Funny enough, though, before taking her leave, Anastasia asked me about Danica. With my suspicions on high alert, I at first said I had never seen her before in my life. Anastasia fired a strange look at me. I then told her that Dah-Nee-Tza is a lost soul who finds comfort in going to festivals, hangs out with Celtic and Viking men, bought her way into this group by purchasing a Dublin Cream Bun, and became a full-on groupie. I added that Anastasia may wish to do the same. Thankfully, she had a good laugh at that!

On second thought, I am going to look up her name here and see what it says. It is of Greek origin and comes from the word *anastasis*, spelled ἀνάστασις, which means ***resurrection***. Perhaps she can use her goddess-like looks and powers to resurrect the mannequin currently guarding Michael's golf cart. It would frighten the shite right out of him, which would allow me to get a look at his notes and see where he's at in his own investigation. Hmm. I will have to keep that thought at the back of my mind until a bit later. I may be able to pull something off just yet.

Frig. That distraction worked perfectly. Anastasia left but forgot something on my table - a business card from Michael with his cell phone number on it. I wouldn't have thought much about it until I read the back. I don't know who wrote it but it reads, *"Tell me what he said."* Therese is gone again. I wanted to see where she went this time, but she has been swallowed up by the large crowd. If she is going to meet someone, I need to find out who that is.

I have never revealed this to anyone before this, Diary. You are the first. We learned a game called I Spy in my social work interpersonal communication skills course. Thus, I spied with my wee eye that Ann was quite covert during the filming of the song, *The Ballad of J.P. Sexton* last night back at the Embassy Suites. A video was recorded which serves as proof of their involvement. But why were she and Michael on the road this morning when I called to let them know Arthur was missing? Did he not say to me he was ten miles out? Where were they going or coming from? That's the question.

Before Michael completes his investigation, I need to beat him at his own game. Now if I were to open my own private investigation company, I would call it *I Spy With My Wee Eye.* I will need my approach to be much more cautious. On that note, here goes nothing I guess . . .

Suspect One – Jim McVeigh

I first met Jim three years ago. He hails from one of the toughest of areas, the New Lodge Road in Belfast. Coming from Norn Iron, we gain a sixth sense, learn how to read people, suss them out and what they are about. Jim spoke to me about where he grew up, only for the conversation leading to me informing him where *I* went to school, in Glengormley up the Hightown Road. I wondered which of us got the upper hand on this exchange. Anyway, I hated that torture chamber; it became my place of study for three gruelling years. Enough lads like myself suffered cruel fates, beaten half to death by bastard teachers hell-bent on the destruction of our senses of self.

One wee lad I went to school with shared Jim's last name – it is his younger brother, Anthony. What are the chances I would meet Jim several years later on the other side of the world? The crazier thing is he went to school with my cousin, Morris. It makes Jim even more of a suspect now! Perhaps Anthony was feeding information to his older brother about me.

Thus, the plot to knock off several writers within the Irish Authors' Corner may have been planted as a seed years ago and is now reaching its moment of release. Could Jim be our murderer? Bloody right! I noticed he had a leftover sausage this morning at the breakfast table as an instrument of torture for any poor, unsuspecting fellow author! In his younger days, Jim would have watched many episodes of *The Goodies* thinking this was the next best thing to the forgotten Lancashire martial arts practice of *Ecky-Thump!* His several years of involvement at the festival gives him the upper hand on planning out the removal of his fellow authors so that only his *Farty McFee* books could be had.

A place near to my heart as my own neighbourhood was Newtownabbey or almost, but not quite Belfast if you ask McVeigh. As he writes books about having the largest fart heard around the world, he blows a plastic trumpet to elicit such sounds for the kids who stop over by his table, although most times they sound half-winded. I guess it takes guts to do that. Or perhaps eating several tins of baked beans. Ack, but sure who am I to question his choice of writing. He plays a decent guitar. He's not a bad singer either. I guess two outta three ain't bad. But this does not negate the fact that he is suspect number one in my books!

Suspect Two – J.P. Sexton

John Patrick Sexton. Born in New York and moved to County Donegal as a child. His memoir *The Big Yank* tells tales of sorrow and survival. Regardless, if my suspicions are true that he is The Last Jedi: *"Use the Force, Sexton!"*

While writing our Irish memoir with myself and Mark, who mysteriously failed to show up for the Dublin Irish Festival, an assassination attempt was made on the collar bone of J.P. to prevent him from forwarding his final submission for our co-authored book. Or so the story goes. I have my suspicions about that, though. If you ask me, looking back on the bottom of page 113 on my diary entry titled *"Breaker, Breaker . . ."*, I think the truth lies within it. He was having a grand old time, getting himself nurtured back to a clean bill of health. It was to seek some sympathy and all of the lovely benefits which go along with that.

Later, J.P. took a trip to Malin Head to work on another manuscript titled *Drawn to Danger*, which was meant to be featured at the Irish Authors' Corner. It's based on his life experiences after leaving Ireland, many of which were too close for comfort. The book never made it to the festival. Neither did J.P. His excuse was using his Irish passport to cross the ocean. A likely story if you ask border agents. As his ballad says, *"I thought I would pass, by the skin of my ass!"*

I think J.P. had inside information that a disappearance was going to occur at the author's tent. He could then incorporate this into his book as part of his courageous approach to save us from impending doom. I believe this will be written into his Curriculum Vitae using Jedi ink:

- Author of a 400-plus-page personal memoir;
- Learned survival skills by cooking pigs, milking goats, and fishing like a Viking;
- Intravenous consumption of Malin Head medicine (Inishowen Peninsula Poitín) just for fun;
- Commandeered a jetliner after his Irish airline interview went arse over heels;
- Child smuggler of Kerrygold butter from Derry to Donegal, evading British checkpoints;

- Became an International Man of Mystery (so much so, he doesn't know himself anymore);
- Fabio / Fionn Mac Cumhaill figurine model: Chiselled looks. Size. Hair. Sans the muscles.

As for dynamite brains here, I wonder if J.P. fed a story to others after informing me he would indeed be in attendance. Could this be part of his set up? And what about that lad of surf and sand, Mark Rickerby? Enquiring minds want to know. This leaves me asking which one plotted the disappearance of our fellow author and which was the accomplice? I will get back to Mark in a moment.

Suspect Three – Michael "Magnum" McCarthy

Retired from the Rochester, New York Police Department, Magnum could plan the perfect execution and cover his tracks. I imagine the report he would do about how the disappearance occurred in the author's tent would be meticulously prepared and to his own benefit as a result of him gathering select information. Not even his lovely, methodically stealthy wife, Ann, knows what he writes about. He keeps his notes so close to his vest, I'll bet he's on the poker circuit. I suppose I will have to try to piece together his case notes like a puzzle.

I imagine they would read something like this . . .

"Jim is currently my top suspect. He likely had several accomplices who know the inner workings of the festival: Barbara, Laura, Kay, Alison, Lisa and Nick. I bet his wife, Shelly, along with their son, Pierce, were involved. Who brings an old wash basin to a festival, complete with parachute cord, masking tape and broom handle, claiming it is to record a newly composed song called The Ballad of J.P. Sexton live, along with other authors in room 429, on a Saturday night, while everyone else listens to prestigious, glorious harmonies as made on various stages over at the Dublin Irish Festival? Their song was written on the same day it was recorded! How does this make any sense? Then again, nothing makes sense with these Irish fellas!"

"Jim tried to poison our minds to death by erupting cannons of disharmonious sounds, including his genius, notorious marketing specialty of providing whoopee cushions to encourage mothers to buy his books. This to keep their wains "quiet" as to enjoy music, workshops, and of course, do all the shopping they could at various vendors, including the Galway Bakers."

"At breakfast, Ann, who has specialized, methodical, and stealthy training in how to play the game of I Spy, noticed that Jim sat directly across from the unassuming Arthur, who all the while was concealing an uneaten sausage. I must review video footage on YouTube. Does Jim know the full martial art practice of Ecky-Thump?"

"I recall the day information was privately shared with me by the Belfast Child when I first met him on the grounds. He mentioned Barbara had spoken about Jim when she invited Greg. He spoke about a man of mystery, J.P. Sexton, and got him invited. From my observations, J.P. is no "wain" as I had been informed. The lad is about eight feet tall, and quite possibly a love child from the romance novels Ann reads. A Celtic Warrior who has Viking blood coursing through his veins, he could pass as a figurine model for Fabio and Fionn since he has wavy hair and chiselled looks. Sad as it is, he suffers from a serious lack of muscles and could use head-to-toe body conditioning."

"Barbara said Jim was "a hoot". It is possible she got a natural high from his Belfast humour, most of which is based on the bodily functions he chooses to write about. It is plausible Greg misunderstood her in that Jim's books actually revolve around "a toot". If that is the case, I believe I now know where the story of Farty McFee originated from – its author is full of shite."

- Michael Magnum McCarthy. ~~Author turned librarian~~ (ummm, scratch that last part). Private Investigator.

Suspect Four – Dah-Nee-Tza Richardson

The sarcastic, fun-loving, green-eyed, professional cat herding, bartending fair maiden sister of RoboCop simply known as Danica first used her devilish charm, infectious giggle, and pronounced wiggle to capture everyone's attention. Forgive me, Diary, that was as a result of a gymnastics accident she suffered a few decades ago.

She likes laughing, especially after inflicting her endless sarcasm on her unsuspecting victims, especially me. If I am to be honest, it is more an evil cackle than an infectious giggle. A temptress, paired with those seductive green eyes of hers, it all sounds too good to be true. It is!

Sourcing the sweet delicacy from the Schmidt's food truck and bringing it into the author's tent, she knowingly left many with ravenous looks and mouths drooling. The deed almost caused murder! This inspired the story behind the Dublin Cream Bun, one of the best pastries an Irish palate could wish for. Since they hold a special place in the stomachs of many authors and among the festival masses, this makes her a suspect, even if she doubles as a manager!

Her predilection for books leaves me to wonder if this is her way of stalking each author, finding out about them so she can plan the best ways for each of them to mysteriously disappear during the festival. As Danica has a lot of time on her hands, no one really knows what she is up to when she says she is checking out various vendors.

What we do know, however, is how cautious, yet extremely meticulous she is in her approach to making an Old-Fashioned. She has it down to a fine art by using sugar, but never syrup, freshly-cut orange slices, 7-Up, not Sprite, and ice, not smoked but instead precisely drizzled with the perfect measurement of bitters. Finally, her main component, Guckenheimer whiskey, because of which J.P. cunningly gave her the title *The Guke Slinger*. If nothing else, the name fits the crime!

Another weapon in her arsenal is her muddler. I heard her tell Sinead Tyrone it is for the maraschino cherries she mushes into the bottom of each glass, giving the wooden tip its deep, red, blood-soaked tinge. I watched how she crushes the mix together using blunt force strikes, ensuring every ingredient at the base of the glass is pummelled beyond recognition, squeezing each drop of flavour out of them. The sugar lies battered beyond its crystal form. Ingredients, once full of life just seconds before meeting this grisly fate only to be hastily discarded after the last drops of each Old-Fashioned has been tipped into the awaiting mouth of those who so hungrily seek the pleasurable mixtures within it. Devilishly licking their lips, their eyes widening, their ears anticipate Danica's tongue to curl and whisper, "Would you like another?"

If this does not make her suspicious, then tell me how many women travel to an Irish festival with a muddler in their purse instead of mascara, eyeliner and scarlet red lip stick? Wow! That paints an extremely vivid image, so it does! Where was I again?

To my dismay, a Dublin Cream Bun is now involved as part of the mystery surrounding the disappearance of Mr. Colaianni, especially when these are paired with foreign whiskey from Northern Ireland. Insider information, as provided by fellow author Ben Anderson, saw Danica go on another one of her infamous shopping trips, spending her paycheque on jewelry, scones, and a library of books. Perhaps a diversionary tactic, she may have used this opportunity to sneak foreign whiskey into the author's tent to accompany the cream bun instead of the refined, much preferred Guckenheimer brand.

Once the overseas venom of *Wee Millie's Bush* touches the lips of an unsuspecting author, the effect is awful to witness, especially if the chosen victim is a devout Kafflick, attends Sunday mass, or hails from the Republic of Ireland. Withering in agony, their senses obscured, their minds drowning in a foggy dew, the intended target is then parted from their belongings. This includes their stash of books, which were previously waiting to be sold and signed. Some might even say I put her up to this.

In saying so, only two people could possibly know that an Old-Fashioned, when made with Wee Millie's Bush and paired with a scrumptious puffy pastry, can be used as a seduction tactic to elicit abduction. Danica is one. The second is someone who would be able to tell the difference when handed his first glass, careful not to touch a drop while circling the rim of the glass below his nose and taking a slight whiff to ensure the liquid within is not tainted. And that someone is J.P. Sexton! Knowing he has a "no limits" approach to what he calls Gukes, he is an established accomplice of The Guke Slinger.

Suspect Five – Mark Rickerby

By way of his father, Mark hails from County California, Northern Ireland; a Protestant lad who surfs waves, dances to the Beach Boys, and writes screenplays just for fun. Establishing himself as a fierce copy editor, he could easily make us all disappear into the pages of this book and no one would even blink an eye. His careful wordsmithing could effortlessly carve a path for us into oblivion. I think he is the Alfred Hitchcock of writing!

This makes him a huge suspect, as he and Michael, who also methodically prepares his written notes for his investigation, keeps them under lock and key until they are summoned by the courtroom. Bulletproof in their presentation, Michael's notes and Mark's editing skills may very well be in cahoots with each other, knocking off authors one-by-one so they can bring *The Other Belfast – An Irish Youth* to the author's tent for its debut release.

Another thing critical to capture is that this year, there were seventeen of us, yet there should have been nineteen.

Funny enough, J.P. and Mark were missing in action. Yet, when I flew to California and met Mark in February, I planned how we were going to get him to Dublin. This involved me setting up an author signing for the three of us and our debut launch prior to the opening day of the festival. I was in talks with the store manager at the . . .

Suspect Six – Julie Burgess

Wait a minute. I can't forget Julie. She had an orange X placed in front of her cash station at the author's tent that wasn't there the previous two years. It was made with the fabric used to make the sash my father never wore which J.P. nicked from County Derry. Julie mentioned setting up a full Celtic display at The Book Loft and having a living, breathing, life-sized lad within her interactive display.

The plot is getting thicker by the minute. It is almost as thick as when I was a child and my ma told me if my brains were made of dynamite . . . ah, those words are as fresh in my mind today as the day she told them to me. Then again, it wasn't just one day that she told me that, it was every day. We always did love the Irish terms of endearment and loving comments she directed toward us when we were children, such as, *"I should have ate the lot of youse while your bones were still soft!"* Aww.

My ma backed that wee statement up by saying, *"Gregory, if you had two brains, you would be twice as thick."*

Bless her poor soul. She was never one at a loss for words, including when she would tell me to go and eat one of her arses. All with love from an Irish mother!

There you have it, Diary - a list of suspects conceivably responsible for the disappearance of Arthur Colaianni. But why him? He is our Elder Statesman. A Leprechaun King Godfather. What sinister secret could he know which might lead to his disappearance? Is there something amongst Celtic folklore or mythology he maybe uncovered which should have been left alone?

Looking up, I noticed Magnum McCarthy was busy putting a military uniform onto his bodyguard mannequin. He also had made a sign for the passenger side of his mini-putt golf cart that read, "Reserved for Colonel Patrick O'Rorke." Did he call in the military and ask for their assistance? After that, it seemed he was creeping around Sinead's table and creating a bit of a disturbance. How he and Ann got her away from there is a mystery in itself as Sinead seems to be surgically attached to it. Although they call me out repeatedly for going off and networking, whether she realizes this or not, Sinead stays put and does the exact same thing. Until now!

Hopefully, Diary, my next entry will be the conclusion of this whole mystery . . . unless . . . hold on just a second - I swear I just saw Michael a moment ago. Where the heck has he now gone and disappeared to?

Chapter 27: Libraries, Lunatics and Leprechauns

While continuing my investigation and talking with Sinead Tyrone, a potential customer came strolling by her table and Sinead gave her usual spiel regarding her heartfelt Irish calamity *Walking Through the Mist*.

"Oh, I am not a reader," said the browser.

"Really?" said Sinead as she reached under the table and pressed a button. In an instant, the orange X marked gopher hole opened and down went the non-reading browser with a swoosh as if a toilet flushed. Plop went the browser into an easy chair on the seventh floor of the Dublin Branch of the Columbus Public Library, known to the reading population as the DPL (Dublin Public Library).

"Here comes another non-reader," said the attending librarian.

"Quick, get the Dick and Jane series," said another librarian.

"No, no, no," said the browser. "I *am* a reader. I just have too many books on my nightstand. I just said that to leave the table without buying a book."

"Send him to the fiction section," said the first librarian.

"No, that's what he's good at," said the second. "Send him to the Ethics Section."

"No, not the Ethics section," pleaded the defrocked browser.

"That's where we sent the Italian Irish writer," said the head librarian.

"Oh, he's not here anymore," said the first librarian. "He learned his lesson about an Italian writing Irish stories. Now, he's writing a murder mystery in the Vatican."

"I'm sure he learned his lesson in the Ethics Section," the second librarian said. "And where did he go?"

"Paroled to The Book Loft," said the Head Reader. "He must report back every six weeks with his sales total. A portion of his sales of Irish stories must go to the **I**rish anti-**D**efamation and **I**mmigration **O**ffenders **T**eam, also known as I.D.I.O.T."

"How appropriate," said the first librarian.

Back at the Author's Tent, I focused on Sinead and her button. I wanted to crawl under her table and find that button, then follow the wires to the source. But Sinead guarded her table fiercely and wouldn't budge from her firm stance in front of where the button lay underneath. I tried the old trick of yelling, *"Look at that! Amazing"* while pointing away.

"What is it?" said Therese, who had a good view of the empty space I was pointing to.

I made up an excuse. "It's a miniature grasshopper," I said. "You should see it." Therese stepped over but Sinead never moved.

"I don't see it," said Therese.

"Oh, it just hopped away," I said.

"Yeah, sure," said Sinead.

Maybe I could get Ann to take Sinead over to the cream bun wagon for a delicacy. I walked down the row of tables to where Ann was sitting.

"Hey, Ann," I said in my best ventriloquist voice without moving my lips so Sinead could not intercept the message. "Would you take Sinead for a walk to the Schmidt's truck. I need to examine her table."

"Stop mumbling," said Ann. "I can't understand you."

"I said, tak she-aa to the shh-mits truk."

"What?" she said, louder.

"Oh, never mind," I said, again turning away from Sinead, then whispered, "Just get Sinead away from here."

"Sure," said Ann. She went over to Sinead, said something and then they both left. "That was easy," I said to me self.

Once out of sight, I went over to the table in question and crawled under. No button, no wires, no mechanical device. "Dang it," I said, "Another wireless Bluetooth operation."

I went over and stamped my foot on the orange X. No door opened; no latch released. Stumped, I thought for a moment and whispered, "I too am not here to buy Sinead's books." Looking back at her table, I noticed Greg's manager was now standing there keeping watch. She had been quietly observing what Ann and I were doing. She also saw what Sinead had done to the previous visitor who was there to kick the tires with no intent to purchase anything. Danica give me a steely stare, raised one eyebrow, and smiled at me before putting a finger to her lips. Just as I was on the verge of shouting "I'm innocent!", swoosh, down I went and right into the seventh-floor easy chair at the DPL.

"Another non-reader!" announced the librarian.

"No, I am an investigator, turned author, turned investigator."

"What are you doing here?" said the librarian.

"I am looking for a tall Italian midget who thinks he's Irish," I said.

"Oh, he's gone. He was here but we paroled him," said the librarian.

"What? When? Where?" I said.

"One question at a time, Mr. Investigator. You should know that."

"Okay, where is he now?" I asked politely.

"I don't know," said the librarian.

"When did he go?" I asked.

"I don't know," said the librarian.

"What *do* you know?" I asked.

"He was here and now he's not," she said.

I said to myself, "Oh dear, I should have stayed retired." However, aloud, I said, "Where do you think I should look for him?"

"I would look for him at The Book Loft," said the librarian.

"Ah, good lead," I said. I left the library but found myself in downtown Dublin, Ohio without my golf cart. How was I going to get to The Book Loft without my energy-efficient, single-cylinder cart? Then I realized I had a ready-made answer with me. I pulled out my investigator's smart phone and pulled up the Uber App. Shortly, I was chauffeured to the massive Germantown book outlet by a moonlighting taxi driver.

With my main connection to The Book Loft safely absent and over at the Dublin Irish Festival (that is Julie, of course), I perused the rooms full of stacked literary gems. Could Arthur be hiding behind James Joyce's *Ulysses* or my own *Flight of the Wretched*? No, too obvious. I tried to think of the most likely place to proceed – Room 13 - the room where special though possibly trapped spirits resided. When I arrived, nothing materialized at first glance. What should I do, wait for an extra-sensory flash of light? But ghosts and goblins come out at midnight, and that would be a problem because I go to bed at ten p.m. every night or I turn into a werewolf myself. Hmm, maybe I should look some more.

Just then, I heard a noise, a moan, or more likely, the eerie cry of a banshee, but it was fainter than a banshee apparition. Even so, it was more than this tough guy wanted to hear. Room 13, as it turns out, is the classics section. Also included is poetry, drama, books on writing, journals, sociology, LGBTQ, and westerns, which is no help because Arthur could be all or part of any of those genres. Well, maybe not western, but he certainly is a classic.

While browsing the collections of books, I discovered a small door. As I anticipated, the door creaked loudly when opened as if the banshee was escaping for an early evening flight. A set of stairs went up to the attic, which I could faintly make out had bookstore equipment.

I climbed the stairs slowly, reminiscent of my police SWAT days, always ready to be surprised by some criminal type looking for a last hoorah. But I wasn't looking for a desperado, I was looking for my lost friend and colleague, Arthur. Then again, he was not only my colleague but my competitor as well. Nonetheless, he was my friend.

This was a search-and-rescue mission. I found a dark attic and wished I had my investigators bag containing my tiny but bright LED flashlight that I got for free from the Harbor Freight store. "Darn," I said to myself. I did have a second option, my super-smart Apple phone that had a built-in flashlight, but before I could bring it out and punch in my code number (that I will not mention here) and light my way, I fumbled through the pockets, mumbling to myself. "No, that's my keys. Not that either. That's a pen. Ah, here it is."

I punched in 1, 2, 3, - oops, I almost mentioned the remaining numbers. Now, I could climb the rest of the well-worn wooden stairs with dusty crevices and corners, and a few cobwebs to catch any airborne smog floating around. No detail was missed as I soaked in my environment. At the top step, I gazed to my right to see stacks of old and new books, some hardcover and some softcover, and some incredibly thick. *Who can write that much for one book?* I thought. Next to them were some thin volumes. *Who put out a book with such little information in it?* There are some crazy writers out there. Then I looked to my left, which had office-type machines on a long table. I had no idea what they were used for, but they had the recognizable "HP" logo on the side.

I made the last step onto the attic floor when a large stack of books came crashing down on me - well, next to me - which would have hurt if it hit my shinbone or something like that. I jumped back, narrowly missing falling down the stairs and having to start over again. The books landed, and when the avalanche was over, a second rumbling of books were pushed aside, making a further mess of colorful book covers and photos of handsome male authors and pretty female authors on back covers, and there laid Arthur curled up in a fetal position, shaking uncontrollably. I knew Arthur could not see me because I was the one with the light and it was shining on him.

"Arthur, it's me - your competing colleague, Mike."

Arthur slowly gained his composure but, still shaking, said softly, "Oh, it's you. Don't hurt me."

"I won't, Arthur. I'm here to help," I said.

"I didn't realize it was you, I'm sorry for pushing the books on you," he said.

"No worries, little buddy. Here, let me give you a hand," I said.

I cleared away the likes of William Faulkner, F. Scott Fitzgerald, Jane Austen, Charles Dickens, Leo Tolstoy, Maeve Binchy, and of course, Ernest Hemingway, as well as some lesser known writers. I had to look – none of my novels were in this mess. They must have sold out all of my historical fiction books. Under this chaotic heap laid Arthur. I helped him to his feet.

"What happened, Arthur? How did you get here?" I said.

"I'm not sure. I was on my way to Mass this morning and stopped at the tent to prepare my stack of books. There was this shadowy figure I noticed back at the hotel. Suddenly, a strange sensation came over me. The next thing I heard was your voice saying something about keys and a pen. That's when I pushed on the stack of books."

"Ah, my voice broke the spell," I said.

"My head hurts," said Arthur. "I guess I had too much of the Old-Fashioned."

"I see. Drinking on Saturday night and Mass on Sunday morning. You really are trying to become an Irishman," I said. "And having blackouts and memory losses, too, so you are."

"One drink is all I had," said Arthur, "and to tell you a secret, I didn't like it that much either."

"Well, my friend," said I. "You needn't worry about it. You can still be an outstanding Irishman without the drink. After all, you've got the gift of storytelling, and you're as short as a leprechaun. You need nothing more."

"I want to go and sell my books," said Arthur.

"Do you want to see a doctor?"

"No, let's just go to the festival."

"Okay, let's go then," I said.

Down the creaking steps to the main floor and out the side door we went. The Uber ride back was quiet, as neither of us wanted the driver to hear the fantastic legend of Author Arthur and the night at the Old-Fashioned table. Instead, the radio played *Into the Mystic* by Van Morrison.

I was swaying to and fro, the raspy voice of Van Morrison belting out of me. "And when that fog horn blows, I will be coming home, mmm mmm." I closed my eyes to absorb all the meaning and message of the words. When we stopped at a red light at the corner of South Third Street and East Livingston Avenue, I opened my eyes to check our whereabouts and saw a little old lady waiting to cross the semi-busy thoroughfare of South 3rd Street. I jumped out of the Nissan Rogue to help the senior citizen in distress. I thought, "What was I doing being transported by a vehicle called a Rogue? I would never be taken by a Rogue." That aside, I hustled over and grabbed the arm of the woman and said, "Let me help you."

"Oh, you're such a gentleman. You know, I don't see much chivalry anymore, and for you to take time out of your day to help an elderly lady - with no money, by the way - to cross the street, is such a refreshing thing. You made my day."

"My pleasure, and gentlemanly duty, madam," I said.

We walked slowly, even though the light had changed and we were only halfway across. The cars were inching forward in an effort to zoom away as soon as we cleared their path. She was undaunted and continued her slow pace, saying, "I had a hip replacement on my left side last year, and now I'm thinking of replacing my right hip."

"Oh, I hope you have good medical coverage," I said.

"Yes, don't you worry about that," she said. "When you get to my age you'll get Medicare."

"I am that age," I said. "I'm turning seventy this year."

"Really?" she exclaimed. "Well, I'd like to take you to dinner."

"Oh no. I'm married to lovely Annie," I said.

"Oh, too bad. Is she in the car with you?"

"No, that's Arthur, the author."

Just then, the cars behind the Uber started honking to move out of the way.

"I gotta go." I ran back to the Rogue and jumped in. We then sped around the corner.

"Wait!" I yelled. "Where's Arthur?" He was not in the back seat where I last saw him. I looked out the window onto the street – no Arthur anywhere. At closer look, the old lady was gone, too.

"Stop the car! Where did he go?" I said.

"Where did who go?" asked the Uber driver.

"You know, the guy in the back seat with me."

"Don't know; wasn't paying attention," said the driver.

I got out of the car and slammed the door, thinking I had been hoodwinked by the Rogue and that some larger conspiracy was at play.

I ran back across the street to where I had left my elderly potential suitor standing. She could not have traveled far in those few seconds, so I looked into Katzinger's Delicatessen to see if she wandered into the shop for some imported Gouda cheese or Braunschweiger Liver Sausage to treat her next picked-up boyfriend. Maybe I was being a little rash about her, but her quick disappearance was unnerving. Even so, I turned my attention to finding our missing author, Arthur.

Not seeing either in the chic artisan deli, I ran back down 3rd Street for four blocks to The Book Loft, a likely place for Arthur to re-appear. Stopping at each intersection to check the side streets for either Arthur or the elderly hipster, I caught my breath due to the exaggerated pace that would out-do even my roaring golf cart.

Arriving at The Book Loft, I searched everywhere, including the mountainous book pile in the attic where Arthur was hiding under earlier, all to no avail.

Dejected, the only thing to do was to return to the festival site. I didn't want to contact Uber for another ride after the bad experience I had just had. I instead grabbed the bus schedule, walked back down 3rd Street, cut over to South High Street, took the number two bus, and transferred to the number thirty-three bus for the slightly more than two-hour ride back to the festival site.

I called ahead to the festival volunteers and had them put my golf cart on standby, but I did not mention my failed attempt to rescue Arthur, then losing my poor little buddy on the Uber ride back.

When that fog horn blows
You know I will be coming home
And when that fog horn whistle blows
I gotta hear it
I don't have to fear it.

Into the Mystic
Van Morrison

Chapter 29: With Love from an Irish Mother . . .

As planned, Nick and Skip came over to meet me at the Spoken Word Tent just before I completed the last of my presentations on Celtic folklore and mythology. Since this would be a wrap for my festival commitments, I decided to add a wee send-off for the audience members based on what we would have been exposed to as children. It was a poem based on many of the lovely childhood experiences I had, even if it meant we were cut to shreds afterward at the hands of our mothers and their fierce Irish tongues. There was no escaping their wrath.

Settling into their seats over by Melissa, I gave a quick check to make sure I could pull this off and not go over my time limit. She was enjoying my presentation about Irish Giants, including the legend behind Fionn Mac Cumhaill as seen through my eyes, and a storytelling poem I composed about Maeve Roe in how she had become the Banshee of Dunluce Castle. I had launched into another poem about the basalt giant resting on top of the Cave Hill overlooking Belfast, and the landscape beneath it, scarred as a result of *The Troubles*. Melissa gave me a nod to say I still had time and could go ahead with one final piece, although she had not been made aware in advance of what this was going to be. At the time, I had no idea either.

Since I did not want to finish off the festival with a reminder of the fearful climate we grew up in during those extremely dangerous and difficult times, I figured some heartfelt humour was needed – especially as we were still dealing with the disappearance of Arthur. Although there were some possible yet unsubstantiated sightings of him, including my suspicious engagements while I was over at the maintenance shed, he still had not surfaced. Funny enough, Michael had also disappeared. I asked Danica about this before starting my presentation. She simply replied, "I don't think you need to fret about him for a while. Let's just say he learned a lesson in that he should have bought *Fragility*, Sinead's book of poems."

Startled, I didn't dare ask what she meant by this.

"Don't worry," she continued. "I made sure you won't be interrupted or interrogated. He will be able to find his way back here by the time your presentation ends. Enjoy this moment in the limelight and dazzle your audience!"

Giving me her infamous one raised eyebrow look, I took a deep breath before giving Melissa the nod to start timing me to ensure I kept pace with their tight schedule.

"Ladies and gentlemen," I began. "I would like to take this opportunity to personally extend my deepest and sincerest thanks to every one of you for coming out to this tremendous celebration of all things Irish, and for bearing with me and my brogue. Although I stand up here before you all, I notice those of you who get lost within the lilt of my voice as heads often turn sideways, faces have looks of shock, or there are fits of muffled giggles. It's all good, though, as I haven't much of a clue as to what you say about me due to your beautiful and robust Ohio accents!"

As anticipated, the audience looked at each other with surprise, then whispered to each other in unison that they weren't the ones with the accents. I have learned to appreciate this over the years. Folks think only the Irish have brogues, yet we think the same about them. It's a no-win situation. I tried my best to explain what I meant.

"As I have come to appreciate, if you don't understand me, just shake your head like this - back and forth. This means *no* in Ireland. Or, if you shake your head like this - up and down - this means *yes* in Ireland. It's the same at home as it is here in America. Head shakes are universal!"

Laughter rippled through the crowd, as many people were guilty of doing just that as I was explaining this to them. There were times throughout my presentation when they had absolutely no clue what I said and turned to the person next to them to ask for a translation. Occasionally, I would pick up on this and ask them what part they didn't understand. Some people had never encountered hearing "yer ma's yer da", a common Belfast phrase. I translated it into, "Your mother is your father" but that caused more confusion, so I slowed down to the speed of Michael's golf cart and spoke the phrase phonetically. Receiving another blank stare, I gave up entirely and moved on. It happens!

"Now, I'm sure there are many of you who had mothers who would 'tell it like it is' - good, bad, or in my case, that and everything in between. For those of you fortunate enough to have your mum with you today, cherish every moment available and thank them for their brutal honesty while you were a child. Only the creator knows how much I would give of myself to have that opportunity once more with my own wee mum. She was my editor, my confidant, and my protector. Although, she was also the one who would crush me to bits with her wicked wordsmithing abilities. So, without further ado, this is for you, mum . . ." I immediately launched into the poem which I had composed and filtered into the same book as my take on Celtic folklore and mythology called *One Cross to Bear: Humanity through Narrative Prose.*

With Love from an Irish Mother . . .

Having been raised by an Irish woman,
Their endearing qualities no stranger.
For each day upon our arrival home,
We would put our lives in danger.

Famous for the lilt in their brogues,
Or how they speak to their young.
Driving our ma around the bend,
We'd learn a new native tongue.

Their mastery of 'Norn Iron' slang,
By mummy's, just like my own.
Loving words, or so we thought,
Would cut us straight to the bone.

Doomsday always on the horizon,
Punches, she was not one to pull.
Awaiting to see what our fate was,
When she called our names in full.

My siblings, "Jesus, Mary, and Joseph,"
As our ma called out to thee.
Only to realize we were fatherless,
"Parcel of wee bastards, aren't ye?"

"God curse and roast yis' all,"
When committing a mortal sin.
"Is it a dig in the gub, yer after,"
Ma battles, we would never win.

"Close the door and keep it in,"
When told our noses were runny.
"You can't get knickers off a bare arse,"
Her response to us asking for money.

"Your arse is out the windy,"
When we tried to make a fuss.
"You're full of hobby horses' shite,"
If she did not agree with us.

"Ack, away and eat one of my arses,"
This accomplishment, I've yet to do.
But what I have yet to comprehend,
Since I've one arse, how'd she get two?

"I'll put my toe up your hole,"
"Get your feet on you before you go out."
"Shut your gub and eat your food,"
The art of osmosis without a doubt.

"I swear to God, if you'd two brains,
You would be twice as thick."
For us who couldn't solve problems,
We would receive some terrible stick.

"If your brains were made of dynamite,
You couldn't part your hair."
Perhaps my ma had forgotten,
My parents' DNA was up there.

"Here. Do ya see if you break a leg,
Don't you dare come running to me."
The menacing warning provided to us,
When climbing or swinging from a tree.

"I'll give you something to cry for,"
While in our quest for sympathy.
"You'd drive a bloody saint to drink,"
At least we'd have holy company.

"The dirt in those ears could grow spuds,"
Those words did make us go quiet.
For roasted potatoes, boiled, or mashed,
Made up much of the Irish diet.

Even after licking our plates clean,
Or seeking another crumb to score.
"That one would ate the Lamb of God,
And would come back for more."

No matter our strict religious upbringing,
According to Paul, this wasn't in the gospels.
"He'd eat Christ off the cross,
And come back for the Twelve Apostles."

"Shite and sugar", "stewed bugs and onions,"
The Great Hunger much to our dismay.
"Now take yerselves off by the hawn,"
Time for us to get out of her way.

"Thon bake is like a busted sofa,"
Terms of endearment were here to stay.
"I shoulda ate youse while your bones were still soft,"
Political correctness never saw the light of day.

Not only did we face her wrath,
The neighbours did without hope.
"She'd steal the milk from your tea,
He's a stranger to the soap."

But her weapon of mass destruction,
Frightening, and made us all groan.
Uttering those six petrifying words,
"Wait 'til your father gets home."

Right there, our lives were done,
A fate worse than death lay ahead.
Praying for salvation and redemption,
Before our souls were offered to the dead.

Yet these memories of my childhood,
Are beyond comparison to any other.
Some of the happiest days of my life,
With Love from an Irish Mother.

* * * * *

As I finished the last words of my poem, I looked skyward and blew a kiss to my mum. It was an emotional moment for me as here I was poking fun at the wrath we faced as children, yet I would not have had it any other way. Looking over toward Melissa, Nick and Skip before turning back to face the audience, I said, "There you have it, folks. Thank you for sticking with me here in this incredible heat. Please make sure you stop by the Irish Authors' Corner and pick up any books I may have left. My lovely assistant and manager, Danica, will take care of you. If anyone questions this, tell them, 'For better or worse, there is a certain security in indentured servitude.'"

I looked over to Danica. She had stepped away for a moment, checking to see if Michael had indeed returned from wherever it was he had gone to – with her assistance. Sure enough, he was back but looked completely deflated. Whatever it was he was sent to do, or meant to do, it had not worked out in his favour. He quietly stood off to the side, hugging his military uniformed mannequin. Seeing this, I felt sorry for him but I could not let my guard down.

I continued talking: "While you are at it, ask Michael McCarthy what he knows about Arthur Colaianni. I am sure he will be delighted to answer your questions and hear everything you have seen and heard here at the festival since he has appointed himself as the supposed investigator trying to find him. Make sure you bombard him in the process. Without a doubt, he will appreciate all the extra attention and your insights. You may also wish to buy one of his books. Now, if you could please follow our lovely volunteer, her name is Melissa. She will guide you over to him and get things rolling. Sláinte mhaith!"

With that, I looked over at Nick and Skip, who gave me a wink and a smile. They knew I was trying to find a way to run a diversionary tactic to set up my next move, which would be far away from both the Spoken Word and Author's tents. Before I jumped onto the Paddy-Only Wagon, I leaned into Melissa and whispered, "Mo chara, could you please ask Jim McVeigh to bring his guitar to the Celtic Rock stage, along with his son, Pierce. Tell them the musicians requested their presence and musical talents for the grand finale tonight. Ask Pierce to start taping his fingers. He will know what he must bring, even though it is not a conventional Irish instrument. Cheers and thanks!"

With that, Melissa paused to look at me, as if trying to say she knew something else was seriously up about the formation and handling of the investigation. She had spent more time than anyone else chasing and informing other volunteers, all the while handing out copies of the photo printout given to her by Michael. From directly observing the nervousness in everyone's else presentations that afternoon, she knew how important it was to give them less to worry about. She quietly said, "Greg. You go and take care of what you need to do. I'll help look after things on this end. Don't worry. I've got your back."

I didn't say anything else to Melissa after that, other than to give her a barely noticeable nod of my head. She picked up on this immediately. Melissa knew I had to be careful with who I was associating myself with, and did not want to breach our trust. Since there was much chatter around the Author's and Spoken Word tents that another author was being considered as the culprit behind the mystery that was clearly showing zero signs of slowing down, she too erred on the side of excess caution.

Melissa continued to maintain her role as a festival volunteer with professional integrity. And, since most of my books had already been purchased, it added extra fuel to my comment about hoping to be the bestselling author amongst my fellow writers. Even if this meant my sarcastic suggestion to reach such a unique status was completely blown out of proportion, and except for a few who are closely linked to the festival including Laura, Nick, Kevin, Kay, Alison, Lisa, Skip, and Wendy, no one else seemed to be listening. Michael had accomplished a remarkable feat of planting and nurturing his seed of suspicion against me.

I motioned to Nick and Skip that we needed to make a move to my next location. Both lads adjusted their shamrock-shaped safety goggles and sat silently beside each other up front. As I took my familiar spot at the back, Melissa began moving the folks from their seats and over toward the Irish Authors' Corner, swelling the tent to capacity. I took a last look back and said, "Go n-éirí an t-ádh leat agus go mbeannaí Dia duit. In case you do not know what I just said, it means Good luck and God bless."

Using her hands and fingers, Melissa made the shape of a heart, which disappeared from my sightline. Within mere seconds of that, we arrived over at the Embassy Suites where I set about to get what I needed if I was to try and solve this mystery once and for all. Although I knew how important it was for me to clear my name, quite a few hours had gone by without anyone knowing if Arthur had been seen or not. If they had, no one was saying anything.

Once I emerged from the hotel, a fellow who sat in a Nissan Rogue by the front driveway called out to me and said, "Hey, are you part of that Dublin Irish Festival?"

"Yes, I am indeed," I replied. "Why do you ask?"

"Do you know a fellow with a Rochester accent?" he said. "He wore a tag which said Author on it. I picked him and an Arthur up from The Book Loft. They bailed on me."

Thinking this was possibly another trap set by Michael, I replied, "Sorry, but I have no clue who that is. I can't help you out." With that, Nick, Skip and I made our way back.

Chapter 31: Message in a Bottle

"Greg, perhaps the fine folks at the Wake House might be able to provide you with some much-needed assistance. Stop over there. I am sure there you will find a clue or two . . ."

Those words continued to rattle around in my head. After a busy afternoon of capturing multiple diary entries, signing a plethora of books in Gaelic and English, conducting a presentation, and making a hasty trip on the Paddy Only Wagon back to the hotel only to then be met by someone claiming to have seen Michael and Arthur, the Professional Cat Herder took this as an opportunity to not have to chase after me and asked if I wanted a break. She had checked to see if my fellow authors could watch over the remaining balance of my books, which were few in count. I was extremely grateful to her for such thoughtful efforts. Underneath it all, though, I was sure the yellow caution tape, which remained exactly where it had been placed several hours prior by Shannon, would suffice.

We decided to take a walk up to the green room for some late lunch and a few refreshments. The mixture of blistering sun and intense humidity from the rain showers overnight left our clothes hanging from us and drenched in sweat. Although I took every opportunity to drink as much water as possible along with a citrus drink for the sweetness of it to feel somewhat quenched, the heat inside the tent, along with the hot, moist air blowing through it, quickly expelled it. It was a battle I was rapidly losing.

I was wearing a blue golf shirt, its unmistakeable logo brightly displaying **Belfast Child.** I had decided to get a dozen of these embroidered using brilliant white thread. Normally proud of this fact, I now stuck out in the capacity crowd like a sore thumb. At first, I noticed that folks looked down at the paper in their hands and pointed at the picture of me before lowering their voices in the hopes of blocking me from hearing the unmistakable chatter singling me out.

"Hey, isn't he the guy who is behind that Arthur fellow going missing?" one said.

Another, much more candid in their remarks, spoke at an audible level, ensuring that everyone in their immediate vicinity would get the message.

"What did the translator say over at the Wishing Tree? Something about the fact that there's going to be one less author today?"

Further up the road, a group asked if my books had made it onto the New York Times bestseller list yet. There may as well have been a large target painted on my head, because every which way we walked, comments were cast in my direction. It was as if I had committed an act of betrayal, imprisoned without cause or trial. Although I was doing my best to ignore the comments, I had enough of being the suspect. I finally spoke up and shouted back.

"Perhaps you need to get the facts before passing judgement. This wee lad is innocent! You shouldn't judge a book by its cover. My dialann entries will prove it, so they will! Ask Magnum what his latest trap was all about."

Hearing me say this, Danica looked over at me, pulled my hand into hers and squeezed it, then said, "What did you mean by that, Greg? The word *dialann*? What is that? Who is Magnum? Why did you say there was a trap?"

What she did not realize is that I had been working on a diary throughout this whole ordeal. She had assumed I was creating the sequel to my *Silly Billy Sillogy* and had been feverishly working away at it, which is the norm for me. Once hockey season starts, my book writing begins. Anytime I take myself to task and step (run) away from her to get something done, especially when I set my mind to it, she says she's entering a state of viduity. There is no stopping me during moments like this. When ideas grow, words flow. It's like a leaky faucet of sentences pouring from my mind. And without realization, I often write until the point of complete exhaustion.

In all honesty, there have been more than enough times when my eyes have begun closing on me during the writing process, yet my fingers continue their methodical rhythm of tapping the keys, putting paragraphs onto the pages of the screen, which sometimes serves as the only light around me. Being a social worker, it was something I taught myself to do while in the position of supervisor; this way, I could multitask, partake in discussions, and listen to the person opposite me as they shared their deepest, most delicate, and sometimes darkest thoughts. It ensured their voices were heard, their words captured in intricate detail, and their story was told without being questioned or judged.

I looked over, smiled, and said to not worry about it. Not one to let things go easily, she pressed me again on this. I maintained my stance and said I was a little tired of folks singling me out as a result of the investigation being done by Michael, which seemed to be squarely focused on me. Countering my comment, she said that she too had been interviewed by Michael. Trying to not be offensive, I asked how he pulled her into all of this.

"Well, Greg," she said. "Perhaps you don't remember this, although with your photographic memory, you never forget anything - but you talked to Michael at length about me. He figured you were giving him clues on who else he needed to interview, since I am usually either at your side, chasing after puff pastry and tea for you and the other lads from back home, or trying my best at cat herding you on your wild and wondrous adventures. You could say he considers me as your accomplice in all of this although I think he knows I am on to him. Are you going to answer my questions? Who is Magnum? What trap? The dialann?"

I paused only for a second to pull my thoughts together before responding. "I appreciate that, so I do, but I think Michael is either grasping at straws or trying his very best to direct any attention away from him. If I am to be completely honest with you, I think Magnum is too serious to be a dilettante and too much of a dabbler to be a professional. However, what I would still like to know is, where was he going when he left the festival earlier? He only made his way back after I called him to explain what was going down here. Since then, he has taken every opportunity to try and dispel my thoughts on this being attached to The X-Files, but placed a massive spotlight over my head. He doesn't seem to know or understand how Arthur operates beneath our noses, yet is always the first one to the Irish Authors' Corner to secure his table. Being a man of many identities, I think Arthur has given us all the slip, but I don't know for what reason."

At that, our conversation fell silent. We made our way to the green room only to be pressed for our credentials. I looked at the lady at the table, who was allowing entry only if we had these with us. Showing my identification, I said, "She's with me, so she is. She's my manager."

It didn't take much more than a split second for her eyes to go from my badge over to the logo on my shirt before saying, "Oh. I know who *you* are, *Belfast Child!*"

The photo Michael had asked Melissa to hand out to as many people as possible was sitting on the table in front of her with the words "Be ever vigilant but never suspicious" written on it in bold, permanent marker. "Wait here just a minute, will you?" she asked. "I'll be right back."

The next thing I knew, the volunteer sitting beside her took out a roll of yellow caution tape and began cordoning off the area. So much for the direction provided by her colleague. I asked where she managed to get a hold of the tape. It seems that Michael had carelessly left it there while retrieving a Gatorade earlier; he had been basking in the spotlight of being mistaken for a famous banjo player.

"The nice gentleman from Rochester, New York forgot it here. Mr. McCarthy. Are you familiar with him? He is a crack investigator turned author. He sounds extremely important. He has such a warm and caring personality."

Seizing on the opportunity, as you do, I said, *"Yeah, I know all about him. Although, I would say he is more a* ***craic*** *investigator than anything, so he is. I call him the NY SPOIL SPORT."* Looking at me with curiosity, I borrowed her permanent marker and wrote it out in detail:

Michael "Magnum" McCarthy: **N**ew **Y**ork **S**pecial **P**olice **O**perations **I**nvestigations **L**ead **S**acrificing **P**ersons **O**f **R**ighteous **T**estimony.

The volunteer looked at me, slowly got up from her chair, stepped back gingerly, and disappeared into the green room. I could not believe what I was watching. She returned with two security guards who were there to escort us into the dining area and over to a table off to the side where a private conversation could be held without having to whisper or attract more unwanted attention. She was probably even more shocked when I saw who our escorts were and let out a yelp of joy, then stepped around the table to throw my arms around them. They were Ray Fean from *Jiggy* and Brenda Willis from *The Willis Clan*. Kay McGovern had seen and heard more than enough to fill her day and mind about the events unfolding at the Author's tent, and asked if they would be kind enough to sit with us during our lunch break to help take our mind off things. She saw how fatigued I was, which was not like me whatsoever. Always as full of energy as Tigger (as Danica says) – or piss and vinegar in the eyes of others – Kay had never seen me dragging myself along like this, even after participating in festivals in previous years that were just as jam-packed as this one. Although I was trying my best not to show it, I was beyond depleted.

As soon as we took our seats, hoping to muster up the strength to go to the buffet line and select some of the wonderfully prepared dishes we received as participants of the festival, Lisa and Wendy came out from the kitchen area and put trays down in front of us. Everything had already been selected and prepared on our behalf. This included a bottle of Five Farms Irish Cream for us to try, courtesy of Johnny Harte, who had also come out of the kitchen and brought it to our table. I couldn't believe my luck. I'd finally get the chance to savour this extraordinary liqueur. Lisa always went to strenuous lengths for us, giving me the warmest of welcomes. I stood up, shook hands with Johnny, and threw my arms around Lisa, thanking her for this wonderful gift. She surprised me by saying she had another gift for me, before handing me a small bottle that this time had the same logo on it as the one I saw back at the hotel room. I knew exactly what this was since J.P. had told me about it during our telephone conversation while I was over at the maintenance shed.

Looking me directly in the eyes, Lisa said, "Hang on to that for now; you are going to need this in a little while. It's a wee tipple of Irish holy water as Philomena Lynott used to call it. You will know when and where to use it. Let me say it will give you a much-needed awakening. I promise you that!"

Saying "Go raibh maith agat, mo chara," and without further question, I took the miniature bottle from Lisa and slipped it into my front pocket. I did not tell her, however, that the reason for my express trip back to the Embassy Suites with Nick and Skip was to pick up the other bottle of this, which had been left in my room prior to my arrival. My shamrock senses told me I was going to need to use it at some point but for what or whom, I honestly didn't know. Better to be safe than sorry, I suppose.

With that, I felt so much more at ease. We all sat together in casual conversation; our minds finally separated from the madness which had been occurring since the early morning hours. Ray spoke about his tour with Celtic Women, his current gig with Jiggy, and more shows in the future with Horslips. Brenda talked about her work in Tennessee and her plans to get her talented children back onto the stage with her in preparation for several live shows during the Nashville Irish Festival. Brenda went on to explain how Nashville has now become the sister city to Belfast, bringing Irish music and dance to and from both cities inspired by each other's experiences with and love for them. Banter and laughter flowed as if nothing had been going on other than long-lost friends getting together to enjoy each other's company.

We spoke about our musical influences and tours we had followed, shows we had been to, and bands we had met. I found it interesting that Ray was just as intrigued as I was about a lad who took the rock world by storm with his drumming abilities: Tommy McManus. Ray recalled seeing him practice and marveling at his talent. He fondly reflected on how he watched Tommy continually develop into one of the most revered and celebrated drummers the rock world has ever seen, all the while hoping to one day model his own style after him. It was nostalgic to hear this, as Tommy was the drummer I too had hoped to grow up and be just like.

We laughed about the time Tommy had been asked to audition for Ozzy Osbourne, a story as was shared by his brother, Pat. Not only did Tommy nail the audition, he landed the gig on the spot and immediately turned it down, saying he was "only coddling". Tommy explained he had his own band with his two brothers, Pat and John, and were in the process of recording their fifth album – *Power and Passion*. The Prince of Darkness asked who the band was, to which Tommy replied, "Mama's Boys."

According to Tommy, and at this point, Ozzy almost imploded. Sprinkled with colourful language normally heard in Irish circles, Ozzy said all he ever hears on his tour bus is Mama's Boys. His guitarist, Jake E. Lee, was a massive fan of the band and listened to them constantly. Thankfully, Ozzy took it all in good spirit and humour.

I asked Ray if he was familiar with Pat McManus's album *Blues Train to Irish Town*. "Ray," I said, "the chorus that Pat wrote in that song is perfect for this moment as we all gather here together as friends and family reflecting on childhood heroes, loved ones and mentors."

Ray knew exactly where I was going with this. With that, we all poured a shot of Five Farms Irish Cream and, in unison, said, "Now won't you raise a glass, and we'll gladly drink to Absent Friends."

We did just that. As our glasses clinked together, we nodded and smiled to one another before raising a toast: "One day, far away, I know, I know we'll meet again. Here's to Tommy . . . Sláinte!"

Chapter 33: Is This Where the Dead Man Lives?

The atmosphere in the green room provided a fantastic sense of calmness, allowing for personal reflection and celebration of those who have since passed. I noticed a few tears being shed while we were lifting a glass and proposing a Gaelic toast in honour of Tommy. He was always the life of every party, determined to have as much fun as possible because he knew his very life was never guaranteed as a result of the legacy and lingering effects of his childhood bout with leukaemia. In my first book, *Through the Eyes of a Belfast Child: Life. Personal Memoirs. Poems.*, I was able to partially capture his life with John and Pat in their early days, after the band was renamed Mama's Boys, in a piece titled *The Pulse of Derrylin.*

Along with the footprints and cherished memories he left behind, for many of us, it felt like it was only yesterday that such friendships were struck. Laughter rippled throughout the room amongst the lot of us – I'm sure there were those wondering why we were so jovial, knowing the circumstances outside of our circle. Although it was too easy to start wondering what may have been unfolding with my fellow authors while watching Michael being pelted with unrelenting questions, it was the relief I desperately needed. It did not, however, prevent me from having to take on the next task which awaited me – a visit to the Wake House. Since we would be passing this on our way back to the Irish Authors' Corner, I figured this was as good a time as any to go and see what I could find out.

The presentation was ten minutes out but the crowd who had amassed were now being told they needed to come back because the dead "bloke" they were there to celebrate was missing. Word rippled throughout the crowd that Nick and Skip were going to run back over to the Embassy Suites to gather up some bedding and stuff it into the wooden coffin, even though this would create a faux pas of an unforgettable nature. One joker remarked, "If this is indeed the 'pillow' case, can we say there was a 'Serta' fiable Wake at the Dublin Irish Festival?"

As could be expected, groans echoed throughout the crowd at such a dreadful pun. Regardless, my shamrock senses started tingling once again. I knew something was seriously amiss and began thinking who might be behind such a devilish deed, even though I was sure all fingers would eventually be pointed in my immediate direction.

Saying I needed to speak with the undertaker about this, I showed my credentials to the lad guarding the front of the Wake House. Inconceivably, it was none other than the last great High King of Ireland who, quite possibly, was believed to have amassed the mightiest of military leadership our wee country has ever known, and is steeped in both legend and saga. His name was Brian Mac

Cennétig, otherwise known as Brian Boru. Since his own battleground presentation was not far from the Wake House, he decided to come over to have a chat, a cup of tea, and to split a Dublin Cream Bun with the undertaker after seeing the ruckus which unfolded earlier.

Knowing his love of women, and having had several wives, Brian was of the opinion that if he repeated my now infamous display at the Celtic Cross the day before, it would help him secure another wife or seven. Hearing this, I asked Brian if he wanted to take Danica's hand in marriage instead to save him the hassle. I realized that, by doing so, my own execution at Boru's battleground would be arranged the following year by redirecting her merciless sarcasm toward him instead of me. That is, if I made it past Danica, who would also take extraordinary pleasure in planning my immediate demise for offering her up.

To get me out of his way and to give his head peace, Brian took one step to the side to allow me to enter the Wake House. About to step forward, Danica said she would rather wait outside because she wanted to find out what happened - and if the person, or thing, involved in Arthur's disappearance had taken the dead bloke we were to wake in their hopes of deepening this mystery further and causing additional chaos. Raising her voice, she then asked if Brian could help have me chained up in the lower dungeons of Carrickfergus Castle for presenting her hand in marriage to him in the first place. Fearing for his own life, he hastily agreed!

While all of this was going on, the crowd, uneasy about what Nick and Skip were in the process of doing to try and rectify the situation, became rowdy and started protesting "Give Us Our Wake! We Don't Want Your Fake! Give Us Our Wake! We Don't Want Your Fake!"

The somewhat fearless High King, Brian Boru, took measures into his own hands and asked Danica if he could go into the tent for his own safety. He followed this up by saying she was welcome to join him if she wished. Instead, Danica turned to him, cupped his cheeks, looked square into his eyes and said, "Honey, ask Mr. Belfast Child. I am known in these parts as the Professional Cat Herder. I have a way of quietly and effectively setting things in order."

Hearing this, without thinking twice, I said, "Oh, Jesus Murphy, may the good Lord grant mercy on their souls" before bolting into the tent, only to hear Danica emit her crowd control measure, which involved her bellowing, "HEY! LISTEN TO ME! I HAVE THE FLOOR! AND I ALSO HAVE ACCESS TO DUBLIN CREAM BUNS!" all the while holding up the partially-eaten puff pastries that were being shared by Brian and the undertaker over a wee cup of tea.

With that, silence fell amongst the masses which had gathered, including those who came over from other tents to check out what all the fuss and ruckus was about.

Perhaps it had more to do with the latter part of her statement, although knowing how she means business, with that look of destiny locked in her steely eyes, the one eyebrow raised, along with the deep sigh she takes before unleashing her incensed fury, I wasn't about to hang around to find out.

Safely inside the Wake House, the undertaker recognized me immediately but figured he would play his role, as he did throughout the Dublin Irish Festival, and introduced himself.

"Welcome, my friend. My name is Robin Graves. I am your Master of Ceremonies for this Wake. Join me inside the house of our beloved friend, Mr. Rigor Mortis, who will remain here in repose until the closing of the festival. Afterwards, we will move his remains to the Celtic Rock stage. During the grand finale, we will celebrate his legacy as a mortician, even though he was quite the stiff!"

His voice then trailed off into a somber tone. It was easy to tell that something had gone seriously awry.

First, he asked if I had brought a puff pastry with me to munch on during the celebratory process like I did the last time I stopped in, and if I had, I was out of luck. I asked what happened? He then asked me if I knew about the mysterious disappearance of one of the authors. I said I was fully aware of everything and was conducting my own investigation. He looked aghast and begged that I do not take any of his props. I asked what he meant by this.

He told me that a lanky man with what sounded like a New York accent opened a wallet with a badge on one side and a library ID card on the other. Sure enough, the New York SPOIL. He said Michael had told him he was there to look for clues. Scaring the wits out of the undertaker, Michael then informed him that he too was a suspect and to not move. Once complete, he took out a powder kit, one of which he had removed from Ann's makeup bag and began dusting the Wake House with Crimson Rose blush for fingerprints. Michael said this may be the last place Arthur was seen, so every nook and cranny had to be searched, including that of the cadaver.

Struck by this, the undertaker asked why an Italian wrote books based on Celtic topics before saying, "I am aware the Irish have their ways and are full of craic and banter, but tell me how an Italian gets thrown into the mix? I know there is a love-hate relationship between your two cultures, as seen between the gangs of New York and their rivalry during the mid-1800's. Is that why the library security guard from Rochester came here? My poor mannequin! He took it saying it needed to be examined as the clothing resembled that of what Arthur the author was last seen wearing. I don't understand it, though, because the picture I have in front of me here shows him wearing a Hawaiian shirt, khaki shorts, socks, sandals and a baseball cap. I can assure you my Rigor Mortis was wearing attire more appropriate for a funeral, and unless Arthur is skin and bones and made of nothing but stuff and fluff, there is absolutely no way the clothes would fit him. How am I going to have a wake without a body?"

Seeing how distraught he was, I thought I would use this as an opportunity to try and cheer him up, bursting into an impromptu performance of a legendary song written by Roger Graham and composed by Spencer Williams. Swaying left and right, I began waving my hands back and forth, all the while trying to kick one leg in front of the other, singing:

Now I ain't got no body,
And no body cares for me!
That's why I'm sad and lonely,
Won't some body come and take a chance with me?

The undertaker did not look impressed whatsoever. It was obvious choreography, and singing was not in my repertoire of skill sets, which reminded me of my mum always telling me when I was younger to "stop actin' the eejit". Upon seeing his reaction, I pulled myself together and went back to being dead serious. Dwelling in deep thought, I didn't dare inform him that I was told another body had supposedly been pulled from the pond, and perhaps he could use that instead. In saying so, I realized there was no information shared about that either, which left me wondering if yet another distraction, or a trap, was set into motion by the pond to throw people off Arthur's scent.

With that, while listening raptly, I let my hand fall from my chin, which it was supporting, and down toward my front pocket. I startled myself as there was a large lump there. I forgot I had put the shot glass here earlier, waiting to make its debut appearance; it was the same one Lisa had given to me back in the green room. Removing it from my jean shorts, I held the glass up. Just as the undertaker stared at me inquisitively, I recited the words Lisa had said to me:

"It's a wee bit of Irish Holy Water. You will know when and where to use it. Let me say, it will give you a much-needed awakening. I promise!"

Removing his prop glasses, squinting at the bottle and back toward me, the undertaker asked if I was there to bless the Wake House using an Irish prayer, and if I attended confession and mass before taking on this risk. I responded, "Absolutely not!" to both questions. "There is a much greater need for this right now. And besides, if I did or even thought of doing what you suggested, this place would go up in flames! Bear with me a second; let me think about exactly what it was that the International Man of Mystery said to me about the contents in here."

Startled by this, the undertaker jumped and said, "Are you talking about J.P. Sexton? His name is renowned around these parts. We have heard he is the lovechild of

Fabio and one of the dames from the front of the book covers. It was a love at first sight romance story. He stands at eight feet tall, has long, flowing locks of hair, and looks out over the North Antrim coast. Word has it he could pass as Irish giant, Fionn Mac Cumhaill, except he lacks the required muscles."

I was shocked how he knew who J.P. was. What was even more disconcerting is that it was I who had first described Mr. Sexton in this manner as part of the backstory of the Dublin Cream Bun, so how did it become cemented into the history of the Dublin Irish Festival? Putting this out of my mind, I refocused on the task at hand and continued concentrating on what the "legend" said while we were on the phone earlier.

"I didn't ship you any extra of that, other than what was strictly for our *Funeral for a Viking* presentation. Or perhaps I did send a wee bit more. How did you happen to get your hands on that?"

There was another part to this which I needed to recall; something about me taking a journey. Since my thoughts were scrambled as so much was unfolding before me, I took out my diary and began searching my notes to find what I needed to know.

"D.H. Holy Frig Nitro Boost? You only need one jar of that as it is extremely flammable; it burns for days. If you drink one shot of the stuff, it causes what some think are hallucinations. However, I can tell you from my own experimentation, it places you into a deep trance, your spirit travels, and you end up conversing with some dead Irish legend from decades gone by. It is different for everyone, though, based on your deepest desires of who you would most love to meet but never had the opportunity.

There are implications though. You MUST have Irish or Viking blood in you to do so. Otherwise, you get severely blootered.

Secondly, the dead come back in your thoughts without any advance warning and will call you out to meet with them, although only you can see them. It has been said many a person was seen speaking into darkness and were put away for reasons of insanity. Meanwhile, they were conversing with the one they brought back from the spirit world. This is not something folks should take lightly."

I shared this snippet of information with the Wake House undertaker. He looked bewildered. As J.P. said, I could be put away for reasons of insanity, especially if I were to try this as an experiment. Mulling my options over for a moment, I figured this needed to be done if I were to try and get to the bottom of Arthur's disappearance, as well as proving my own innocence in the process.

I uncorked the miniature bottle of Danny Houton's Sextuple Distilled Poitín and raised the glass above me before saying, "Robin Graves, care to join me on this trip? I am going to find my fellow author, Arthur Colaianni." He replied he would end up blootered, so it was likely not a good idea for him to be participating in this and added that he would keep his eyes peeled like a night watchman. Lowering myself and knocking on the lid, I quietly asked, "Tell me something. Is this where the dead man lives?"

Slowly, the undertaker removed the lid. I saw that the plywood coffin was nothing more than a void space. Just as he had said, there was no body to wake.

As he was doing so, I tippled the contents into my mouth. The burn from it was immediate, knocking my senses for a trip into an unknown abyss. I could feel the liquid pulse through my veins, coursing its way over and throughout my body. However, because the hit was so fierce as I mostly drink nothing stronger than a Shandy - beer mixed equally with fizzy lemon-lime – for which my mate, Paul Simmonds, regularly laughs at before he refers to me as being an amateur - my legs went to jelly, causing me to stumble backward and fall into the open coffin.

Hearing the ruckus in the tent, Danica stuck her head in to find out what was going on. I could hear her voice and that of the undertaker talking above me; it felt like I was in a pool of shallow water. As much as I wanted to respond to them, and could hear myself doing so in my head, I couldn't. I tried to move my arms and legs, but they too failed me. Danica tried shaking me and calling my name loudly, but I still couldn't speak or process anything other than my own thoughts. The shot glass remained by my side and under my hand where it had fallen. My eyes remained open, yet there was no movement.

The undertaker looked at Danica and said she should maybe kiss me to see if that would help snap me out of my state of rigidity. Her response was exactly what I would have expected: "What? Do you think this is the story of Sleeping Beauty? Although the young fellow lying there is extremely handsome, I don't think that is going to work right now. I forgot my lipstick."

Taking out his cell, the undertaker looked sheepishly at her and said he would call me an ambulance. Danica stopped him and said to hang up his phone since I was still breathing but in a state of paralysis. She explained what was going on.

"My brother, Rusty, said one of two things might happen at some stage throughout this day due to everything that is going on with the disappearance of his fellow author. It has deeply affected Greg. Quite often, as Rusty and I first thought, the onset of cataplexy is prompted by strong emotional reactions to events, including excitement, fear, anger, stress, or laughter. It produces a sudden loss of muscle tone while the person lies awake. I researched it earlier to see what it meant. Since Greg went into maximum overdrive experiencing these emotions while trying to figure out what happened to Arthur, and in his efforts to clear his own name, this was bound to occur to him. However, although he will be fine, he is actually experiencing a different symptom which I should probably explain as well.

I did additional research because I know how active he is in his daily life, personally and professionally. Although he goes at 189 miles per hour, he does take some time to self-meditate every day to calm his mind down, and listens to music through earphones, which allows his mind to travel to destinations unknown while rejuvenating his spirit. Even though he multitasks while doing so, it also allows him to literally work himself to death in the process. He will only stop once his body forces him to as a result of being on the verge of absolute exhaustion. What he is experiencing right now is called hypnotic catalepsy, a muscular rigidity usually affecting the arms, eyelids, fingers, or, in rare cases, the entire body. Magicians use this hypnosis as part of their stage show to balance people between chairs. Obviously, Greg took the full hit."

The undertaker lifted my still hand to point out to Danica the one thing she had missed – a now empty shot glass of Danny's Distilled. "He asked me not to tell you this but said to me privately that he was going to look for his fellow author, Arthur, and then drank it to the last drop. The look on his face was one of pure determination."

Danica looked at me, then back at the undertaker, raised her one eyebrow before taking a deep breath, sighed and said, "This is not good. He rarely takes an alcoholic beverage. I was surprised he drank several of my Old-Fashioneds, as a Shandy is usually his choice of beverage. Oh, boy . . ."

The undertaker asked what they should do. Thinking for a moment, Danica smiled and said, "Greg is always one to go off somewhere networking. He never wants to waste any opportunity, even if it means I am left waiting for him. Since this is a welcomed break from my Professional Cat Herding duties, I say we save the day and have an almost Irish wake here!"

Horrified by her cynical statement, the undertaker looked at Danica in a state of shock and asked if she wanted to instead take me back to the Milwaukee Public Zoo and put me in a cage on display for everyone to stop at stare at instead. Sharp and witty with her answer, she protested and responded, "Huh? Seriously? Are you kidding me? That is so extremely cruel! Do you really think I would do that to the animals?"

With that, she stuck her head back outside the Wake House. Once again deploying her crowd control measures of "quietly yet effectively", she put her fingers in her mouth, whistled loudly enough to literally awaken the deceased, and let out an eardrum-piercing "**OI!**" before bellowing, "Mr. Robin Graves is proudly debuting his Not-Really-Quite-Dead Belfast Child Wake! Come and see this once in your lifetime event. Happening today only!"

Cheers erupted amongst the crowd, who began lining up with Abraham Lincoln's. Danica looked back at the undertaker, smirked and said, "See, what did I tell you? The show must go on!" It was obvious he was not aware that the so-called "gentle, loving" Danica relished and never missed an opportunity to have a blistering laugh, especially at the expense of my poor, exploited soul! With that, the undertaker lowered his head in disbelief and blessed himself before placing two pennies above my eyes and a Charon's obol on my chin, just for the craic. The customary belief was these were placed on the eyes and in the mouth of the person who had crossed over in order to pay the ferryman taking them on their spiritual journey.

Taking a cantor flask from his pocket, he raised it above his head and whispered, "Godspeed, my friend. I'll hope to see you upon your return. Thankfully, I did see the other two folks who came in here in the early hours of this morning, although they only took a few dabs of that same Poitín potion." He emptied his flask in one long draught.

Still unable to respond, and with darkness now beginning to descend upon me, I heard voices whispering in the background, two of which were quite distinct. They were not part of the crowd who gathered to wake my wee arse, either. Separated from my paralyzed state of being, and now looking around me, it was only then that I realized I was no longer at the Dublin Irish Festival.

Chapter 35: Paradise or Purgatory

Date:	Tuesday, August 6, 2019.
Entry 8:	Into the future, back to the past.
Location:	Folklorama – United Kingdom Pavilion.
Time:	Start of the first of three shows.

Dear Diary . . .

Or is it "Dear Brain"? I honestly do not know the difference between the two any longer. I believe I am in a darkened, convention-size room right now. Or am I? Things have become a complete fog within my tormented thoughts. Am I trapped, or simply stuck within a shifted moment of time while perhaps crossing the threshold between life and death? Is this the meaning of having to spend time in purgatory, as instilled during my strict, Irish Roman Catholic upbringing?

A digital display on the wall says this is Tuesday. How can it be? I spoke to Laura Nelson on Sunday night at the performer wind-up party. What am I saying? That event has not even occurred just yet, so how do I know about it? This can't be real. Nothing makes sense.

I could swear that moments ago I was at the Dublin Irish Festival, an enchanting gathering which celebrates everything from Irish dance to dainties, music to mothers, and overall is one of the largest and absolute best festivals in America, bringing people together from all sides of the globe to have a party in the form of a Céilí. If my memory serves me correctly, I was at the Wake House meeting with Robin Graves, the undertaker. He was explaining how he was also being investigated by Michael regarding the disappearance of our fellow author, Arthur Colaianni, and that I was going to go in and find where he is through a spiritual awakening and journey.

Yet I now hear voices saying, "Welcome to the United Kingdom Folklorama Pavilion." The McConnell School of Irish Dance is on stage, directed by their beautiful, intrepid leader and dance instructor, Shayleen. Originally founded in Ballymena, I'm sure they went home to compete in the World Irish Dance Championships in County Killarney. Is this real? Or have I become entombed inside of my own memories and am writing this entry as if it were my diary when it is actually the voice inside my head telling me all of this? I supposed that last Old-Fashioned I had after the two pints of Guinness while chatting with Charlie Lord and Jim McVeigh was not such a good idea afterall.

Wait a minute, did I just write the last jar of Old-Fashioned? How did that even get into my room on the ninth floor? We did *The Ballad of J.P. Sexton* in the Guke Slinger's room on the fourth floor. That was last night – Saturday. I didn't have any whiskey in my room. There was the bottle of Four Farms Irish Cream that was mysteriously left outside of my door with the shot-glass size of Danny Houton's Sextuple Distilled Poitín placed within it. I gave the Irish Cream to the tour bus driver and kept the shot glass for myself. Lisa handed me one other. Other than practicing J.P.'s ballad with Jim prior to Danica taping the live production, why do the rest of these seem to be events I have already attended? Did I somehow pass through a time warp?

Perhaps my overactive mind is steering me toward one of my nightly escapades where I find myself reliving my childhood or visiting more recent events, including what is unfolding before me. This time, things are different. I am not having night terrors, nor am I presenting prose and poetry about my experiences growing up during The Troubles of Northern Ireland from 1970 to 1985 – from the moment I was born to the day we emigrated out of my homeland, although I have gone home repeatedly ever since. That presentation, which left many of the audience members in tears and me on the verge of them as well, was back on Friday night.

In saying so, my other presentation based on Celtic mythology and folklore was much easier to get through, except for when I shared an ode to my wee mum at the end. I told the folks in attendance how her loving Irish tongue cut my siblings and I to the bone through the use of her wee sayings such as *"if you break your leg, don't come running to me"* or *"thon bake is like a busted sofa"*. So much for the loving terms of endearment uttered effortlessly by Irish mothers into the ears of their unsuspecting offspring. We were unknowing participants in being told like it is. Ack, the poor things. Wait a second, I was one of them!

I shared stories of Irish giants like Fionn Mac Cumhaill, along with the basalt giant who, while he should be overlooking Belfast Lough, has done nothing but sleep. In all the years he's laid there, the frigger never once blinked an eye or gave several politicians and other individuals a deserving, giant-sized toe up the hole for being involved with the political unrest afoot at the time. I never knew if he had a name or not, although his face makes up what we know as the Cave Hill. It was Jonathon Swift who drew his inspiration from and then wrote about the little people, him being one of them, walking in the shadows of such giants. I should just refer to him as Napoleon since that's what we call Cave Hill's "nose".

Then again, I compose tales about wailing, Irish female ghosts who mourn their impending deaths. The one I am aware of sits beneath the ruins of Dunluce Castle in the Mermaids Cave on the North Antrim coast. Maeve Roe is her name. A banshee, her spirit walks straight through you after stepping foot onto the grounds of her once mighty fortress – it's equivalent to having artic ice slice itself through every inch of your body, starting at the ends of your hair all the way down to the tips of your toes. The flush of full body goosebumps has never been so prevalent.

Even though I spoke about Maeve in my presentation, I never thought death would befall me. Or did it? I am trying to figure out the difference between reality and the possibility of being a newly created spirit, living in what I perceive to be happening around me, even though no one seems to be aware my presence amongst them. If I am a ghost, I will have to make sure I remain clothed as my Irish arse will be much brighter than the rest of me since the sun never shone there.

I am surrounded by glass displays of sweets, crisps, chocolate bars and familiar faces. A surprise to my salivating taste buds is the dairy flavour from an ice-cream cone, often referred to as a "99" or a "poke" back home, even though it is missing the final touch. A poke is not a poke without the red raspberry sauce drizzled all over it. I can picture it now, oozing down the front of my bake, making it look as if I was bleeding from my gub. I must remind myself to be careful. Nowadays, it is misconstrued as being an inappropriate proposition when simply asking for one. Political correctness in a world gone mad and where meaning can be easily misinterpreted. But I digress.

I recognize the lady standing in front of the machine filled with soft whip ice cream, and behind the glass counter protecting all the Wispa bars, bags of Maltesers, Double Decker's, and Fry's Chocolate Cream. Her name is

Sandy – I will call her the Wee Sandy Sans. It is equivalent to having a cup of tea with no milk and sugar. Friggin' hell, the blasphemy of it all! Still, the miniature flake which has been shoved into the soft whip ice cream casts my curious mind back to a carefree, long-lost time. But why can she not hear me asking for one? Sigh.

I wonder if this is a tease since I often gurn about not having the luxury of eating our glorious sweets, foods and baked goodies from home. Maybe this is a part of my unfulfilled bucket wish list in saying, "Here is what you've been waiting for, but good luck in trying to get it." If I am indeed dead, I must have ended up in hell, for these visuals are sheer agony. I can feel my mouth hungrily watering in vain anticipation for what I cannot have.

Along with cultural presentations which prominently feature locations all throughout Northern Ireland, Scotland, Wales, and Eng . . . wait, is that a Punch and Judy puppet show I'm hearing? I remember his oul creepy, raspy voice from my childhood. If I am to be honest, those critters terrified me with their rosy cheeks, daft red hats, and polished noses. Uncomfortable memories of two puppets, both of whom had the unfortunate luxury of having someone's hand firmly shoved up their holes while hiding behind the booth to bring them to life, torturing wains in the process. The mere thought sends shivers up my spine! I swear Punch must be trained in the forgotten practice of the Lancashire martial art of Ecky-Thump. He and Jim McVeigh would get on like a house on fire.

I would much rather sit quietly while listening to the strings of the Celtic harp just to my left being plucked in unison by . . . whom? There is no one near this beautiful wooden instrument. I sit in awe, watching this unfold and clearly hearing the music. Is the one responsible for Arthur's disappearance here with me right now, stalking my every move and playing on my fears? Why can I not see a human soul behind the dulcet harmonies echoing throughout the display area, although I can certainly see the shadows cast by their hands and fingers, plucking the strings. Is this what they call vengeance of the missing?

Stepping back and trying to refocus, these eerily familiar scenes and memories seem to be all too real right now. My own voice sounds much the same as Punch's. Either I have a case of laryngitis from talking to much at the Dublin Irish Festival, or the spirit of the puppeteer has peered into my thoughts and decided to enact his punishment on me for my shenaniganism's.

I am fighting with my thoughts although I am sure I spoke to Laura Nelson on Sunday night at the wind-up party. She organizes the authors, takes care of us, ensures we are sorted, advises when our speaking engagements occur, and all else needed. She checks in while we are engrossed in our works, signing copies for those remarkable individuals who stop at the Irish Authors'

Corner, taking time to listen to us waffle on about each book. I sign mine in Gaeilge and English. I guess the Irish language lessons I was forced to take in secondary school have their merit, even though I'd never use it on the streets of Belfast. Better to be safe than sorry.

Where I stand right now, I see old cars which are in the process of being restored to their previous splendour and beauty. A forest green Morgan which would have cost £100,000 from the factory brand new, built by hand, taking forty-five months to complete. I only know this because I heard one gentleman explain it to several dignitaries in his thick, London accent. He tells them that he was a Sergeant in the British army back in 2000, fifteen years after my own family left as a result of The Troubles. He explained how he had been dispatched to Northern Ireland and was stationed in Dungannon. The worst seven months of his life, unless you consider when he was sent to Iraq for the same timeline. That then became the worst seven months of his life. A difficult career choice by all accounts.

He hated Northern Ireland due to the ongoing war we had there. He sat waiting for a bomb to go off. When it was his turn to take to the turret, he found himself missing his own family, hating the place, as those down below ate chips and burgers, and drank a pint or several. His job was to sit still and watch everyone else enjoy themselves until some eejits, regardless of what side of the conflict they were on, decided to cause friction, prompting him into action. The mere thought of this brings sweat to his brow to this very day.

Beside the Morgan are two more vehicles - a Triumph 250, the other a Triumph TR6, bringing back memories of my ma telling me stories about the first car she received from James Devlin, my granda, back in the seventies. I was only a baby then. I don't remember him because he died when I was four years of age. I don't even remember my ma driving his car. Perhaps my mind is failing me now, and maybe that's why my head is in such a fog. Maybe this is a review of different segments of my life.

The Celtic harp is here. British cars surround me. Cadbury's chocolate, which was my biggest weakness growing up, is represented, coupled with the partial pokes. But where are the rest of my authors right now? What happened to Jim, Mary, Ben, Jeanne, Cindy, Laura, Sinead, Brenna, and Patricia? What about Dah-Nee-Tza the Guke Slinger? Where might Ann McCarthy, Ralph Bentley, Shannon Briggs, Shelly and Pierce McVeigh be? None of them are anywhere in sight.

Sitting directly ahead of me on the other side of the hall is a replica of The Tardis as used by Doctor Who during his own time travels. That reminds me, a fellow author of mine has who spent his life working in conflict resolution was recently indoctrinated for his endeavours. He is a massive fan of the show and quite literally lives and breathes it. His name is Tony Macaulay. A brilliant author who loves his family, literature, changing lives, and now bringing his books live on stage as well as through audio production, was a massive fan of the Bay City Rollers, among other musical legends from his childhood, including ABBA.

Tony told me he would like to take a trip back through time and relive those days of wonderment. What are the chances The Tardis went through its own malfunctioned warp using the Time Rotor, picked him up, and brought him here to the UK Pavilion? And if that is the case, why did no one believe me when I said I thought this has something to do with The X-Files?

Pausing for a moment, the next wave of unanswered questions took me once again by surprise, rushing over me like a tidal wave. The two voices I heard within the Wake House have now come back into focus again. They are clearly those of the *undertakers* - Robin Graves and Danica. They are not speaking to me directly but are explaining to individuals the purpose of a wake ceremony in Irish family circles. I must be separated from mind and body and am indeed caught between parallel dimensions.

Hang on a second . . . are they seriously hosting a wake in my honour? Am I dead? That can't be, although as I understand, the hearing is the last thing to go, so maybe I am. Why is it, then, that I can also hear Michael McCarthy and Therese Gilardi clearly speaking to two folks within The Tardis? Since those are both male, I notice a distinctive characteristic highly idiosyncratic to their personalities. As I make my way forth to investigate, I realize they both have heavily defined and unmistakable Irish accents: one is from County Cavan, the other from County Dublin.

With each step, I begin to hear a distinct, third accent in amongst the rest. I recognize the voice which clearly comes not only from Belfast but comes from the Shankill Road area. It's the wee peacemaking fella who started off his career as a paperboy, so it is. Finally, a friendly face, one who lives and breathes science fiction!

Maybe I will finally get the answers I seek, including "How the hell did I get here?" and "How do I get back after finding Arthur Colaianni?"

Chapter 37: Time Enough at Last

Walking up toward The Tardis, and before I could reacquaint myself with my old friend turned Honorary Doctor, another voice which I had not previously heard started to come into my range and stepped forward toward me. I noticed everything else within my direct vision was in full colour, yet the fellow who emerged from the shadows appeared as if he was from a black and white film or had come through from another decade. I tried to engage him, but he did not introduce himself. I tried to shake his hand, but he did not acknowledge it. I tried to say hello, but he did not respond. I tried to ask him where we were, but he instead walked back into The Tardis. I wasn't sure if he was being ignorant or if he couldn't see or hear me.

Seeing I was not going to get anywhere using this approach, I followed him inside, only to find myself in a room filled with electronic contraptions, including the Time Rotor Column and a progressively enhanced version of a robotic dog; the design was modeled after the original one I knew from my childhood days. Everything around me looked as if I had walked straight onto a television production set. Something about it looked out of this world and not normal. Then again, ask yourself if anything is normal about this book – if you didn't already notice, even the chapters are odd! Anyhow, the model number on the dog was K99. A bottle of red raspberry sauce, the same one which was missing from the ice cream machine behind Sandy Sans, was attached to the collar beside her nametag. Called *Wee Milly*, she answered questions or responded to commands given to her *only* when they were accompanied by lyrics from the Bay City Rollers or ABBA. Obviously, Doctor Macaulay was the mastermind behind this creative invention, trying to relive his own carefree and youthful days at the Westie Disco in Belfast – this was *his* escape from The Troubles.

The fellow who stood before me finally turned and spoke in an authoritative voice:

"There is a fifth dimension beyond that which is known to man. It is a dimension as vast as space and as timeless as infinity. It is the middle ground between light and shadow, between science and superstition, and it lies between the pit of man's fears and the summit of his knowledge. This is the dimension of imagination. It is an area which we call The Twilight Zone."

From his unmistakable introduction, I realized it was Rod Serling. Wondering how the godfather of imaginative creativity from my television screen was standing right here before me, I realized I had watched a lot of The Twilight Zone in my youth and was enthralled by his ingenious talent to create each segment. Since Rod had lay trapped within my subconscious thoughts for years, this gave him the opportunity to come forth and play on my own fears.

I carefully followed him. In the blink of an eye, he stepped into a shadow and was gone. Figuring since he had said that this *"is the middle ground between light and shadow, science and superstition"*, I closed and opened my eyes rapidly to clear my thoughts, only to have several scenes unfold; short snippets based directly on the show. I began with Season 1, Episode 8 - *Time Enough at Last,* which first aired on November 20, 1959. I could clearly see Arthur Colaianni, but he was not within my reach; rather, the scene showed him outside of a building while everything around him lay in ruin; columns toppled over, with scaffolding and bricks. I watched Arthur begin to climb out of the devastation. Stopping to view the lettering on the pillar directly in front of him which read *Public Library*, he began ascending the steps.

"Where is he off to?" I thought. I followed his footsteps back into what I believed was the UK Pavilion. Looking around me and blinking my eyes to make sure this was real, I realized none of the patrons who were in attendance for the show could see either one of us. It was obvious we were in another dimension; theirs was parallel to ours. I could cross back and forth between the two, but Arthur could not. He was imprisoned. What I did not realize is that every time I rapidly opened and closed my eyes to

ensure this wasn't a dream, they did the exact same thing back at the Wake House. My state of hypnotic catalepsy was slowly wearing off. At first, the patrons were flocking in to participate in the wake, but as soon as they saw my eyes blinking, they screamed and ran out, believing I had been brought back from the dead!

Shouting out to him and asking him to come back to the Dublin Irish Festival with me, Arthur did not look at me or respond. Instead, he started reciting the manuscript word for word that had been previously laid out for the actor in the scene now unfolding in front of me. Arthur replaced both roles. It is then I realized that he too couldn't hear anything I was trying to say to him. He had been placed in a black and white production, his clothes from the same era, and glasses I had never seen Arthur wear in the few years I had known him. These were obviously far too big for his face, but since he was in character, he had no choice other than to follow the production directions to a tee. Climbing in amongst the ruins in front of him, with volumes of encyclopedias and hard covers discarded like yesterday's newspaper, I both watched and carefully listened as he began speaking, shuffling himself from one book to the next:

"Collected Works of Dickens. Collected Works of George Bernard Shaw."

As he continued doing so, I noticed Arthur was now looking toward the upper end of the steps. It was almost as if he was trying to convey his message, but to whom I could not see. The next part took me by surprise.

"Books. Books. All the books I'll need. All the books, all the books I'll ever want," said Arthur's onscreen character, all the while throwing some off from one of only two bookshelves that remained standing amongst the ruins. The scene which was unfolding before my eyes was bizarre, to say the least. It was like Arthur was trying to find his way out, but from where exactly? The next thing I knew, he was walking down the steps, after having stacked piles of books and sorted them first by each month of the year, then by following years. It was a striking pattern to behold, one which I could only describe as being a librarian's apocalypse.

In the next scene, Arthur began hugging a massive clock he had found amid the rubble, all the while continuing to recite the script exactly as it was presented before. He did not seem to deviate from the character he portrayed. The clock read 12:21 p.m. What was uncanny is that was the exact time I had made my way back over to the Spoken Word tent to do my final presentation on Celtic folklore and mythology for the awaiting audience. Could it be possible those dimensions were also aligned with each other, thus making Melissa believe I was well within my allotted time to do my *With Love from an Irish Mother* presentation? This all seems to be quite peculiar, so it does.

I was sure Arthur looked directly at me, so I called out to him. I told him to stop wasting time, which we didn't have, and that we needed to get moving if he wanted to alleviate the mounting pressures and concerns of every author, festival participant, and staff member involved in the large-scale search for him. If he came with me now, we might be able to use The Tardis to get us back to Sunday afternoon in time for the grand finale over at the Celtic Rock stage. If nothing else, it was a shot in the dark. Here, I would be able to introduce him to the throngs of people who would be flocking to see all the acts on stage together - and prove my innocence in the process. This was the best scenario I could pull together. He could also add this to his chameleon personality of Italian Godfather turned Irish Leprechaun King writer, and now an actor in *The Twilight Zone*! "Quite the wild introduction that will be," I thought.

I opened my eyes only to see that Rod Serling stood watch, sizing me up to become his next character for whichever script he chose. Shutting my eyes as tightly as I could, I went into where Rod had described in his introduction as being the middle ground - *". . . the dimension of imagination."* I went back as far as I could to my bedroom, in my aunt's house, upstairs on the second floor, and onto my bed. The light was out, the television on, The Twilight Zone was playing. Season 1, Episode 10a, November 29, 1985. My thoughts aligned with what the show brought forth that night. I could hear the music and his hard breathing as the scene unfolded.

"I am The Shadow Man. And I will never harm the person under whose bed I live."

It was only then that I realized I could now see Rod in two different dimensions in my mind. In the first, if I looked at him straight on; he was fully dressed in black clothing. But when I looked at him using my peripheral vision, he became a shadowy figure and could move from one location to another with stealth-like precision. The icy chill I felt during my visit at Dunluce Castle from Maeve Roe's presence pierced through me all over again.

Striking my mind like a lightning bolt, I realized Rod had come for me and this was his way of enticing unsuspecting writers. This is how he managed to make Arthur vanish without a trace. Transforming into one of his own scripted creations, Rod had the ability of moving from one darkened location to another without ever being seen. We weren't suspects after all. We were targets! The first one from Chicago, Illinois - Arthur. The second was from Belfast, Northern Ireland - Greg. A third writer from Rochester, New York - Michael. Rounding out the first part of his collection, the fourth coming from Los Angeles, California - Therese. We were to become scriptwriters for the next series he had laid out called *Ebullience in Delirium.*

Completely forgetting that he was still playing his onscreen character, I opened my eyes and once again started shouting to Arthur, telling him his presence was needed back at the festival and that he needed to stop what he was doing.

"You've got to get out of there, NOW! Arthur Colaianni, I need you to listen to me. This is a trap, so it is. We need to go."

Looking around, I couldn't see him. I found myself back inside the UK Pavilion. Shayleen had moved on to the next set of her stage production, which happened to be about Northern Ireland.

I closed my eyes tightly to concentrate harder and pull myself back in to see if Arthur had finally heard my voice or followed my direction. Anything was worth a try at this point. Instead, he sat down, pulled a book close to him, opened it up to the middle, hugged it and said, "And the best thing, the very best thing of all, is that there's time now. There's all the time I need and all the time I want. Time, time, time . . . there's time enough at last."

My cries went ignored once again. I figured if I waited patiently enough for him to finish, he could possibly break free from his character and speak to me. On the other hand, Rod remained where he was standing, relishing in the fact that The Twilight Zone was playing front and centre within my imagination, as well as in the dimension in which I travelled; my fellow author playing the lead and only role. There was no one onscreen who could help him, and from what I could tell, no one offscreen either.

Waiting for this to end so I could pull Arthur out of it and make our way back, the next part was something I could not have expected whatsoever. He had dropped his glasses, which broke both lenses, rendering his vision useless. Not only could he not see the books anymore, he would not be able to see me either. Arthur was despondent that he had all the time in the world to enjoy his books, wherever that may be, but now had no way of reading them. It was as if Rod Serling knew well in advance of writing that episode that this would end up happening and ensured no one could reverse the events which he had set into motion. With that, he turned away from me and began speaking, closing out the scene as he did at the end of each episode:

"The best laid plans of mice and men, and Henry Bemis. The small man in the glasses who wanted nothing but time. Henry Bemis, now just a part of a smashed landscape. Just a piece of the rubble. Just a fragment of what man has deeded to himself. Mr. Henry Bemis, in The Twilight Zone."

After the screen faded from stars to black, Rod moved back into the shadows again but continued to speak to me with a sense of satisfaction.

"I hear you calling to the fellow as Arthur Colaianni. Has no one ever told you, my dear man, that that is an Italian surname?

The man in front of you is a famous sopranist and has been chosen to join The Irish Tenors in my Menagerie of Music. Michael Bublé is next. I am eagerly awaiting his arrival. I believe their voices to your written words will be harmony to my ears!"

I froze. Didn't Nick tell me the exact same information when I met with him much earlier on Sunday morning at the maintenance shed? According to Rod, the man in front of him was a famous Sopranist. But to my eyes, it was the same author I met three years prior when I first attended the Dublin Irish Festival. At hearing this, I yelled, "Can someone tell me who the hell is the real Arthur Colaianni? The man is a chameleon of a thousand faces!"

Rod spoke again, *"He is indeed just that and tried to give me the slip at The Book Loft. I brought him over there and was going to use him as Romney Wordsworth, The Obsolete Man whose occupation was that of a librarian. He was to be liquidated and then placed within the Supernatural section, creating a spectacle of want. Every time people come in and touched any one of my books, they would purchase the entire collection of my written works. Arthur was to move my books around each night. That way, when Julie Burgess, Gary Lovely, Bryan Boylan or Sean Boley came back the next day, every publication of The Twilight Zone was in different sections, sitting by the front door or down by the cash register. By doing so, I would become a New York Times bestselling author and my show would go back into syndicated circulation. That show, in case you are curious, was from Season 2, Episode 29. It originally aired on June 2nd, 1961."*

At this moment, it became extremely clear to me that Rod Serling was an absolute genius who, in my opinion, came from some otherworldly place. Not only was he a stellar narrator, screenplay writer, television producer, playwright and author, he could recreate himself over and over again, captivating the minds of adults and children, playing on their fears, bringing them into their imagination, exploring their knowledge or lack thereof, as well as casting a spotlight on superstition versus science. I realized he was a mentor to me and my own writing.

Rod continued. *"I was almost successful in doing so, but one of your other author's came snooping around, found Arthur where I had left him up in the attic, and tried to bring him back to the Dublin Irish Festival. So, into darkness I went once more as The Shadow Man. When your fellow writer decided to be Mr. Nice Guy and left the vehicle to help some senior citizen, I pulled Arthur into the veil of darkness. The detective, as he likes to call himself, passed us both on 3rd Street. If he had of looked down, he would have seen three shadows instead of just one. So much for him being a sleuthhound. The best way for me to keep this author friend of yours is to put him into my scripts and have him play the role of each character. Today he is Henry Bemis, tomorrow he might be Adam Grant. Season 2, Episode 26: Shadow Play. Original air date May 5, 1961."*

As a result of this, I decided to make my way back inside The Tardis. Wee Milly was buzzing around, looking for miniature Flakes to make a poke with. I asked her if Arthur's onscreen character would remain trapped in decades long-past. Since I did not accompany my question with lyrics from a Bay City Rollers or an ABBA song as required, Wee Milly ignored me. Even though I was not wearing a pair of tartan trousers or disco fever flares for that matter, I tried again while singing

"We sang Shang-a-Lang
And we ran with the gang
Doing doo wop be dooby doo ay

We were all in the news
With our blue suede shoes
And our dancing the night away . . ."

The only thing I got back from Wee Milly was not what I wanted to hear.

"Affirmative."

Chapter 39: Free Based Irishmen

I jumped as Doctor Macaulay approached me and offered a ha'penny for my thoughts. Taking it as a very generous offer, as they certainly weren't worth that much, I explained to him what was going on - with Arthur being missing, the search for clues, my diary, interrogations of innocent people, and everyone being made out to be a suspect, especially me. I spoke about the Wake House, taking the shot of Danny Houton's Sextuple Distilled, and somehow then ending up between dimensions. I mulled how I was going to get my message to Arthur to join me before the effects of Inishowen Peninsula's Purest Poitín wore off, sending me back to where I was supposed to be.

"Ack, but surely I can help," said Tony, "but you need to see something first. By the way, Therese and Michael are here but I must warn you – do not breathe a word; you are entering into their dimensional shift, so you are! They too are over at the Wake House – in a time different from your own. However, since you are already there right now, lying in the plywood coffin supposedly being waked, and are currently frightening the Dickens - pardon the pun - of out everyone by opening and closing your eyes, you need to be careful. If they find out you are there intruding on their wee interludes, Arthur will never get back to the

Dublin Irish Festival. In fact, the four of you will become locked forever within Rod Serling's *Menagerie of Madness*."

I looked at Tony, wondering what he meant by this. In an exasperated tone, I said, "Tony, I just met with Rod. He brought me in to see what Arthur was currently doing, but he was stuck inside the screen. I asked Wee Milly, your robotic doggie, if Arthur will remain trapped in short snippets, perpetually acting the eejit by taking on other roles which have already been filmed. She gave me an answer which I didn't want to hear. But what about this *Menagerie of Madness*? Rod had told me about a Menagerie of *Music* which is to feature my fellow author, Arthur Colaianni, along with The Irish Tenors, and supposedly Michael Bublé will become part of this creation as well."

Tony gave me a look of extreme curiosity. I should have known what was coming next.

"Greg, are you talking about Arthur Colaianni, the famous sopranist? Sure, he is one of my favorite Italian crooners. Well, then again, nothing comes close to my all-time favourites - Agnetha Fältskog, Björn Ulvaeus, Benny Andersson, and Anni-Frid Lyngstad. Do you happen to know who they are? They were quite famous during the seventies and eighties, so they were."

"I do indeed know who they are, Doctor Macaulay," I replied. They are a Swedish pop supergroup which was formed in Stockholm back in 1972. Taking their name from the first initial of each of their names, they went on to become one of the most successful of bands – ABBA."

"Very good, my friend. Well done," said Tony. "Obviously, you know the classics. Now, to get back to your question, did Rod not tell you the details behind the Menagerie of Madness? You are all to become part of his newly-created festival featuring Irish and American novelists, which is to directly compete with the Dublin Irish Festival. But it doesn't end there, so it doesn't. The Shadow Man is going to continue with his escapades of kidnapping each one of you until the Irish Authors' Corner and Spoken Word tents are void of your presence at the festival. Instead, this will evolve into a feature each day of the year, becoming a permanent installment within the attic of a newly created place in Columbus, Ohio, called The Book Loft Pub and Hotel!"

Hearing this, my already overactive and saturated mind fell into an even deeper meltdown. "I know the Irish can talk the leg off a stool at the best of times, even those of us who have not kissed the Blarney Stone, but believe it or not, this is a bit much even for me! I wonder if Julie, Brian, Gary and Sean are indeed the ones behind this? They always said they hated when the Dublin Irish Festival comes to an end because so does the mad craic and banter; in saying that, we all have to part ways with one another for a full year. We always have the time of our lives and laugh like there's no tomorrow. I guess the end is nigh."

Tony snapped me out of my moment of hysterical thought and said, "Greg, enough of tormenting your mind further; get back to the storyline. People are waiting to find out what happens next!"

"Oh, all right then, Doctor Macaulay," I said. "Sure, if they are creating what you have just mentioned, I imagine there will be room service, exit doors, pints, and probably a front desk reception. Perhaps they will take to serving up wee variations of the Dublin Cream Bun. Otherwise, there is absolutely no way Rod is going to be able to keep us there indefinitely, so he's not."

With that, Tony handed me a Sony Walkman cassette player before asking me to put on the foam-covered earphones and press play. Since my curiosity always did get the best of my better judgement, what little there was of it, I looked down to see a cassette tape inside that read, "The Eagles Greatest Hits! If found, please call 867-5309. Property of Danica ♥ Shaun Cassidy ♥ Richardson."

"Danica sure fell for that Shaun Cassidy fella, whoever *he* might be," I said, before pondering how Tommy Tutone had kept finding ways to crawl into my battered thoughts, planting Jenny's number again and again. Pressing play, I instantly knew the message Doctor Macaulay was trying to not so inconspicuously relay, saying the words in unison:

"You can check out any time you like, but you can never leave!"

As my eyes went wide with fear, now knowing the plan was for us to remain trapped once The Shadow Man carried out his sinister scheme, Tony played the best air guitar solo of Joe Walsh and Don Felder ever seen. I, on the other hand, was not yet finished with my questions.

"Tony, how in the green fields of Eire did you manage to get a hold of this? Do you know who this belongs to? I haven't seen one of these things since . . ."

I didn't get a chance to finish my sentence as he was expecting I would likely ask this of him. Interrupting me, he said, "As I was passing back through time – it was a midsummer's night dream in July '85 to be exact - The Tardis took me over to the Delavan-Darien High School. I noticed a younger version of your fair maiden was in the schoolyard, walking along and bopping her head to the music. She was going to be driving up to a Mama's Boys concert that night over in Milwaukee. It was none other than their Power and Passion World Tour. While she was distracted at the concert, I "borrowed" her Walkman. But don't worry, I will drop it back off again. She won't even notice it was missing to begin with. The past, present and future remain the same."

Pausing for thought and strength at the same time since my creative imagination often runs away and gets me into trouble, I wondered if the creation of this story among a small collective of authors from various walks of life had greater purpose or meaning, or if there was perhaps a connection between me and The Shadow Man, Doctor Who and The Tardis; or with Captain Kirk and The Enterprise; or with my fellow author and dear friend, Tony Macaulay, and his own youthful escapades throughout parallel universes.

Even if these creations were only in our besieged minds to help us escape from our days growing up during The Troubles, or as adults surrounded by relationships and the never-ending challenges which come with them, both good and bad, our imaginations were a place we could run to, be safe, hide, play in, and become like our heroes as their roles unfolded on our television screens. It was a place I ran to while working in difficult conditions, or when made to feel like these efforts of putting together a whole new story were "going off track and down a hole" as I was told. It was difficult to separate my mind from fiction and reality with all that has been going on lately and things that were said. Perhaps I was now like the character portrayed in Season 2, Episode 26, called *Shadow Play* – and am reliving episodes of my life in a recurring dream – or possibly an ongoing nightmare – as a result of making preposterous choices!

With that statement, I snapped out of this temporary mind paralysis and realized Doctor Macaulay had more time travels to get to, so as to not interrupt any sequencing of events which already took place and may inadvertently cause a stir across the universe. Since he also realized this, he was ready to now move me into the next phase of events, which I needed to know if we were going to get to the bottom of this mystery, or forever be doomed if I failed.

"Gillian and David," said Tony. "Can youse walk Greg's mind back a few days?"

For a moment, I thought my eyes and ears were deceiving me. Standing right before me in all of their Golden Globe glory were Agents Fox Mulder and Dana Scully. I knew I was right! My brain began racing because I sought answers to an abundance of questions. My next plan was to follow up with them about what had been said to me on the phone earlier on the Sunday morning shortly after Arthur vanished – to ask them about Page 47 of the Presidential Diary.

David Duchovny stepped forward, extending his hand in a warm, friendly handshake, but introduced himself as Agent Fox Mulder.

"I already know you are aware this moment was coming, Greg. Or do I refer to you as Agent Mad Dog? Since you are standing in front of me, you obviously received the package we sent with Mark Rickerby in California. Nice lad, he seems to be. A brilliant screenplay writer as well. He is looking forward to the production of the disaster you and Agent Striking Viking are working on right now. What is it about you Irish lads having to set everything on fire? Do you not think you would have both been better pursuing career choices in the field of pyromania? It seems to be in your wild warrior ways."

Looking first at Agent Mulder, then over at Doctor Macaulay, my mouth fell open, but no words came out. If truth be told, it was a miracle in the making as I had been left completely speechless!

Gillian Anderson was the next to step forward and give me a warm hug, all the while telling me it was time I took a deep breath and ventured into their worlds and modes of escape. Moving into her role as Agent Dana Scully, she said, "We didn't have much time to get a sense of how or why Therese and Michael were speaking to people from the past, but they are of an exceptional and notable status. It is up to you, Greg, to try and figure out how they got there and if they are going to help or hinder you with the momentous challenge which lies ahead."

I gave Agent Mulder and Agent Scully an all-knowing nod before reciting the words they would have told others before me:

"To find the truth, you must believe . . ."

Chapter 41: A Wilde Interlude

Fellow author Arthur Cola's gone missing from the Dublin Irish Festival and a New York SPOIL is leading the investigation into his disappearance. The SPOIL has drawn up a list of suspects that includes every author at the festival. Every author, that is, except me. Either the SPOIL is very sloppy or very sly. My money is on the latter. Surely, a former New York copper would know I was the only writer next to Arthur in the Irish Authors' Corner this weekend. The SPOIL must also be aware that Arthur and I have enjoyed the craic every year. And certainly, an investigator would have noted that I, like Arthur, am a bit of an interloper amongst all these full-blooded Irish, with an Italian surname and Latin heritage.

The SPOIL overlooking me can only mean one thing. He believes I'm the culprit. That I will lead him to Arthur. He probably has a tail on me right now, here in Coffman Park. The park is peaceful in the bewitching hours before dawn, after the last banjo chord has been played, the books, jewelry and souvenir stalls tucked into canvas blankets for the night, and the food trucks shuttered. The cool air tastes of trampled grass and cotton candy. A handful of stars sprinkle the sky, though their light is not enough to pierce the darkness shrouding the sloped lawn beneath the oak trees. I'll bet the SPOIL's tail is hiding in one of those sheltered spaces.

"I see you." My voice echoes.

"As always, you're the only one who does," a male voice replies. His Irish accent is soft, like butter melting atop a warm scone.

I take a step in his direction. He's reclining on a small slope, leaning back on his elbow, his left knee bent, his right hand resting on his chest. It's a familiar pose. The same position his granite likeness assumes in the far corner of Merrion Square, in that other, far-off Dublin across the Atlantic; the place where we first met.

"Oscar Wilde."

He stands, straightens the garnet fur trim on his deep green velvet jacket, pushes back the rings on his left hand, and leans toward me.

"Therese Gilardi, Ma Chérie."

He kisses me, once on each cheek. Oscar's very continental. Perhaps it's because he's slated to spend eternity as an honorary Frenchman, his body entombed in Paris's Père Lachaise Cemetery.

"How are you, love? It seems like only yesterday . . ."

"It's been almost sixteen years."

Oscar shrugs. "To me it feels as recent as this morning. Memory . . . is the diary that we all carry about with us. Of course, it also helps that I'm operating on a bit of an 'otherworldly' clock." He pats the gold pocket watch dangling on a long chain from his vest pocket.

"What are you doing here, Oscar?"

"The same as you - soaking up a bit of Irish culture. Enjoying the Yank nod to the old sod. Although I must say I'm a bit disappointed the Wake House is not livelier. And I didn't see any of my books for sale at the Author's Tent. Very troubling. But I saw your titles. Have you sold many books?"

"It's been my best year. Probably because my table is next to Arthur's. He's a top seller. Or he was."

"Did he leave the Festival early?"

"That's one way of putting it. Arthur's missing."

"Missing?" His eyes widen. "And here I thought this Dublin was the safe one."

"I'm not so sure that's true."

Oscar pulls an engraved silver flask from the lining of his jacket. "You've had quite a shock. You need a shot of liquid courage."

"Thanks."

He tucks his hand through the crook of my elbow. "Take me to the place where Arthur was last spotted."

"Oscar, if we knew where Arthur was last seen, he wouldn't be missing."

"Apologies. It's the absinthe talking. Let's walk and you can tell me about this author, Arthur. What does he like?"

"He has a fondness for cream buns."

"A man after my own heart. He can resist everything except temptation. Do you think it's possible he's been poisoned with one of these cream buns?"

"No. The buns are enormous."

"Ah, American super-sized as it were."

"Exactly. A box of them was handed round the Author's Tent. Because they're so big, the buns were all cut in half. If Arthur had a tainted bun, the person who ate the other half would also have fallen ill."

"Suppose there were left-over buns? Perhaps one of them held the other half of the poison?"

"Trust me, there are never left-over Schmidt's buns."

"Fair enough. What else do you know about Arthur? Does he have another job besides author?"

"He used to be a principal. You know, head of school."

"Education is an admirable thing, but it is well to remember from time to time that nothing that is worth knowing can be taught."

"Oscar, you sound like my high school self. Or maybe my college self, after that intro to philosophy class. I wish I could drown the memory of that humiliation."

Oscar passes me the flask. "An educator. Shaping young minds. Or not . . ."

"I know what you're thinking, and the answer is no. Arthur's not the type to have an old student with a vendetta. More than likely, he has a drawer full of thank you notes from former pupils."

"And yet he's missing." Oscar pulls an enamel cigarette box from his pocket. A handful of small cigarettes lay inside. "Hand rolled. From Turkey. Amazing what people leave on my tombstone. Would you care for a smoke?"

"No, thank you."

Oscar places the cigarette between his teeth, then sets it aflame with a ruby encrusted lighter.

I glance around Coffman Park. Surely the SPOIL's tail will notice the rings of smoke rising from Oscar's cigarette? Or smell the heavy tobacco? I brace myself, but no one appears.

For the first time, I'm afraid. A potential body snatcher is on the loose, possibly targeting Irish-Italian authors, and I'm strolling through a deserted park with nothing but the ghost of Oscar Wilde for protection. I cross my fingers for luck, just like my mother's cousins do in County Donegal.

"This is quite the challenge. A missing man, and no clues. You're certain, Therese, that you noticed nothing amiss with Arthur this year? Nothing's changed since you saw him last?"

"Actually, there is one thing. Arthur always brought his wife to the Dublin Irish Festival. Until this year."

"My God, woman, you've buried the lead!" Oscar waves his arm wildly. "Cherchez la femme." Find the wife, you find the man. Or vice versa. How can a woman be expected to be happy with a man who insists on treating her as if she were a perfectly normal human being?"

"You've got it all wrong. Arthur was laughing when he told me he'd texted his wife to say she'd chosen the wrong year to stay home, since the author accommodations were so posh this year."

"So, Arthur's wife is not missing as well?"

"No."

"Reluctantly, I rule her out. What of the other authors? Any chance one of them has done Arthur in?"

"I've been invited to the Dublin Irish Festival for the past five years. Most of the authors are the same people, although there have been a few who dropped out or have joined us recently. From what I can see, they're nice enough."

"Do they like you?"

"I think so. Except for the SPOIL."

"The SPOIL?"

"One of the authors is a retired investigator. I have the impression he believes I'm behind Arthur's disappearance."

"Bad people are, from the point of view of art, fascinating studies. They represent color, variety and strangeness; bad people stir one's imagination."

"I don't know if the SPOIL thinks I'm bad. More likely, just guilty."

Oscar and I walk past the Celtic Rock tent. We sit on the dewy grass, our backs against the fence.

"This suspense is terrible. I hope it will last."

"All well and good for you to say, Oscar, but I'm afraid of what might happen when the sun rises."

Oscar passes me the flask once more. "A dreamer is one who can only find his way by moonlight, and his punishment is that he sees the dawn before the rest of the world."

Overhead, pale streaks of light make their way across the sky. I don't know how long we've been traipsing around Coffman Park, trying to figure out the riddle of Arthur's disappearance. Interludes with Oscar Wilde are always timeless.

"I hope I can see my way to solving this mystery before I'm wearing a pair of locked silver bracelets."

"Handcuffs will look fetching on you."

"Oscar!"

"Apologies." Oscar snaps his fingers. "I've got it! I am so clever, sometimes I surprise even myself. Your man Arthur has taken a page from the book of Oscar Wilde."

"Does that mean you know where Arthur is?"

"Not quite. Rather, I know why he went missing. *The Importance of Being Earnest*. It's Arthur's modus operandi. His model. Arthur has staged his own disappearance. Consider this. He leaves his wife at home even though he knows this year's accommodations are much fancier than in years past. Why would he do that? Because he knew he wasn't going to spend the whole weekend at the Dublin Irish Festival."

"But he loves the festival. Why would he do that?"

"Because he wishes to avoid his social obligations. Perhaps he wanted to write. Maybe he had another pressing engagement he wished to keep private."

"That doesn't sound like Arthur. If he couldn't be at the author's tent for some reason, he would have sent word. He's very loyal to the festival. No, Arthur wouldn't disappear from the Dublin Irish Festival for no reason."

In the distance, several car engines sputter.

"That, my lovely, is my cue." Oscar stands. He extends me his hands and pulls me to my feet. Again, he kisses me, once on each cheek. "*A bientôt mon amie*. Until we meet again on another starlit night."

Oscar takes five steps, then disappears into the early morning light. I rub my eyes. Much as I'd like to, I can't tell any of the other Dublin Irish Festival authors about this. They already think I'm a dreamy poet from California with a fondness for absinthe and a penchant for Oscar Wilde quotations.

The sun climbs higher. The first volunteers will soon arrive at Coffman Park. Until Arthur disappeared, this year's festival was my favorite. The food, music and craic were top-notch, as was the hotel. I enjoyed my speech and seeing old friends. Once again, readers came by to snag copies of *Narvla's Celtic New Year, Matching Wits with Venus* and *Isabelle the Imaginist*. And they loved my new book. The one rushed to publication for this year's Dublin Irish Festival. The one with the clever title, which I now fear may prove quite damning in the eyes of the SPOIL:

The Arsenic of Archangels.

Chapter 43: The Colonel's Voice

"I, too, had a weird calling on Sunday morning," I said. "I woke up out of sound sleep thinking it was time for my nightly trip to empty the bladder, but that was not what woke me. No, it was a voice with an Irish accent, a young man's voice - well, younger than my sixty-many years. It said, 'Get up, come follow me.' Now, I have had many a weird dream and I thought nothing of it. After the obligatory visit to the bathroom . . ."

"Too much information, Mike," said Mr. Robin Graves, exasperated, "so please continue on without the bathroom visits."

"Okay," I said. After doing what I just said I did, I went back to bed only to be disturbed again by the same voice with the same instruction: 'Get up and follow me.' I looked over at the clock that said it was three o'clock in the morning and this is what happened:

"Now, get dressed," said the voice. "Grab your keys. You are going for a ride."

"What about Ann?" I said. "She'll be worried when she wakes and I'm not here."

"Bring her with you, if you like," said the voice.

"Who are you, anyway?" I asked.

"You'll find out soon enough. Just hurry up. We don't have much darkness left."

Darkness? I thought. *What are we going to do in the darkness?*

I woke Ann and said, "You need to get up. Some voice is talking to me."

Ann blinked a couple of times as if to clear her head of the cobwebs that had assembled during her sleep and said, "What voice are you talking about?"

"I don't know," I said, "Some voice told me to get up, get dressed, and go for a ride."

"And you woke me up for that?" said Ann, my trusting and devoted wife.

"Oh, come on," I said. "It sounds like an adventure."

Within a few minutes, we both were ready to go, and headed for the elevator. While passing through the lobby, the night clerk, resting on two elbows, waiting for his shift to end in about four hours, just looked.

"It's a calling," I said. "We have to go."

"Not another one," said the clerk under his breath. "I've seen everything on this job. I should write a book about the bizarre adventures of a hotel night clerk."

"I heard that," I said. "And yes, you should become a historical fiction writer."

"No fiction here," he said.

Out onto the darkened parking lot we went. For some strange reason, the streetlights went out so I had to click my key fob to make my lights flash to find my car. Once inside, while warming up my 3.2 turbo engine, the voice returned.

"See that bright star in the southern sky?"

"Yeah, that's pretty bright. I 've never seen a star so bright. Are you sure it's not some used car lot having a sale and using a search light to draw us in?"

"No, it's not," said the voice. Just then, a faint figure came into view in the back seat. It was a young man, just as I thought, and he had on a Union army uniform on, complete with a kepi hat, and a crossed rifles emblem, indicating he was from the infantry. He had a fresh scar on his forehead.

"Let me introduce myself," the voice said. "I am Colonel Patrick Henry O'Rorke of the One Hundred-Fortieth infantry."

"Oh my," I said. "This can't be true. I know who you are. I'm a member of the Patrick O'Rorke Society in Rochester, New York. You're a West Point graduate, first in your class, and killed at the Battle of Gettysburg."

"Yes, 'tis true," said Patrick. "I know who you are too, and that's why I am here. You have been chosen for a special mission."

Ann said, "Who are you talking to, and why are you looking in the back seat?"

"Shhh," I said. "It's Patrick O'Rorke and he is taking us somewhere."

"We should go back and get the night clerk," said Ann. "He can add this to his book."

"No fiction, Ann," I said. "It's true - Colonel O'Rorke is with us."

"Better than the devil," said Ann, looking out the window. "How come it's so dark?"

"Patrick turned off the lights so we could follow that bright star."

"Christmas in August is it?" she said.

I followed the light, which took us onto Interstate 270 going south. I blinked, or I think I blinked, but suddenly we were in southern Ohio near Cincinnati. The star had us turn east along the Ohio River into a little town called Point Pleasant.

In the center of town, Patrick said, "Turn left and stop."

I turned onto Indian Street, which runs along Big Indian Creek before it empties into the Ohio River, and stopped the car.

"You see that little white house there?" said Patrick.

"Yeah, the house the star is shining onto," I said. "What's the big deal?"

"That's the house where Ulysses S. Grant was born," said Patrick. "If I hadn't lost my life at Gettysburg, he would have been my Commander-in-Chief. I would have served under General Grant through the end of the war."

"And admirably, I'm sure," I said.

"I brought you here, away from the others, to give you a message. I joined a new army."

"A new army? The Confederacy?" I said.

"No, not the Confederacy. When I died, many souls came with me from the battle, and we joined many more that already perished. We were joined by many more before war's end. We have formed a new union with all souls to forego any new war and avoid needless bloodshed."

"The message I want you to give to the world through your writing is the necessity of listening, compromise, and unity. You cannot allow division like we had in 1860 before the war's start. When President Lincoln was elected, he was vehemently hated by the south for his values and principles, especially around slavery. Therefore, they seceded from the United States, causing a war that took over six-hundred-thousand American lives. All because Congress could not compromise a legal settlement."

"I was born in County Cavan in Ireland, a country similarly divided in the 1800's. My family moved to Rochester, New York, only to experience more division. I attended the United States Military Academy at West Point to protect my adopted nation, not to fight within it. Now I see the United States is on the edge of another similar division, and because of a few bad and angry words or incidents, is on the verge of another civil war."

"We have seen the Irish diaspora spread across the globe more than any other country through the vast spread of the British Empire of long ago, for good or for bad. Nonetheless, we Irish have learned the brutality of war, oppression, torture, and mere harassment from person to person. Our group of departed souls, who have witnessed these atrocities in the past and who continue to see it today, want you to send this timely message."

I was flabbergasted at the message. "Why me?"

Colonel O'Rorke said, "You are a writer of Irish stories from Rochester and you have a vast outlet through the Dublin Irish Festival."

"I'll do my best," I said.

"Remember," said the Colonel, "compromise and dialogue is difficult. It's hard work to go beyond one's hardened opinion and be willing to listen and forgive. It's even harder to change one's own attitude for the sake of the greater good. I have heard sayings like 'never compromise' or 'stick to your guns no matter what.' Words and feelings such as those cause stalemates in a democracy. Everyone shouting leaves all sides in frustration and isolation. Be as kind as you wished your parents had been to you."

"Interesting concept," I said. "I hope to carry the message as well as you did."

With that, the image in the back seat faded away. The Colonel was gone, even though I wished he would stay longer to chat. I took a deep breath and sat motionless for a few moments.

Ann saw the change in my demeanor and allowed the momentary reprieve until I reached over and started the car again. We rode several miles back to Dublin in silence before Ann asked, "What happened back there?"

"I was given a task by a group of our forefathers to send a warning. They foresee trouble ahead in our country and they want we authors of the Dublin Irish Festival to help avoid it."

"What are you going to do?" she said.

"Let's keep this quiet for now, until we figure out how to proceed," I said.

"This is your task to handle as you see fit," said Ann as she looked out the window, watching the darkened fields of southern Ohio pass by. "As Luke in Chapter Twelve said, 'To whom much is given, much will be required.'"

Ending my conversation with the undertaker, before taking my leave, I said, "Shortly after that, I received a phone call from Greg saying that Arthur was missing."

Chapter 45: Ebullience in Delirium

Watching as the two scenes of Therese and Michael drifted away from us all, I turned back to Doctor Macaulay with a look of concern on my face. "Is Therese having an illicit affair with Oscar Wilde? Mon Cherry? Handcuffs? What does *'share she laugh am'* mean? I know we Irish are a bit full of the romance and all, but good grief, he sure turns into a wee charmer, so he does."

Laughing, Tony said, "Ack, Greg. We are indeed just that, but you need to work on your pronunciation of the French language, so you do. Oscar said, 'Ma chérie. Cherchez la femme.'"

"Sure thing, Doctor," I replied. The only French I knew from back home, as my ma would tell me, were swear words, so they were. Anyways, what was that all about? How did Therese and Michael both end up at the Wake House on different occasions on Sunday morning? What led them there? What am I not seeing here? I had to figure this all out on my own, so I did!"

"Greg, what you did not see is that three bottles of Danny Houton's Sextuple-Distilled Poitín had been dropped into your room, along with instructions on how to use and not use it. But, when you went out to check to see who had knocked on your door, only to discover that a

Dublin Cream Bun was sitting at your feet, The Shadow Man slipped into your room and replaced the instructions. You invited him in by opening the door. That was your first mistake."

"Tony, that can't be true," I replied. "There was only one small shot-size glass bottle left there for me, and the only thing on it was a Skull and Crossbones. It also had a four-leaf clover emblazoned onto it as a bowtie, and a note beneath it saying to drink it only if of Irish or Viking blood, and to enjoy your trip or something to that effect. Authors and other participants began questioning this gesture because not everyone got gifts. I heard only a few of us did."

Putting his hand to his forehead in disbelief, Tony said, "It all makes sense now, Greg. I know exactly what has gone on here. The bottle you got was NOT meant for you at all. If you received a glass with that kind of a caution label on it, it was meant – that was supposed to go to J.P. Not only did you receive his shot glass of the stuff – it is known as the purest of the pure in Irish circles and used only when joining the Viking fishermen after a day of drinking. It gives the courage one thousand men strong to handle the trek. It is used to toast a feast fit for a king. Danny was known for this. He would take a live crab, smash his fist into its back, and suck the juices before ripping out the meaty flesh and feasting as he conquered the wild Atlantic waves. What you got was Danny

Houton's DOUBLE-Sextuple-Distilled Poitín – twelve times the potency!"

I looked at Tony in disbelief. "Well, I guess that explains why the Guke Slinger and Robin Graves are having a bit of craic with my body at the Wake House, making a small fortune off me in the process. The cheek of the two of them! To be completely truthful, Doctor Macaulay, I am surprised they have not called in a priest to give me my last rites after what I just drank. That stuff burns! I hope no one chances a cigarette while waking me. The place will go up in flames, so it will. The most I usually drink is one lemonade Shandy and that usually takes me well over an hour to finish."

"Greg, you will be just fine, so you will," said Tony. "The only thing you might have when you get back from here is a blistering headache, although you can rest assured your insides will be one-hundred-percent cholesterol-free. But if you start glowing, you may want to get checked out. Then again, you could very well require a complete organ transplant. If not, the good news is that you are of Viking heritage! The not-so-good news, depending on how you want to look at this, is that you are a close relation of J.P. If so, it makes perfect sense. The two of you are completely out of your minds, so you are. Who goes about collecting pallets from the City Council to ship them to the Dublin Irish Festival to have a presentation on how to have a Viking funeral? And what was that part about Belfast Riots on Tour? Plus, on top of all that, I saw that you and Jim McVeigh wrote and performed a song called *The Ballad of J.P. Sexton*. Do you get my drift?"

Looking to my left, I saw David Duchovny taking all of this in, shaking his head in disbelief at the shenaniganism's that were unfolding. "Doctor Macaulay, would you be able to bring the two of us to that point in time if it ever happens again?" asked David. "I would pay to watch this in person myself, so I would! Although we do so much time travel, it would be wonderful to come back here to have a laugh while watching what this craic stuff is all about, so it will."

Gillian Anderson smirked at hearing David use the Norn Iron lingo at the end of his query, as everything ended with so this or so that. "Yes, I too would very much like to be a part of that, so I would," said Gillian. "I was in Belfast and filmed a show called The Fall, so I did. It was truly dead brilliant, so it was. The North Irish are mad but have fun with it, so they do. It was a fantastic experience, so it was. Their accents are ninety, so they are!"

Laughing at Agent Mulder and Agent Scully doing their best to speak like the two of us, Doctor Macaulay brought things back to a critical moment that we had not yet addressed.

"Greg, you mentioned that there were a few of you who received gifts at the hotel. I will tell you why. The second time you received a knock at the door and ended up finding the bottle of Five Farms Irish Cream at your feet, The Shadow Man was behind that as well. Arthur had startled him while he was in the process of setting his trap and caught a glimpse of him moving through the hotel. That's why he was targeted first. As you were looking around, he slipped back into your room and removed the remaining shot glasses. Do you know who the other two are that received them?"

Before heading out together as a group for supper at the Dublin Irish Tavern, I thought back to a meeting of the festival participants and realized the others had arrived at the hotel much later than I. It was at this point that Therese shared with Danica that she had received a small welcoming shot glass gift in her room, with a specific set of instructions. When asked what it said, Therese responded, "You are cordially invited to the Wake House this Sunday morning at 6:30 a.m. Come and a**wake**n your mind, your body and your soul. Bring this offering with you!"

Overhearing this conversation, Michael came over to say he had received the same gift but was to come over at 7:00 a.m. As explained by Doctor Macaulay, what they did not know is they were being targeted by The Shadow Man. He planned to capture Arthur at 6:00 a.m. as he knew he didn't drink. Since Arthur had drunk his first and only Old-Fashioned the night before, the trap was easily set. What better way to distract his attention than by leaving a Dublin Cream Bun for him in secret the next morning at the Irish Authors' Corner? How could he resist? As the two others most likely do the same as Arthur and get set up for the day, they would also go missing.

Frantic in my response, I said, "Tony, this makes no sense to me whatsoever. How did we all suddenly become targets? Why is it Therese and Michael did not get as far as I have in trying to find Arthur? Case in point is I am here with you, Agent Mulder and Agent Scully. I met with Rod Serling. I can see my fellow author, Arthur Colaianni who, from being told this twice now, also moonlights as a sopranist. That is a secret he kept from all of us - well, until now that is. But he is trapped in the screenplays out there. He does not seem to see or hear me. What can I do?"

"The answer is simple," replied Tony. Turning to Agent Mulder, he then said, "David, can you walk his mind back earlier on Sunday morning? He needs to see this. Remember, do not say a word in here, Greg, for you are going back into *their* dimensional time shift, so you are. There is no room for error. Do the same as before – quietly observe until we come back out again."

Entering the Wake House, I watched as Theresa and Michael had both gone in and left on separate occasions that Sunday morning, following their scheduled times. When Therese went in, she offered a gift – the shot glass of Danny Houton's Sextuple-Distilled Poitín. Pouring a small amount into her hand, she dabbed it with one finger and placed some under her nose. Another small portion was poured into a dish with a candle in the middle, which was then lit.

As it burned, Mr. Robin Graves joined her in the room and asked if she was ready for her journey. Knocking on the lid of the coffin, Therese said, "Is this where the dead man lives?" and drank the balance. With that, Robin opened the coffin. The room transformed with thoughts from deep within Therese's mind, taking her to the location of where she most desired to meet the man of her dreams – Oscar Wilde. It was here I learned that the undertaker was much more than a role-playing character for the Dublin Irish Festival. He too, had his own secret in that he was a medium who could speak to those who have passed, and who could make the connection when the time and mood was right. However, since Therese drank less than half of the shot glass, her journey lasted for a short time, but it was enough time to make her connection and fulfill her dream of seeing Mr. Wilde again, and try to find answers to the mystery of where Arthur had gone to.

When the car horns sounded, it was to signal to her that she needed to leave Oscar and get out of the Wake House since Michael was now nearing the scene. If he stumbled upon this, it would have made her out to be not just a suspect as he thought, but the culprit responsible for his disappearance.

Running from this scene and heading out to the Irish Authors' Corner to gather her books, The Shadow Man was lying in wait for her. From here, she too would have then been brought to the attic of The Book Loft, along with poor Arthur. Two down, two to go.

As for Michael, he took a little more time getting into the Wake House since he wanted to first search the location to see if perhaps there were any clues there, and stayed back at the hotel a little longer than expected to make sure he groomed himself fully. He noticed the mannequin and felt this played an important role in his search, possibly providing extra clues into Arthur's disappearance. What he did not want anyone to know or see was him causing a disturbance so early in the morning, so he hatched his own deviant plan to get the mannequin later in the day. This covered his tracks in case anyone saw him going there that morning and questioned his intentions, both good and bad.

Michael followed the same process as Therese. However, as he had shaved before he went out, which caused him to be late, and rather than dabbing a little under his nose to clear his senses, he poured a handful and rubbed it over his face thinking this could be a new cologne. Not the wisest of choices, as he got more than he bargained for. He then tipped the rest of the contents into his mouth, knocked on the lid of the coffin and repeated the words, "Is this where the dead man lives?" But Michael did not take the trip alone, as he had hoped. His lovely wife, Ann, was brought into his journey. Michael had to explain who he was talking to in the back seat of the car. Had he followed the same process as Therese, this would not have been a requirement. It explained why they left the festival early that morning. Michael became so influenced by shenaniganism's and Old-Fashioneds, Ann was doing her own intervention and got him out of there!

Stepping back from that, I could hear Danica, Nick, Kevin, Skip and Robin Graves all speaking to each other. Looking into the Wake House, Tony realized I was starting to make my way back because of my more pronounced body movements. If I lifted my hand or walked around while trying to sort all of this out, my body was doing the same movement I was making in the coffin. I was slipping out of my current, time-shifted dimension of Tuesday and heading back to Sunday.

"Greg," he said, "it is time for you to go back. You cannot stay here any longer. You must go back. Otherwise, you are going to remain stuck between two dimensions. It is not pleasant."

Protesting this request, I said, "Tony, I have to bring Arthur back with me. No one, other than J.P. - well, yeah, then again, ummm, never mind - no one is going to believe me. I am going to be certified and committed after this one if I tell people where I was, who I met, and what all went down on my journey out. You must help me get Arthur back with me, Tony. He has a gig at the Celtic Rock stage. No one other than me knows he moonlights as a sopranist.

If he doesn't show up for the grand finale, people are going to think that two people mysteriously vanished from the festival. Can you imagine the panic this will cause? It will be complete pandemonium.

On top of that, if I try explaining how the Wake House is also a place for dimensional journeys with assistance from Robin Graves, or whatever his real name is, how is that going to look? Plus, with everything I know about Rod and his wanting to have us all become scriptwriters for his new series *Ebullience in Delirium* at The Book Loft Pub and Hotel in Columbus, the Dublin Irish Festival is going to lose all of us as part of their cultural display. Just think what that entails. No more Irish Authors' Corner. No more Spoken Word tent. We simply cannot let this tragedy happen, Tony. You have got to help me, so you do. I am begging for your assistance."

Turning to Agents Mulder and Scully, I repeated these same pleas to them. Gillian pulled David off to the side with Tony, and then came back to me to say there was only one way they could help fix this, but it would involve wiping the mind of Arthur and bringing him back with them to the Celtic Rock stage. Nonetheless, they would have to first travel back in time to Malin Head to pick up some supplies prior to J.P. sending them over to the festival, but they did not know how long that would take. With precious seconds slipping away, time was not on our side. The risk associated to this was of galactic proportions.

I put my hands in my pant pockets while taking a wee dander, trying to think what we could do, when I felt a lump. Once again, I had forgotten I had a second shot glass of Danny Houton's Sextuple-Distilled Poitín. I only knew this since there was no Skull and Crossbones on it. It was the one Lisa had given me. Pulling my hand out of my pocket, I said, "Tony, take a look at me in the Wake House", and as I began lifting my hand and arm up and down, my body did the same.

"Slow it down, Greg. I can't see." he said. "You're going too fast right now, so you are."

Bringing my tempo down, Tony could see that the shot glass bottle within the coffin did indeed have the skull, crossbones, and four-leaf clover bowtie on it. This meant the one with me right now would leave Arthur completely blootered if we were to use it on him, and would do exactly what Gillian had hoped for – it would wipe his mind of the event which had occurred.

"I hope this works," said Tony.

"It will," reassured Agent Scully. "I have watched many of my fellow cast members in Belfast not remember a thing while having drinks after the filming of each episode of *The Fall*. As the stuff you guys drink over there does that, this poor man doesn't stand a chance of remembering any of this. The last thing he may recall is seeing a shadow running through the hotel lobby, and he'll blame it on the Old-Fashioned. Everything beyond that point will be erased from his memory.

If anyone asks if he vanished from the festival grounds, he will only know he was at his hotel and was making his way to the Irish Authors' Corner. Tell him he ran into the Godfather of Leprechaun Kings and they went for a long trip to meet up with the faeries. He will probably find inspiration enough in that and will start writing a new book based on those adventures."

Handing the shot glass over to Doctor Macaulay, I thanked him for the journey and experience into this otherworldly dimension, and for bringing Agents Fox Mulder and Dana Scully with him. Preparing myself to leave this dimension and re-emerge within the Wake House, I stood, shook hands and shared one closing thought before I bade them farewell.

"I need you to know that this reminds me of having to leave Belfast back in 1985 all over again. As much as I want to say I will be back, I don't know when that will be. The last time took seven years. Although I thought time had stood still and that everyone would be exactly the same as I had left them as that is where my memories kept me all those years, I came back to a place which I loved and hated. People did not stay the way they were – they grew up. In my mind, we were still the same kids who ran around together. When I got back, lives had changed, friends moved on, nothing was the same. I cannot take that heartbreak all over again, so I can't. Once was enough. I am still chasing those same childhood ghosts thirty-five years later. It's not fair."

Placing a kiss on my cheek and taking a step back, Agent Scully looked me in the eyes and said, "Greg, the road to hell is paved with good intentions. Remember what Enya wrote:

May it be, an evening star
Shines down upon you.
May it be, when darkness falls,
Your heart will be true.
You walk a lonely road.
Oh, how far you are from home."

"Greg," said Agent Mulder, "remember what you reminded us of. This is not the end; it is only the beginning. We will see you much sooner than you think. We are going to need your help with this one if the Dublin Irish Festival grand finale is to be saved and you are to tell your story in the Spoken Word tent. You better get a move on. There are people waiting for and counting on you. Now make your way back. Godspeed, mo chara."

Chapter 47: The Investigator's Epiphany

During my two-hour-and-fourteen-minute bus ride back to the Dublin Irish Festival, there was a little traffic tie-up as we went through **THE** Ohio State University campus because, apparently, the football team was returning to campus for early season practice. There is such a frenzy over college football.

"Go Notre Dame!" I thought, but dared not speak it aloud.

Other than that diversion, I was putting together my thoughts on poor Arthur. Arthur is not dead - I know that now - but he is missing. Why? The other "why" is, why did I have that apparition with Colonel O'Rorke? The two must be connected, and if they are, this abduction and mystery is about a message or messages dealing with Irish-related authors. Colonel O'Rorke called it a "new army" but I think it is more connected to a team of Irish ancestral spirits. After all, Ann believed my hand was guided by the McCarthy ancestors when writing my first book, *From Cork to the New World*. A new team has appeared and reached out not only to me but probably other authors as well, so that we may send a message to the world.

There it is: Arthur is missing because he is the only one in the group who does not have a direct heritage connection to Ireland. Everyone else was either born there or came from Irish ancestors, including Therese, who has connections to Donegal. So, he was used and removed from the group to get our attention, so we would think and challenge our purpose as writers. Arthur is not an outsider; he is a catalyst to get the message through. Ah, the spirits are at work again.

I didn't want to mention my Colonel O'Rorke apparition to the group before this happened as they would think this over-the-hill investigator was now out-of-his-mind. But not so! On the contrary, age and experience have given me clarity. My mind is as solid as the stack of books that buried poor author Arthur. Well, before the stack came tumbling down on me, that is. Anyway, Therese had said something to me this morning that I stashed away and did not reveal, thinking she may be as crazy I was. She mentioned an apparition and was visited by Oscar Wilde; and as wild as that may seem, it now makes sense.

Therese quoted Oscar as saying, "Education is an admirable thing, but it is well to remember from time to time that nothing that is worth knowing can be taught." Wow, what a kick in the pants. Wilde is telling us not to teach but to shape or predict future ideas, values, or events. W.B. Yates did it in *Cathleen ni Houlihan,* which was followed up by Tommy Makem in *Four Green Fields.* They were shaping the reunification of Ireland. Many other notables such as Becket and Joyce were shapers of thought.

But who are those voices of today? It's us! It is their call to arms for us. The ancestral spirits are saying we are the new shapers, each of us with our own slice of expertise. I write about immigration, Greg writes about The Troubles in Northern Ireland, Jeanne Crane looks at the spiritual side. The murder mysteries are a slice of humanity we must deal with. Irish dancers are future cultural artists, etc. Jim McVeigh had it right, I am sorry to admit: we need to be thinkers, and promote thinkers, not just tell the story.

I felt energized to return to the group and explain that Arthur is safe and would be returning to us shortly, not that his work is done, that no one is a murderer or abductor, and that all is well. Before the sun sets on this Sunday afternoon, I will say, Arthur will reappear, and I am sure even he has his marching orders to give a foreigner's perspective, or maybe his writing with the Vatican. That direction is for each of us to choose, as it was for Yates, Joyce, Wilde, and the rest of them. No need to put ourselves on the same plane as our ancestral spirits; that's too lofty of a goal. We each have our audiences with whom we speak.

The bus dropped me off in front of the Embassy Suites, where I waited for one of the festival shuttle vans reserved for the entertainers to take me to the green room at the festival, which added another thirty-five minutes in returning to the Author's Tent. The driver, who I had interviewed earlier, had obviously been thinking about the goings-on with the authors and said, "As the saying goes, 'Idle minds are the devil's workshop', and that certainly describes these authors who attend the Dublin Irish Festival."

"Oh, no devil," I said. "Artists they are, inspired by their heritage."

"I do have great admiration for their talent. I read one woman's story. I forget her name but she wrote about a car accident and the aftermath the son and family faced."

"Yes," I said, "that was Sinead Tyrone, and she wrote *Walking through the Mist*."

"That's it, *Walking through the Mist*. I read it shortly after my uncle was killed by a drunk driver. I found it very helpful, and comforting."

I smiled as we passed over Interstate 270 and pulled into the festival grounds.

As I was driving my golf cart back to the Author's Tent, I heard the High Kings singing from the main Dublin stage. Yes, the High Kings. I thought about what a coincidence it would be if they too were inspired by their ancestral spirits when singing their uplifting version of *The Rocky Road to Dublin*. Indeed, it is a rocky road to Dublin, but quite illuminating.

Now I realized that the songs on the radio were intentionally placed by the ancestral spirits, and Enya was speaking to me all along:

Who can say where the road goes,
Where the day flows, only time.

And in the cloudy, mystic air of Sunday morning, Morrison says:

When that fog horn blows,
You know I will be coming home,
And when that fog horn whistle blows, I gotta hear it,
I don't have to fear it.

I was now certain that all of these shenanigans were orchestrated by the spirits.

Chapter 49: Menagerie of Madness

For a fleeting second, my eyes started to focus as familiar faces began appearing before them. Although I was now hearing several sets of voices, I did not want to return. I had found a place of peace, of acceptance, a dimension I could stay trapped in for as long as I wanted to. I could play roles in *The Twilight Zone* and await the arrival of two of my other fellow authors – Therese Gilardi and Michael E. McCarthy.

Since Arthur was already there, finding his way around his first script and acting it out onscreen, I could quite easily do the same. Although I knew I had to go back, I struggled with the idea of it. I wanted to stay, all the while knowing the danger of being stuck between two dimensions. I was going to turn this into an Irish goodbye, and present a reason why I should not go back. I said the first thing I thought of.

"I'm not going back," I shouted. "I've decided to stay put. I don't want to leave, after all! The pokes they are making here are partial, so they are. I am a perfectionist. Unless it gets corrected, I am going to stay right here until it is made proper, regardless of any consequence!"

With that, Tony, David, and Gillian all checked their watches collectively in succession. If I did not make the leap back into the dimension I left behind before my time was up, they would collide into each other and unleash the equivalency of Pandora's Box. Seeing this unfold exactly as he had scripted, The Shadow Man spoke out from the darkness and revealed what his plans were. He was patiently waiting to pounce on this opportunity, and only when the time was right. I had granted him that chance. The scenes began playing out in front of us all.

I was to become three characters – the suspect, the villain, and the victim - every time, all the while trapped within my own nightmare. My diary would eventually drag in all those who were deemed by me to be suspects; my characterization of them determined how they were going to be portrayed on screen. Their fates had been sealed. Using my carefully detailed notes, Mark Rickerby was to become the lead screenplay writer, copy editor and producer of each script. At his own discretion, he chose if a person lived or simply disappeared at the stoke of his pen.

Therese Gilardi was chosen to be the femme fatale in every episode, whether she was being charmed by Oscar Wilde or chased by Wild Oscar. As to be expected, Michael "Magnum" McCarthy became the investigator in all the shows, first capturing villains, only to then turn into the judge, jury and executioner. With him appointing his wife, Ann as everyone's attorney - no one stood a chance!

Legendary musician and vocalist from the New Lodge Road in Belfast, Jim McVeigh, was awarded a record deal and went on tour - of the New Lodge Road. Each day, he went from one end down to the other, playing and singing his heart out. His tour merchandise included copies of his books and, of course, the dreaded whoopee cushions which came with them. It could be said that during his concerts, the sounds echoing around the neighbourhood became their own symphony of destruction.

As for the fair maiden Guke Slinger, she scrambled from vendor to vendor to find items, only to have them sell out as she arrived. Returning to the Author's Tent, Dublin Cream Bun in hand, and waiting for streams of light and heavenly voices to shine down upon her instead of the puff pastry, she discovered that the Belfast Child had left to go to various locations throughout the festival at the same time that he was supposed to do his Spoken Word. As his manager, it was the job of Dah-Nee-Tza to deploy her Professional Cat-Herding skills to locate and bring him back, only to turn around and find he had gone AWOL yet again on another networking adventure.

Watching and waiting carefully to see what was going to happen with J.P. Sexton, I looked to see that the three people I had seen repeatedly checking their watches had suddenly surrounded The Shadow Man. They brought him forward into the light between the dimensions of my imagination, and that of the UK Folklorama Pavilion, where everyone on the production team could see him. He shouted at them by name:

"TONY. DAVID. GILLIAN. YOU CANNOT DO THIS TO ME. I AM THE CREATOR OF THE MENAGERIE OF MADNESS. THIS IS MY SHOW!"

Seeing the commotion unfolding, Shayleen McConnell walked over to the grouping and asked what they were playing at, only to then say, "Doctor Tony Macaulay? Is that you? Fancy seeing you here! I am heading home to Ballymena at the end of the week once my work is completed here to take in the stage production of your first book, *Paperboy*. It is lovely to make your acquaintance."

"Agents Fox Mulder and Dana Scully?" she continued. "Wow! I had a wonderful feeling you might be gracing us with your presence. Each time we bring Greg out to the pavilion here as our featured author, he speaks about you in the highest regard. He did tell me our imaginations are the key to our future, and are so much more powerful than any of us could ever realize. He asked me to watch *The Fall*, saying your acting was nothing shy of brilliant, Gillian. I hear Jamie Dornan is the male lead! You are one lucky lady; Jaime said the same about acting opposite you – how fantastic!"

"David, I see you have Rod Serling here with you! Are we on the set of *The Twilight Zone*? If that is indeed the case, this could only be related to *The X-Files*, so it could. All week, we have been missing a key ingredient to one of our feature products, which has made our dairy whipped delicacy a bit . . . lackluster, shall we say?"

Wee Milly, the robotic dog came out of The Tardis and went straight over to Shayleen. Although she saw it had a bottle of red raspberry sauce attached to its collar and asked if she could have it, she was unsuccessful at getting anywhere with her request.

Looking over and welcoming me, as she always did with a smile that could light up the world, a huge hug and a wee hello, Shayleen said, "Greg, it is so great to have you back again. How has the writing been? I loved the books you provided me last year – wonderful stories coupled with the North of Ireland humour. Thank you for coming out to be a part of the UK Folklorama Pavilion once again!" At that, she pointed over to where I should set up my display table.

"Shayleen," I said, "although I am here, I am not really here. Well, I am, but not at the moment. Never mind. I will explain things to you on Tuesday once I get back here, for it is really only Sunday where I am right now. I am in two dimensions, so I am. I will have to introduce you to a wee shot glass size of Danny Houton's Double-Sextuple-Distilled Poitín. It is a trip and a half, and then some!"

Looking at me sideways for a second as if I had two heads, she knew I always spoke with an honest heart.

"I look forward to giving that a wee go, so I do," she said, before turning her attention back to Wee Milly.

"Shayleen," I shouted as I was being drowned out by the stage production. "As mad as it sounds, and just like everything else you know about me, incorporate ABBA lyrics into your question. I already did one using a song from the Bay City Rollers called *Shang-a-Lang*."

"Alright, let's give this a wee try," she said. "How about I sing *Thank You for the Music*?"

"Mother says I was a dancer before I could walk.
She says I began to sing long before I could talk.
But I've often wondered, how did it all start?
Who found out that nothing can capture a heart
Like a melody can?
Well, whoever it was, I'm a fan."

With that, Shayleen asked if she could have the bottle of red raspberry sauce.

"Affirmative . . ." said Wee Milly.

I called over to visit Sandy, who was both shocked and happy to see me because I had come out of nowhere. I asked if she could pull a dairy-whipped ice cream and be sure to put two flakes into it, making it a Double-99.

"Anything for you, Greg," said Sandy as she turned around and prepared it. "Sorry, but I understand it just isn't the same without the final touch. It's a bit of a dull creation, but it is all we have at the moment."

"Don't worry, Sandy," I said. "It's not for me, but it will help sort things out. I promise it will be perfect, so it will. Just be on the ready for a bunch more orders!"

At that, I brought it over to Shayleen and asked her for a favour: "Could you run a wee distraction for me? Once you have added the raspberry sauce, give this to The Shadow Man. Tell him it is a feast for the gods, and to enjoy the rest of your show. It will keep him occupied. But don't give him any serviettes. He will have to go and find one since the sauce will be running down the front of his face. It always happens, no matter how careful one is.

Agents Mulder and Scully will be able to free Arthur since he is not in the clutches of The Shadow Man. Ask Doctor Macaulay to bring him to the Celtic Rock stage for the grand finale, but to make sure Arthur takes his 'medicine' first to help wipe his memory out. I'll see you again on Tuesday and will tell you all about the Menagerie of Madness, so I will."

Shayleen nodded her head in agreement, gave me a hug farewell, and set about to take care of the deed. "Safe travels, Greg. Ever since I've known you, you've always been a bit of a world traveler. I suppose this takes it to new dimensions. Be safe. I will see you in a few days!"

With barely any time remaining, I turned to David and Gillian and gave them the peace sign, only to switch it for Tony to a Vulcan Salute. He returned the gesture. Seeing this was also happening in the Wake House, I made my way back, only to have the darkened sense I descended into return to light, along with five familiar voices talking over the top of me.

Chapter 51: The Secret of the Sopranist

"You have finally decided to come back from wherever you were? It must have been quite the interesting journey, wherever that may have been," said the undertaker. "Nice of you to join us. I have not seen anyone so animated in action while going on their journey. Your arms and legs were moving about, and your eyes were all over the place. At times, we weren't sure if we were trying to have a wake or a séance. I would love to hear who you saw and what you did. It will be a story for the Spoken Word tent!"

Sitting upright, I knew we didn't have time for conversations that could last hours and well into the evening. There was a bigger mission at hand. Seeing the time on the pocket watch Robin had taken from his waist coat, I knew we were nearing the start of the grand finale over at the Celtic Rock stage.

My response hurried, I said, "We need to move immediately. There is no time to waste. I will try my best to explain everything later at the wind-up party – well, maybe not, because none of you would believe me anyway. Nick, can you and Skip help me onto the Paddy Only Wagon? I need to get to the stage to get ready. There is a concert waiting to be had and much to be done if this is going to occur. More than one person is counting on us to make this happen – but we only get the one chance to make things right. Dah-Nee-Tza, can you join us and then go back with the lads to get the signs from last night when we did the live recording of the song with everyone at the hotel? I think we're going to need a lot more copies, so I do! You probably will want to borrow a set of safety goggles, for you are going to be in for the ride of your life!"

Danica tried asking me what was going on but there was no time to respond as we were at the backstage area within seconds of our departure, which would have normally taken well over twenty minutes to walk due to the size of the crowds. Hopping off so they could continue on and get back in time for the curtain call, I made my way over to speak with the stage manager and the sound and lightning crew. Afterwards, I approached Jim and Pierce McVeigh to brief them for the performance. It was Jim who spoke first, asking where I had wandered off to, and if I was now the Irish ambassador to some other global region.

"Fella's, there is no time for idle chatter. Do you remember your roles from last night at the Embassy Suites? I need the same today, only better. Jim, as you are playing acoustic, we will have you play in front of a microphone. Do you also recall the intro you played and what you lilted? I need that again. Put all of the air from your lungs and elsewhere into it. Pierce, can you tell the sound tech to mic up your washtub bass? Thanks. Follow my cues, lads. This will be the show of your lifetime!"

Turning around, I saw that the Three Irish Tenors were also waiting for direction. They had watched me speak to Jim and Pierce and wondered why the stage call and set list was abruptly changing all of a sudden. I took them off to the side to explain.

"Gentlemen," I said. "The Sopranist you are waiting for to lead today's set is a bit indisposed at the moment, so he is. If am I not mistaken, his name is Arthur Colaianni, correct?"

I had a feeling I would find out this information when I first journaled about it in my diary and had planned to stop by the Celtic Rock stage, before getting distracted several times. This suspicion was further aroused after I met Rod in the dimensional shift, and from his direct observations of who was onscreen playing the role of Henry Bemis. The Irish Tenors nodded their heads in agreement. John McDermott said, "Aye, that is the man indeed. We are delighted to have the honour of singing with him." My suspicions had been confirmed with this response.

"Right," I said, "he is going to be making a magnificent entrance on stage – one which the Dublin Irish Festival has never seen the likes of. I promise it is going to be out of this world – figurately speaking, of course. Although we are entering into unchartered territory, you may wish to wear sunglasses as the stage lighting is going to be blinding once the moment arrives. There will be a lot of stage fog as well for added special effect, and a few other details I would rather leave out at the moment. It will be a spectacle and one of tremendous surprise! As for the song choice, are you familiar with *The Wreck of the Edmund Fitzgerald* by Gordon Lightfoot, or a wee ditty called *Back Home in Derry* by Christy Moore?' You are? Perfect. The fair maiden Guke Slinger will be back any second now with lyric sheets. Or, if you prefer, you can watch a wee video we recorded and put up on YouTube last night. Your lyrics are to be that and the chorus. I will guide you through it once we get the sheets back."

Looking to Anthony Kearns, Finbar Wright then stepped forward and asked if we were going to rehearse first as this would be the proper approach to the show.

"Actually, lads," I responded, "I am so sorry but there really is no time to do so. I can get the lyrics put up onto the stage teleprompter monitor. It will go flawlessly. I promise. Promise me you'll give this all you've got."

I was startled by an unexpected call advising me there were fifteen minutes left until show time. Running around all of the staff, stage, and production crew backstage, I told them a phenomenal entrance would be occurring, and whatever they do, the show must go on. Keep filming, the lights on, the sound full. I assured them that this would be the biggest grand finale the Dublin Irish Festival ever had in its thirty-two years of celebrating anything and everything Irish.

In that moment, Nick, Skip, and Danica, the latter sporting a new hairdo from the speed she was traveling at on the back of the Paddy Only Wagon, came back from the Embassy Suites and started handing the lyric sheets to John, Finbar, and Anthony.

Smiling, I said, *"It's showtime!"*

The musicians who had gone on ahead of us were about to leave the stage when I stopped them and asked if they could also join us. I asked musicians with banjo players, bodhráns, fiddles, uilleann pipes, Irish harps, tin whistles, and guitars to please take their positions, but to leave space at the front of the stage for the display of their lives. In saying that, I had no idea what else had been planned out. I just figured the more musicians and vocalists to add the backing vocals, the better. Looking out from the stage, I saw Danica, Shelly McVeigh and Barbara Cody-Burkholder among the crowd handing out sheets with printed messages on them regarding what we wanted and needed them to do.

The lights came down. Alison LeRoy approached the central microphone and thanked everyone for their efforts to remain calm throughout the festival. She assured the crowd that although they had not yet found the missing person from the Irish Authors' Corner, every effort was being made to do so, and they had received some positive leads. There was still no mention of what the discovery at the pond was, leading me to believe what I had suspected all along – that it was a trap to ensnare the authors, cause further panic, and add more confusion to the investigation.

Along with Jim and Pierce, The Irish Tenors stepped onto the stage. I looked up, around, and behind me to see if the grand entrance I had planned and put into motion was about to occur, but nothing happened. Disappointed that the suspicion toward me was now going to continue, I reminded myself of what Agents Mulder and Scully had informed me. Using this to keep my hopes and dreams alive, I soldiered on.

I introduced myself as one of the authors before explaining the circumstances behind our song choice for this year's grand finale - that another author going missing from the festival had provided the background story to it. Sighs thousands strong deeply echoed throughout the crowd. Perhaps it was not going to be so grand after all. I explained that the sheets of paper with messaging on them which had been handed out to everyone were for them to hold up during the chorus. They read **"FREE J.P."** I informed the audience that this song was in honour of our missing comrade, who was held up at the Irish border because of an expired passport, was being recorded live.

Taking my place and giving Jim a nod, he stepped up to the microphone beside me and began strumming the opening bars. Ray Fean took his place behind the drums.

"Ladies and Gentlemen," I began, "this wee song is called *The Ballad of J.P. Sexton* and was written just this weekend. It was originally performed yesterday by Jim and I before bringing in the rest of our fellow authors, including the one who has since gone missing, to help free J.P. and bring him home here to the Dublin Irish Festival."

Jim began lilting, which was followed by the chorus of Celtic harmonies in accompaniment.

As we went through the song, if it were not for the brilliance of The Irish Tenors, along with the stunning synchronizations from the musicians and other backup vocalists, it would have otherwise been a complete and total disaster. Since I was feeling quite down in my hopes for a grandeur display, I simply mouthed the words as we went along and joined in at the first chorus. To encourage the audience to participate in singing *Oh, I wish I was in Dublin, Ohio*, I began waving my hands around in the air as if I were conducting my own orchestra.

As soon as those words were sung, and before I knew what was going on myself since I was so wrapped up in the moment, the stage began to be consumed with dry ice mist being pumped in. The person operating the controls was somewhat overzealous as we all disappeared beneath the fog. Although the song continued, the lyrics were paused to give the instrumentalists a chance to showcase their outstanding talents, even though they too could only be heard but not seen. Stage lights began casting strobes, beams, and lasers, which flew in all directions. A blue police telephone box appeared, its red cherry light flashing on top, accompanied by a whooshing sound. Deafening silence fell over the crowd. The tenors who were about to sing once again paused their vocals and watched with curiosity, as did the musicians who continued to play at a low tempo. The music now suspenseful, the moment of surprise finally arrived.

Stepping out of The Tardis and onto the stage was none other than Arthur Colaianni, although I personally needed to take a second and much harder look at him. At first, I did not even know it was him. There was no resemblance to the author I knew. He was also not dressed the way he normally did for the festival, missing the khaki shorts, Hawaiian shirt, and ballcap, along with his other attire. Nor did he wear the clothing that I saw him in during the journey from the Wake House to the UK Folklorama Pavilion in his screenplay. Instead, he stood with a Phantom of the Opera mask on his face to conceal his identity, dress pants with Celtic Cross knotwork logos on either side, with more Celtic knotwork in front. His jacket lay open, with gold symbols painted on his chest resembling Led Zeppelin IV.

Looking over to the entrance of The Tardis, I could see that Tony, David, and Gillian all stood to watch what was about to unfold. Immediately, Arthur walked to the front of the stage, posed with one leg in front of the other, began clapping his hands above his head, stomped his heeled foot, and worked up the amassed crowd into a wild frenzy of cheers and chants. I looked to the corner of the stage and signaled to Alison to send out the Irish dancers, who were still in costume, as they too had completed their performance prior to the grand finale. This was about to be the show of a lifetime and one of permanent memory.

With his hands on his hips, Arthur began tapping out a series of steps in rapid succession, which were then to be followed by scores of Irish dancers. Since a secondary stage was lowered in front of us that had the perfect floor for a hard tap shoe, the roar of thundering taps echoed throughout the festival grounds and across the City of Dublin. Ireland was very much alive and represented, with only four of us truly knowing who was leading the group into their dance steps. Look out, Michael Flatley. This man can move like the winds crossing the Wild Atlantic Way!

I stepped back for a moment and over to The Tardis before saying to Tony I was not aware Arthur had cemented himself as a force in Irish Dancing. "Oh, but he hasn't, Greg," said Tony. "In fact, this is his very first attempt at it. I think he is doing a grand job, don't you?"

I looked at Tony in a state of shock and awe. He knew I would be asking how this was at all even possible because when I had seen them back at the UK Folklorama Pavilion, Arthur was still trapped in the screen. Before I could even get the rest of my sentence out, he responded.

"After we rescued him, your dear friend Shayleen asked if we could continue to stall for time by making an abundance of pokes - using the proper technique and method, of course - so she could have the opportunity of putting Arthur through some dance routines. She saw something special in him. And although we got him to drink the shot of Danny Houton's Double-Sextuple Poitín, the effect of it was twofold. The first half he drank wiped his memory out as we had hoped it would – he does not know that he disappeared from the Irish Authors' Corner. The last thing he recalled seeing was a shadow running through the hotel, but he blamed it on the Old-Fashioned he had the night before.

When Arthur drank the second half, he began mimicking the steps of the show up on stage. Shayleen figured that with a few quick, on-the-spot lessons, he could steal the show tonight when he got back to the festival. And, as this might be the one and only time he gets to do this, she wanted to keep his identity secret. So, she sized him up in some dance costumes from the rear of the stage. The rest, as they say, is history, so it is. Now, go over there and announce his introduction before anyone else gets a chance to figure this all out."

"I will do," I replied, "but I ask that you, David, and Gillian all come up with me. I need to put a few final things into motion to clear my name before the festival ends tonight. There are those who think I am stark raving mad, and although it is most likely true, an innocent lad does not need to be a suspect any longer."

Tony agreed and signaled to them to come up front and centre with me. Taking to the microphone, the music played on while Arthur continued to lead his dance troop through their steps and dazzle the crowd.

"Ladies and Gentlemen," I began, "tonight, it is my absolute pleasure and great honour to introduce to you the lead dancer, choreographer, writer and developer of this one-time grand finale called *The Secret of the Sopranist*, Mr. Arthur Colaianni. Who knew this world-famous singer could also dance so effortlessly and gracefully? The next production number is called *Dance for the Jedi*, which will be followed up by *An Ode for a Viking*. With that said, I am dedicating this number to fellow author J.P. Sexton, who should be here tonight with us all to celebrate. Keep those hands going! Arthur, take it away!"

As an outpouring of cheers, screams, applause, and whistles filled the festival grounds, Therese, Sinead, Cindy and the others began repeating what they had just heard. It was Michael who watched this happening, and although he himself was not so sure, looked over to them and said, "How amazing! Will Arthur find out that there is an Italian man out there who shares his name, his love and passion for all things Irish, especially dance, music and singing? I hope he turns up soon so he can get a chance to meet that man on stage. He would be in his glory."

While looking out over the capacity crowd, I saw Michael down in front and continued with my thoughts.

"Tonight, I have been afforded the opportunity, honour and undeserved privilege of introducing to you all three of the incredible individuals who helped me on a journey to search for a friend across dimensions, parallel universes, and places most of us would only find within our imaginations. Ladies and gentlemen, please put your hands together and give a resounding Dublin Ohio Irish Festival Céad Míle Fáilte for my dear friends who inspire me – Doctor Tony Macaulay, Agent Fox Mulder and Agent Dana Scully. They have certainly instilled this tremendous value within me - to find the truth, you must believe."

As applause and cheers reached deafening levels with chants of "X Files", I took this as an opportunity to ask Tony to take Arthur back somewhere safe to drop him off, preferably at the Embassy Suites. This was to ensure that he could sleep off the effects and wake up feeling refreshed the following day, but with the knowledge that he had a brilliant time at the festival, especially after tonight's outstanding performance.

"Can you send him a video of this wherein only he will know it's him aside from us four – something he can share with his wife since she couldn't make it? Let's also close out this show with a bang!"

Tony assured me he had everything taken care of. The set moved back into the initial song chosen, only with a slight adaptation to the chorus. I gave a nod to Jim. He went back into lilting the opening bars. I took to the microphone again and said, "Come on, Folks! Let's get this going! I want to hear you sing this at the top of your lungs!

I wish I was in Dublin, Ohio.
My heart is in Dublin, Ohio.

As the crowd went into a frenzy with this, Gillian waved to the crowd and made her way toward The Tardis, followed by David, Tony, and Arthur. Before disappearing inside, we all took a bow. I asked them to put their backs to the audience and for us to capture a selfie as a memento, but I didn't bother checking it until the following morning. Arthur had slipped his mask off for a split second just as we were in the process of doing this.

The authors who saw this said, "Hey, was that our fellow author, Arthur Cola?"

Michael said, "We see what we want to when we put our will to it. When you use your imagination, anything is possible. The science fiction in this production was mind-blowing. I *so* wish he was here!" The others agreed.

Tony asked his Wee Milly to set coordinates for the next destination. As the stage floor filled with dry ice fog once again, the red light began flashing atop of The Tardis, the swooshing sound began to drown out the musicians, yet the Irish dancers continued in full celebration. As if it were with the Paddy Only Wagon, we made our departure in speeds that were light years beyond that, although we did not have too far to go.

"Doctor Macaulay," I said, "can you drop me off just on the fringe of the grounds, near the pond? I will make my way back over to the Irish Authors' Corner. As for Arthur, it is probably best you bring him back to where Agent Scully wiped his memory out, which was at the hotel this morning when he saw the shadow.

I know this is going to be a bit strange for him as he was leaving at 6:00 a.m. to go to the tent to set up his books. However, when he gets there, it will be 6:00 p.m. instead. We will have to say he drank way more than his fair share of Old-Fashioned cocktails the night before and had been dreaming he was making his way to ready his display. I think that should suffice. And thank you all for your tremendous help in making this journey occur which I will not forget anytime soon. Until we perhaps meet again, my friends, wherever that may be, I say goodbye, good luck, and Godspeed to you all!"

Tony, David and Gillian warmly smiled. This time, however, and without the prompt of a Bay City Roller or an ABBA song, Wee Milly made her own announcement. "This is not the end; it is only the beginning . . ."

Looking at Doctor Macaulay, to Agent Fox Mulder and finally, to Agent Dana Scully as they piqued my curiosity, I was floored when their response was said in unison.

"Affirmative . . ."

Chapter 53: Wholesome

Once back at the Author's Tent, I wanted to talk with the authors as a group to explain my findings, and Greg came out to meet with me.

"Hey, *Mo chara,"* I said to Greg.

"My friend?" he mumbled back. "Are you sure I'm your friend?"

"Indeed, you are my friend, even if I am a NY SPOIL, or whatever you said in front of my back. Can I buy you a cream bun? As a peace offering, of course, seeing that somehow my inquiries hurt your sensitive Irish feelings. I know you like them."

"No, thank you!" said Greg, "I have plenty of ways of getting a cream bun."

"Let's go inside and talk with everyone," I said.

"So, you see, Greg, each of us - you, me, and Therese - have had apparitions, and probably a number of other authors, though they have not admitted to it. In fact, I was a little slow myself in saying so. Anyway, we have had extra-sensory meetings with Irish notables who have given us insights into our labors. They talked about our work. My apparition was a colonel in the American Civil War. He wanted me to write about unity and working things out with all people, not just those we associate with or who think the same as us. He used his heritage in Ireland as well as the cause of the Civil War. So, I need to apologize to all of you because I thought someone abducted or harmed Arthur.

"So, where's Arthur?" said Sinead.

"He's safe," I said. "I have seen him. I talked to him too, but only for a few moments, then he disappeared again."

"Where is he?" asked Danica.

"I don't know, and when Arthur returns - and he *will* return - he won't be able to tell us, either."

"Too far-fetched for me," said Terry O'Leary, who had been listening in the background.

"Too far-fetched for any of us, Terry," I said. "No one will accept this explanation, which is good. No need to make a splash across the tabloids that will discount our messages. When Arthur returns, we'll just give him a hearty welcome and all will be fine."

"Just like that, you say," said Greg. "I went through hell trying to clear your suspicions of me."

"Tell me one instance in history that great change hasn't endured hardships," I said.

"This is too much for me," said Terry. "I'm out."

"No one is forcing you to take on anything, but you have described in your stories great pain, hunger, abandoning one's homeland, and starting anew with great success. In fact, you're a product of that story. All the ancestral spirits are doing is emphasizing our role, our product. Terry, you're way ahead of getting the message out through your stories."

Greg said, "What about the cream bun?"

"Still worried about the cream bun, eh?" I said. "Once again, it was the ancestral spirits that put the cream bun there. You were targeted to get your juices flowing, and it succeeded."

"I see. I focused on the small picture instead of the bigger view."

"Indeed, and I got played, too," I said. "They knew I would fall into old habits in questioning what was going on and trying to figure out the narrow perspective of who, what, where, when, and how, but forgetting about the why. I immediately fell into the aggressive questioning of the inner circle, thinking the answer was in close proximity. You were right, Greg, sort of, when you said there was a supernatural phenomenon at play. In my world, we don't accept crazy talk, but I knew there was a kernel of truth somewhere in your rantings. I just didn't see it early on. But in the end, that helped shape the bigger picture. All of us were involved.

In the past, it was the media with their worldly view that inspired thought, but today they are too busy playing politics on both sides of an issue and have forgotten their true role of truth and accuracy. The ancestral spirits thought it was time to intervene. Some people would argue they do this frequently; others, like myself, scoff at the thought. However, today, it makes sense."

"Now, it has been left to others, like us."

Ann nailed it when she quoted Luke: "To whom much is given, much will be required."

"Ah, look! Here comes Arthur," I said. Arthur was strolling undaunted across the open field between the Spoken Word Tent and the Author's Tent.

We were whole once again.

Epilogue: The Last Jedi . . .

Monday morning came far too early for me since I had networked late into the night at the Wind-Up Party with Charlie Lord and Jim McVeigh, sharing our experiences about growing up in Belfast during The Troubles. It was interesting to hear what Charlie had said while going to school. He had watched a bomb being disarmed outside of the classroom window while in the process of writing his A-Level exams, but was unsure if he should interrupt the teacher to let him know what was going on. He decided to simply put his head down further onto the table, beneath the windowsill, and continue with his writing. So what if it went off and the glass from the building blew in? As horrific as it was, it had become our norm. I assured him this would become part of my own presentation, but that I would use his name and experience.

We finished eating breakfast with fellow authors and other acquaintances, gathered up our belongings, and said our goodbyes to one another before checking out of the hotel and making our way forth. It was another amazing weekend with many friends and those who have become family to us at the Dublin Irish Festival.

I pulled out my phone to hopefully finish up some unfinished business from the night before. During the

Wind-Up Party, Danica and I had met up with Laura Nelson and talked about the next year. Danica discussed recipes and specialty cuisine dishes she thought could be prepared. I suggested seeing acts on the Celtic Rock stage, including the Pat McManus Band. Although only a three-piece group, they pack as much of an incredible punch as we tried to with the grand finale, which turned out to be an unbelievable spectacle of showmanship, and a tremendous surprise.

"So where are you off to next then, Greg?" asked Laura. I looked up and replied that I was on my way up to Winnipeg to participate in the United Kingdom Folklorama Pavilion and would be visiting with my dear friend, Shayleen. I then said Shayleen should consider bringing one of The McConnell School of Irish Dance stage productions to the Dublin Irish Festival, and to send in a presentation package for consideration. They put on a spectacular show, developed using creative displays and Irish storytelling.

The conversation was light but fulfilling. There was nothing mentioned about the body that was supposedly pulled out of the pond. Laura was relieved that the mystery of Arthur's disappearance had come to an end. Many were still stumped by what had happened. Only a few truly knew what went down. Although the four of us who were involved were sworn to secrecy, there was at least one other person who deserved to know the truth about what had happened . . . Arthur. After all that had gone on, I felt I should at least give him the respect of sending copies of the photos to his email.

As they continued to talk, I went back to my phone to try and see what the pictures I took at the end of the show looked like, and was shocked to see what happened. When Tony Macaulay, David Duchovny, Gillian Anderson and I got together, we put Arthur in-between the five of us. Steadying my hand, snapping three separate photos, I saw that Arthur had his *Phantom of the Opera* mask in front of his chest. All of us had huge smiles. Directly behind us, we could see Michael in front of the stage since he is slightly taller than most.

The most curious thing of all is that in the first photo, Michael stood with his arms in the air. It was almost as if he were a referee, making the signal for a touchdown. In the second photo, he had crossed his arms, which were still in the air, making the shape of an X with them. In the third photo, while making the X shape, he also formed the Vulcan Salute with each of his hands.

"Hmmm," I thought to myself. "Perhaps he must have heard what I said on stage. *To find the truth, you must believe*. I wonder if that's what he was on about last night when he pulled me into his group discussion with the rest? Michael Magnum McCarthy – More Than Meets The Eye!"

Just as I was about to send them on to Arthur, Nick and Lisa Bova, Alison LeRoy, Skip Moerch, Adam Parker,

Kay McGovern, Wendy Bell, and Mike Herriot all came over to meet up and say farewell to us all. They had also heard about the events from the previous day and wanted to make sure we were all okay.

"It has been an incredible adventure," I said. "The Wake House has now become one of my favourite locations on the festival grounds; we will have to see what we can do next year about having the *Funeral for the Viking* and the *Belfast Riots on Tour* presentation done. Mike burst out laughing and said he had been filling the staff in on our plans regarding it.

"Maybe that J.P. Sexton fellow will replace the military mannequin, and he can play the role of Mr. Rigor Mortis in the coffin with Robin Graves," he said.

"Are you kidding me, Mike?" I replied. "Have you seen the size of that man? He will put Robin Graves *into* the coffin and then lift the two of them over his head and say, 'This is how a Viking wakes someone up in the morning!' He'll use them as his bench press!" Again, Mike fell into a fit of laughter at my response.

As more people gathered to say hello and goodbye, including musicians who were still buzzing around, reflecting on the stage show from the night before including the incredible entrance and exit of The Tardis, Doctor Macaulay, Agents Fox Mulder and Dana Scully.

I excused myself to go and get the *Sash My Father Never Wore* at the Irish Authors' Corner. I had forgotten it on

Sunday night before leaving to go to the Wind-Up Party back at the hotel. I also wanted to have another look at something I never had the chance to explore as a result of everything else that was going on. I asked Mike if he could bring me over to the site to get it. Adam took me instead.

About a half hour later, Danica came down from her room. The first two people she saw were Ann and Michael, and asked if either of them had seen me.

"I last saw him last night," said Ann. "Michael asked him to join our circle of conversation because he wanted to talk about clearing the air and what went on with Arthur going missing. You did the wise thing and went to bed before that. Afterward, we saw him chatting with Jim McVeigh and another fellow from Belfast."

"That's why I'm here, Ann," said Danica. "Greg had said he wanted to take a walk this morning after breakfast and was going back over to where the Irish Authors' Corner is located. He wanted to have another look at the hole in front of Julie's cash register. Something about it being a trap door to another location or dimension. Adam Parker brought him over there."

What Danica didn't realize is that Adam was among the group and stepped forward to say he had circled back to the hotel and was to go back for me within half an hour. Upon pulling up to the location, he could not find me. Adam figured I had maybe gone for a walk around the grounds and would make my way back to the hotel for the ride over to the airport. I hadn't.

Looking at Danica, Ann asked her, "Exactly what is it Greg is looking for?"

"Ann, you won't believe this, but after he got back to his room late last night, he texted me to say an instruction sheet had been left for him next to the apparent gift of a shot glass. He swears it was not there when he left the hotel earlier yesterday morning. I was sound asleep and did not see his text until just now. He sent me a picture of what was written on it. That's when I came down here to ask if you have seen him – I wanted to see it for myself."

"Really? Are you sure about that, Danica?" she replied. "Did you read what was on it?"

"It said on Page 47 of the Presidential Diary, in order to pursue and find the truth, one would have to wait for a new book to be released in the year 2020. It then said there will be a chapter within that book – 13 – with a heading titled *One Unlucky Viking*, and that information within that chapter would give specific directions regarding where to find two authors who will be considered missing. However, to the naked eye, people are unable to read the chapter because it will be written using the ink of a Secret Spy Last Jedi. Somehow, I think Greg is behind it."

"Danica," said Michael. "Did he perhaps drink one or two of the Guke concoctions you made? I understand you wanted to use up the last of the ingredients and mixed them a little bit stronger than you normally would. I'm not trying to be insensitive, but I must ask since I don't drink much either and found them to be a bit raw, so to speak. Personally, if you ask me, it sounds like something out of *The Twilight Zone.*"

* * * * *

While standing at the empty tent, I received two text messages. The first said, "Greg, mo chara. This is your friend, Rod. Did you really think you and your fellow authors were going to escape your roles in my Menagerie of Madness? Once you enter The Twilight Zone, you remain here. What was that line? *You can check out anytime, but you can never leave*!"

Immediately thereafter, I received a text message with two pictures. I opened it up and looked to see what it was. There was a hole with a five-foot opening leading into an unknown abyss.

"That looks nothing like the hole here in front of Julie's cash register," I thought. "I actually have no clue as to where this is. Is someone playing a sinister joke?"

* * * * *

Fifteen minutes later, Greg's phone was found lying beside the hole on the ground. There was no sign of Greg.

It was Danica who picked it up and showed Michael the two pictures on it.

"I know exactly where that is, Danica," said Michael. "I had gone for a walk prior to Ann and I leaving to come to the Dublin Irish Festival. I was in the low level of Ellison Park back home in Rochester, New York, when I came across it. Since I have such a hard time leaving behind my days as an investigator, I stood over the hole and began looking into it."

Michael's description sounded quite funny. Danica was unsure what else anyone would do with a hole and wanted to collapse with laughter but knew this was much more serious. She did not know that Rod was back again and was probably hoping to use this to recreate another one of his scripts. *Someone* did know, however, and although he was reluctant to speak about it, decided it would be the best thing to do.

"Danica, Greg told me last night he was an avid fan of The Twilight Zone, and that he watched it, for lack of a better term, religiously. Since he was having a few drinks, although he usually only has a Shandy, I thought he was back to his ways of trying to wind me up again. He talked nonstop. As he spoke, I looked for kernels of truth, even if it sounded outrageous.

I have a sinking feeling this may be based on something he told me regarding Season 3, Episode 14 of The Twilight Zone, titled *Five Characters in Search of an Exit.*

Greg said he and three of his fellow authors were to become trapped when he went in search of Arthur. The fifth did not make it to the Dublin Irish Festival; that person is Mark Rickerby, who is mysteriously absent.

Greg said that he, Arthur, Therese, Mark and I were to be given specific roles. Mark was going to become the lead scriptwriter. He is also taking on the copyediting role of a book which Greg co-wrote and took the main author role: *The Diary, The Detective and the Dublin Irish Festival.*"

Danica asked Michael how they were going to address this and what it might take to get Greg back, as well as prevent another author from going missing, even though they did not know who just yet. Michael was hesitant to tell Danica what he knew about finding Arthur Colaianni at The Book Loft, only to then lose him again on 3rd Street in Columbus to The Shadow Man.

"Magnum," said Danica. "When Greg first called you and believed Arthur's disappearance had something to do with The X-Files, you immediately discounted him and said there was no way this was related to supernatural phenomena. Thus, you became his biggest suspect; he thought you were trying to shield attention away from yourself and may have used him as a pawn instead. Look at this other picture on his phone. Arthur is between him, Tony, David, and Gillian. You knew about this, didn't you? The one person who was against Greg the most is the one person who is now making hand signals from the audience. Why didn't you say something? He would have cleared your name in a heartbeat. He was writing a - a dialann - as he called it."

Michael continued, "There was something Greg said last night to me . . . *"To find the truth, you must believe."* I didn't believe until I had my own experience meeting with Colonel Patrick O'Rorke. There is much to explain, but right now is not the right time."

At that, Nick and Skip came racing over to the same location on the Paddy Only Wagon, only to be debriefed on what was going on. It was Nick who spoke up.

"I know he loves to have a bit of craic and banter just like Mad Dog, but I do believe there is one person who can help you find Greg; but it'll involve a trip over to Ireland. I overheard him saying this since he believes this lad is quite possibly The Last Jedi. Now, as you try and sink your teeth into that, he also mentioned something about The Tardis:

"To locate J.P. Sexton, you must summon Tony Macaulay!"

Printed in Great Britain
by Amazon